Our Song
By K. Nies

Our Song

Our Song

1st ed. 2024

ISBN 979-8-218-53781-4

K. Nies

Trigger Warnings:
alcohol abuse, drug abuse, violence

Our Song

Thank you to Ryan and Sarah, my favorite test audience and soul mates.

For you, Dad.

Our Song

Chapter 1
December 2024 - Quinn

I can see the blood drying on his arm as we race down the Pacific Coast Highway. My heart is roaring over my car's engine, pounding in my ears. I pulled the needle right out. I didn't even think twice. It wasn't much blood, but he shed blood for this all the same.

I look over to my passenger seat to see his eyelids opening again. They're glazed like donuts. He smells like he's never had a shower and his skin looks gray, like an upset storm cloud.

"Where are we going?" he asks.

"Do you not remember the last ten minutes?" I ask in response, avoiding answering his question.

I already told him where we were going when I was hoisting his slumped, and near lifeless body, into my car. It was clear the moment I got his voicemail where he was. When he left his very incoherent message, I could hear the balls on the pool tables knocking in the background.

I knew he would be at Whiskey's.

I also knew there was only one place we would be headed from there.

When I arrived at Whiskey's, I didn't know that he would be locked in the men's room with a needle hanging out of his arm and urine soaking his pants.

The bartender was nice enough to unlock the door and look the other way when I told him I would take care of it. Lucky for me, Whiskey's isn't exactly the type of establishment that wants cops around, even if it would've helped in a situation like the present one.

At first, when I opened the door, I thought he was dead. My mind went blank for about ten seconds and I forgot how to breathe. My lungs felt like they were drowning in the tears that my body couldn't figure out how to cry.

Then, by the graces of whatever God's people believe in, he moved. He rolled his head and squinted his eyes open enough to see me and say "Baby, you came!" before falling back to sleep.

Of course I came.

He's in every fiber of my being, my twin flame. If he was on the other side of the world with a flat tire, I would find the next flight to him, just to help patch it.

At the same time, it took everything in me not to scream at him once I knew he was alive. It's conflicting for me that I wanted to kiss him just as much.

I decided on the drive here I don't give a fuck anymore. I don't give a fuck about the band; I don't give a fuck about the tour; I don't give a fuck about myself. I'm implored to say I don't give a fuck about my marriage.

I glance over at the man sitting next to me and I just need him to be okay and right now.

"I remember your hair smelling like strawberries." He grins at me, lazily.

He picks up his weighted hand and slides it across the center console into my lap. His hand takes up its favorite position on my inner right thigh.

"Is that *all* you remember?" I ask.

"Don't be mad at me, please don't hate me Quinn, I fucked up, I didn't mean to. It was one more time, I swear," he pleads, as an answer to my question.

"I'm not mad at you, I could never…" I stop before I let my emotions slip past my words.

I can't let him know I'm sad, or mad, or most of all, devastated. This isn't about me, it's about saving him.

I don't even know if I can say it's his fault or mine. I want to say it's everyone's fault; that we all contributed our jagged fucked up piece to this puzzle. My piece just feels like it's the biggest.

"Does he know you were with me earlier?" he asks.

For someone in his state, he seems to be aware of reality. I don't know if that makes what I'm about to do to him easier or not.

"No, but you can't keep doing this to me…to us…." I don't like how punishing my tone is towards him.

What he seems to lack in memory is what I told him right after we got in the car.

I called his brother and told him he needed to go home and get help. I got his phone number from the emergency contact sheet I keep for everyone as the band manager.

I've never formally gotten to meet him, so I hate that this was the first conversation we've had. Right now he's somewhere making rehab accommodations.

I told him to send me the bill.

"I'm sorry," I continue, "I'm not mad. No one knows. But I need to know…why did you do it again?"

His body seems to have more life in it as he sits up straight and his hand leaves my thigh.

How does my leg feel heavier with the absence of his touch?

My heart physically aches in my chest for the road ahead. His fingers comb through his hair and he rubs at his eyes before taking a deep breath.

"I just…I don't know. I hurt and I didn't want to hurt anymore." His voice sounds weak.

"I don't want to hurt anymore, either." I say.

Chapter 2
January 2022 - Quinn

Fuck moving. Fuck card board boxes and packing tape. I swear I will die in this apartment because I am *never* moving again.

The worst part of moving 1,000 miles away from everything you know and love is having no one to carry your boxes and help you unpack.

Kimball, South Dakota, will always have a piece of my heart, but I needed to leave before I forgot that I could. After my mom died from breast cancer when I was thirteen, I had to step up and take care of my dad.

That sounds backwards, I know, but sometimes parents forget how to be parents, I guess. Dad never had a sip of liquor before then, as far as I could remember.

The day of Mom's funeral, he stopped at the package store down the street from our house on the way home. He came back out with a tall bottle of some brown liquid. *Jim Beam* written in bright red letters across the front.

Our Song

When we got back to the house, we didn't speak. I went to my room to go to bed, and he sat down on the living room couch. We were both exhausted, and it truly felt like no words would make anything better, so we just separated in the unspoken silence.

I woke up at 3a.m. the next morning to a loud bang. When I went to investigate, I found him lying on the kitchen floor, the bottle of liquor in tiny fragments all around him.

Tears soaked his cheeks as he yelled to no one that they took his best friend. I walked across the broken glass in my socks to get to him. I needed to console him and make the dreadful wails coming from him stop.

When I sat down next to him, I noticed freckles of blood starting to stain my white socks. I cradled his head in my lap and felt the weight of his sadness in my chest. It morphed with my own, creating a bigger mess that felt like suffocation.

He turned on his side, shaking, and sobbed into my leg. I sat there softly stroking his head until the sadness consumed him into sleep.

Once I was sure he was out cold, I got up with as little movement as possible, and gently placed his head on the tile. I peeled off my socks and cleaned my feet at the sink.

Only surface level scratches were left when I dried them off. The wound in my heart, however, was a much deeper cut.

I got the broom from the closet and cleaned all the glass. When finished, I stood in the silence of our kitchen, watching the morning light start to leak through the windows. Dad was just laying there like a wounded animal, helpless.

I went back to my room and pretended to sleep until he "woke me up" for breakfast around 10a.m.

Over the years, we fell into a similar pattern of me trying to mend his broken heart, unsuccessful in every attempt.

He learned the healing power of whiskey. I learned how to take care of myself. He learned that my face reminded him too much of Mom the older I got and that it was easier if he was never home.

Google Search raised me if I'm being candid. When I got my first period, Google taught me what a tampon was and how to insert it, then I went to the store and bought pads.

When I had my first crush, Google taught me how to practice kissing on the back of my hand. All for nothing though. Stupid Ethan Swanson ended up taking Lily St Clair to the prom instead.

Google even found me my first job. As soon as I was old enough to work, I did. During the summers, I worked as a camp counselor. During the school year, I waited tables at the local Denny's on Friday nights and weekends.

I saved every dollar from when I was sixteen to now, at nineteen, and finally I have enough funds to execute my escape plan.

I ate through a packed cooler of road snacks and listened to an audiobook for the straight fifteen hours I drove. I didn't intend to make it in one shot. I figured I'd pull into a rest stop and sleep when I grew too tired, but the prospect of my new life kept me alive like a wire.

Five stops for gas and several Diet Cokes later, I was at the Tower Suites in Hendersonville, Tennessee. The front of the twenty story building was nothing but shiny windows and concrete.

Our Song

My new home.

I got my keys from the front office, drove down to the parking garage and have now started the dreaded unpacking of my trunk. One of my biggest reasons for choosing this building, outside of the cheap rent, was that it is furnished.

I would willingly sleep on an air mattress until the day I die before I try to even think of how I would lug a full, human sized bed up to the thirteenth floor by myself.

I allow my mind a quick moment to dream about a world where I can afford movers *and* my own furniture. Then I open my eyes and continue stacking as many boxes as I can into my hands.

Thankfully, I snagged a parking spot right next to the elevators. As I turn on my heel to close my trunk, the roar of a load engine sounds.

"Is that a *motorcycle*?" I ask myself.

There is something about men on motorcycles that I find unappealing. Maybe it's the loud obnoxious revs they love to do, or the dangerous riders that love to weave in and out of traffic on the highway that I can't stand. Silly toys for childish men, if you ask me.

A moment later my question is answered as a man suited up in a leather jacket and acid-washed jeans flies by.

I *swear* for a brief second his bike slows and his helmet turns, looking back at me as he revs up at the bend in the garage. He speeds up and turns out onto the road dramatically. For just a second, I catch a glimpse of a big Kiss sticker on the back of the helmet.

At least the asshole has good taste in music.
Was he showing off by taking off like that?
Why the fuck do I feel flattered?

I chalk it up to my poor history of rejection and need for approval before continuing on with my day. Once all my boxes are upstairs, it only takes me about an hour to unpack them.

I look at the clock on my stove and it reads 7p.m. I don't have the energy to go to the grocery store like I thought I would.

I decide the expense of a pizza for dinner is well worth not having to get off my pre-owned, new-to-me couch. Money's tight, but I deserve a little reward for the grueling twenty-four hours I've had.

I put in for the pizza and then call my dad to tell him I'm settled in. Except, I don't get to say that to him, I say it to his answering machine.

It's Tuesday, so that means that there's a $5 drink special happening at O'Flannagans right about now. He probably won't be home until they force him to be.

I sit in silent peace, waiting for my pepperoni delight. When the UberEATS app shows the drivers two minutes away, I head down stairs to meet him at the front door.

Tipping the driver with the last five dollar bill from my wallet, I quickly head back upstairs. The elevator traps the magnificent smell of meat and cheese and my mouth is watering by the time the doors open.

I approach my door, excited to eat my first meal in my first apartment when it occurs to me.

I didn't grab my fucking keys.

Our Song

I have to be the dumbest person to live. Who forgets the key to their own apartment? It's my first night of independence and I'm doing a horrible job.

My favorite part of this dumpster fire of a night is that the front office closed at 6p.m. I try to call my landlord directly but there's no answer. Of course his voicemail is full too.

I want to believe that I can sit in the hall and eat my pizza while I wait for him to return my call, but my phone is on five percent, so my odds aren't looking favorable right now.

I refuse to knock on doors and ask for help either. I'm an adult now.

Accepting defeat, my back slumps down against my door as I open the pizza box. Before I can even realize what's happening, my tears are raining down onto the slice of pizza in my hand. I eat my tear seasoned slice and all I can think about is how this is what I wanted.

To be on my own and free. Responsible for myself and no one else.

After a while I'm full and bored with my own thoughts. My phone dies promptly after I finish my hallway cuisine.

It's not long after I feel my eyes grow heavy.

I'll close them for just a second…

Just a minute…

***

"Hey, are you okay?" a deep voice says in my dream, only it's not my dream.

I hear it again and my eyes fly open. I forgot where I was for a minute. I look up and am met with brown eyes and sandy blonde waves.

"Are you okay, ma'am?" He says with more panic.

"Ma'am?"

"Yes you, girl sleeping in my hallway with a box of pizza as a pillow."

Only now do I realize I must have fully drifted off and snuggled up to my pepperoni slices.

"Sorry, I...I'm locked out of my apartment." I point to the door behind me.

His face relaxes a bit when he realizes I'm not some random person sleeping in the hallway.

I'm his *neighbor,* sleeping in the hallway.

"The office didn't answer when you called?"

I run him through all my unsuccessful attempts at trying to get into my apartment. While I do, I appreciate his cut jawline and tall stature.

"What time is it?" I ask.

"11p.m."

Well, there's no way I could call my landlord from this guy's phone at this hour. He stares at me for another moment, his eyes feel like lasers of heat across my skin.

"Well you probably shouldn't sleep out here," He finally says.

"I know, I'm sorry, I just-" he cuts me off quickly.

"Why are you apologizing?"

Our Song

I hesitate. I don't know how to answer. The embarrassment of it all, I suppose. I can't let this very handsome man know I'm embarrassed, though.

"Why don't you pick up your pizza and stay on my couch for the night? I live right next door." He points to his door. "There is one condition, though."

My heart races for what he is about to say. He doesn't seem like a bad person, but what do I know? I'm from fucking South Dakota.

I think he sees the panic wash across my face and continues quickly.

"You have to use a *real* pillow. I don't need sauce stains on my couch. I don't own it." His eyes crinkle as he laughs.

I breathe a deep sigh of relief and shake my head in agreement.

As I stand up and grab the pizza box, I begin thinking about that one dateline episode I saw about the guy that murdered girls and kept their toenails in a jar.

My burning questions during that episode was did he cut them off before, during or after.

Snapping back into reality, I look him over again. This guy doesn't *seem* like the type but, how does one spot a murderer with a toenail fetish?

I follow closely behind him into his already open doorway and enter his apartment. I shamelessly admire his frame and broad shoulders.

At least he's a beautiful murderer.

His apartment looks just like mine. Only, every surface is garnished with thrown clothes or clutter. Lots of notebooks and crumbled up pieces of paper line the floor. I notice a small collection of guitars and a makeshift recording set up in the corner.

Not a toenail clipper or an obvious murder weapon in sight.

The overflowing trash can and sink full of dishes tells me that the mystery neighbor man is *definitely* single.

I can't imagine a woman who would live, or even visit, in this mess. He sees me eyeing the apartment, and a small look of embarrassment flushes his face.

"Sorry, it's kind of a mess." He says, clearing off the couch for me to sit. "Band rehearsals have been running late, and it doesn't leave me much time to clean."

How horrible am I that I stopped listening after I heard band rehearsals?

A beautiful musician neighbor who is willing to let some random girl sleep on his couch. I think I'm going to be just fine here.

"So you're in a band?" I parrot back.

I see a small grin on his face and his shoulders relax as he takes a seat on the LazyBoy next to the couch.

"When I'm not slinging espresso at the Starbucks down the street, I am. It's called Compass. I'm their singer."

"That sounds really cool." I say.

What a lame response. Of course it's really cool.

It crosses my mind to bring up my songwriting and it being the main reason I moved here, but that just seems so basic. I'm sure every girl living in a furnished studio in the state of Tennessee is writing their own songs, hoping for a break too.

Our Song

I tell myself I moved here more for my mental health. I'm not sure if that's just to protect myself from inevitable disappointment, though. Nonetheless, it's a fresh start in an environment surrounded by my first love, music.

Even if I never got to hear someone sing one of my songs, being around music in general was a good enough deal to me.

"It's definitely cool," he laughs. " It would be a lot cooler if we could start booking gigs though. We've played a few parties and graduations. It'll be cool the day I get to sing on an actual stage with lights and a crowd of people just there to hear me sing. A guy can dream though."

"Why don't you just call and ask to play?" I ask like it's that simple.

"Yes, because I can just call up Bluebird Cafe and say, hey I know you've never heard of us, but please give us a Friday night slot."

"You could."

"They'll say no," He fires back, surely.

"How do you know they will say no if you don't ask?"

He pauses at my question. I can't tell if he is growing bored with my banter or is intrigued by my optimism.

"How about *you* give them a call and tell them to let us play, if you're so confident?"

"Fine." I say quickly.

"You don't even know if we're any good."

"Oh, you're good."

"How do you know that? Are you my first official stalker? Was this all a ruse? I'm honored. I didn't think my first stalker would be so beautiful. I was honestly betting on a middle-aged rock-bro hooked on his glory days."

Did he just call me beautiful?

I try my best to process everything he just said and still have a cute, educated and witty response.

"I just know. How can a band have a singer who looks like you and not be good?"

Oh my god…are we…flirting?

He arches an eyebrow as if he is questioning his decision to let a stranger sleep in his apartment. Or maybe he's wondering if I'm in fact a stalker.

"So tomorrow you're going to make a life-changing phone call for me and give my band their big break?"

"Yes," I say confidently, "You have some sort of demo I assume?"

"We have three original songs on Spotify!" He says proudly.

I would be remiss if I didn't acknowledge how attractive I find his confidence too. I've never had that.

"Perfect. Text me the link." I say, as if it's just that easy.

"So what, you're my band's manager now?" He asks, and I swear there's a hint of flirtation in his tone.

"Sure, I have nothing outside of waitressing going on in my life at the moment."

Why did I just admit that out loud?

Pathetic.

"Not even a boyfriend?"

"No, not even a boyfriend. Text me the link and I will make you proud to call me your band's manager." I say, pleased by his question.

"Shouldn't I know your name before I go giving you my number?" He asks, "You were just sleeping in my hallway five minutes ago."

"Shouldn't you have known my name *before* you offered me to sleep on your couch?" I question back.

"Touché"

I think his eyes are lingering on my mouth for a moment.

The exhaustion is making me see things.

"Noah Taylor, pleased to meet you." He says, holding out a hand.

"Quinn Finch," I say, taking his hand in mine, shaking it formally.

As we do, I notice something past his shoulder sitting on his kitchen counter.

"Is that…"

He turns to see what I am looking at and looks back at me with a smirk.

"A motorcycle helmet?" He finishes my questions like it's a flex.

It's not *just* any motorcycle helmet, though. It's a motorcycle helmet with a Kiss sticker on the back.

Of fucking course it is, I silently laugh to myself.

Chapter 3
December 2023 - Quinn

The band is in the booth when my phone rings. I look at Mo, the studio's recording engineer, and tell him I'll be right back. I step out to the parking lot of Edward Recording Studios and answer the call.

"Hello, this is Quinn Finch speaking." I say, in my most professional big girl voice.

"Hi Quinn, this is Grant Madison over at Rich Records. How are you today?"

"I'm great, good thank you."

Keep it together, bitch.

"I'm glad to hear. Listen, I just got out of a meeting with the board and they absolutely loved the demo!" He says.

I immediately feel the weight of my fears fly off my shoulders and chest.

"I'm so happy they loved it. We're honored your team took the time to listen to it!."

They absolutely love the sound. Now, obviously, we can't just push this out, it only has six songs, we'll need at least seven or eight more before we officially put the record out."

I stop breathing, mute the phone and actually scream out loud. Not a cute excited squeal either, a scream. Full-blown running from a killer through a cornfield scream.

This means…

"Hi Quinn, are you still there? Did I lose you?"

"Hi, sorry, did you say *record*?"

"Yes, apologies. I should've led with the news, not the details. We would like to officially extend a record deal to Compass. We would like to put out an album as soon as possible and get you guys on the road once it's in stores. My people will send over all the nitty gritty stuff later tonight. Get ready to live your wildest dreams, kid."

"Thank you so much sir. We won't make you regret this!"

"Talk soon, bye."

After I hit the end call button and double check that I definitely hung up, I open my mouth to scream again but no noise comes out this time. Instead, tears start running a marathon down my cheeks.

Is this what being in shock feels like?

It has been a long two years since this journey started. It has felt like a lifetime, frankly.

I'm twenty-one now and Noah's twenty-five. We're not the same people we were when we met, but I couldn't be happier. A day hasn't passed without seeing Noah since that first night he invited me to sleep on his couch.

We stayed up until the front office opened the next morning just talking. It's kind of crazy how much you're willing to tell someone you just met when they save you from sleeping in a hallway.

We discussed our greatest dreams and our biggest fears, our failures and triumphs, but mostly our dreams.

He said my eyes were the prettiest shade of green he'd ever seen. He liked how they stood out from my honey blonde hair.

I just about died inside.

I asked to hear the band and Noah played their three originals. To my relief, they were good.

Really good.

Their sound is a blend of your favorite rock verses and your favorite pop choruses fused together. Rhythmic guitars and pulsating drums married with Noah's warm tone. It was magic. Each song was catchier than the next. They truly made my job easy.

I eventually told Noah that I wrote songs. He said maybe one day I could write one for the band. I haven't yet, but there's always time, plus we're about to have a need for more.

The whole "Band Manager" position really took off for me the day after we met.

I burned a few copies of a CD with their three originals and a few of their covers from Spotify. It was a mix of rock and contemporary, a few pop tracks too.

I thought surely just playing one original song would convince someone to take the CD and listen to the whole thing. Then, inevitably, they would let them play.

Our Song

I try being optimistic because it reminds me of my mother. She always said, "Everything you need is inside of you. Shatter every ceiling until you see stars."

After I got my apartment unlocked and a few hours of sleep, I made my way down to Broadway Street with nothing but determination and Compass's dreams in my hand.

Bar after bar, club after club, no one was interested. They wouldn't even fully listen to one damn song. It was either they were booked, not looking for new bands yet, or flat out were uninterested.

When I started contemplating walking into oncoming traffic, it was clear I needed to take a break. I stopped for lunch at a bar called "Sally's".

It was a bit of a dive, but it was the closest place off Broadway with food and the least amount of dollar signs on Google maps.

I sat in a booth and ordered a Diet Coke and chicken fingers, the best kind of comfort food.

I was scrolling through Facebook when my ears were invaded by the most off-key rendition of "Blank Space" by Taylor Swift.

I turned my head around the corner of the booth and noticed the tiny stage and karaoke set up they had.

That stage looks big enough for five people and a drum set, I thought to myself in a lightbulb moment.

I looked around to see if there was any indication they offered live music, aside from whatever *this* was. When I didn't see any, I charged up to the bartender with unnecessary speed.

"Can I help you?" He asked.

"I sure hope so. Is the owner here?" I asked, trying to sound charming and not desperate.

"You're looking at him."

"Do you ever have live bands playing here?"

"No, this is really just a seven days a week karaoke bar."

"That sounds like the worst Ground Hog day ever." I realized after he was laughing I said that bit out loud.

"You're not wrong, but once in a while there are good singers. I took it over about a month ago from my grandfather and have just kept it this way. The locals seem to have fun with it."

"Well, what if I told you I could fill this place with people and really *really* good live music?"

"Karaoke is kind of our thing, however unfortunate that may be."

"But what if for just one night it wasn't?"

"But karaoke-" I cut him off again with a pleading look.

"You seem reasonable..." I notice a name tag on his shirt, "...Devin, real reasonable. Don't you think that change is good?"

"Well, yes but-"

"Would you agree that this place could use a little more clientele?" I press.

I followed his gaze as he looked around the bar. There were a few pool tables, a jukebox, several empty booths and a horseshoe-shaped bar in the middle, with only a quarter of its chairs taken.

Of course, we can't forget about the two foot high stage in the back surrounded by a few high tops.

"I mean, it wouldn't be bad…"

"Perfect, so you agree bringing in a live band for one night might be a good thing for your thriving business."

"Well, I have been wanting to find a way to make a little more money."

"It seems like it's your lucky day because I happen to know a really good band that will play for you live and free any night of your choosing."

After a little more convincing, Compass had its first gig on a stage that Saturday night, then every Saturday night after.

Devin was, in fact, a very smart businessman. He saw the potential in charging cover fees and playing live music on the weekends while still keeping the regulars happy during the week.

As a thank you for helping him fill seats and sell drinks, he promised the band a permanent, and most importantly paid, 9p.m. Saturday slot.

Noah and I moved into a one bedroom down the hall together a month later.

Our connection was instant, and our passion for the band amplified that. It was clear from the second I heard Compass that even if the Band Manager title started as a joke, Noah wasn't taking it back. They were going somewhere, and I was going to be a part of it.

Noah, being the kindest soul I've ever met, made falling in love with him effortless. When he mentioned the unit down the hall was open, I didn't even bat an eye before I was getting up and grabbing a cardboard box from my recycling.

He said, "What are you doing?" and I replied, "Moving in with the hot lead singer of a band."

That was the first time in my human experience that I felt love for someone like that.

I wanted him to be the first and last thing I saw every day and night, and so he was.

He told me he was in love with me a week later. I told him it took him long enough.

The two years that have followed the Sally's gig have been filled with a non-stop hustle and grind.

I found out that I genuinely enjoyed being the band's manager. I started networking more and playing their music for anyone who would listen to it in between my shifts at the diner.

Noah and the band practiced every free moment they had too. We were all chasing the same dream. Together we were unstoppable.

After about a year, they had played a few paid gigs outside of Sally's. Myself and the rest of the band invested in studio time and made a new demo CD with six songs. I burnt one hundred copies of the CD. That's how confident I was.

I mailed it to every record label and radio station in the city of Nashville and its surrounding boroughs. I sent emails and made phone calls until I couldn't bear to look at my phone anymore, too anxious to see if someone was going to reply.

No one took interest.

That was, until about a month ago. The band was playing their regular slot at Sally's when Grant Madison showed up.

Our Song

Sally's has become quite the music scene despite being outside of the main music strip. It was only a matter of time until labels started sending people to check out the talent.

He approached me after the band's set and gave me his card. I gave him mine and one of the many copies of their CD I keep on me at all times, and yes, I did make myself official Band Manager business cards.

I'm an adult.

It's been a long few weeks of hoping and waiting. I honestly thought he wasn't interested. I told Noah that we just needed to keep making music and our time would come. They say it takes ten years to become an overnight success.

That's why we're at the studio right now, spending more of our own money to make a new single.

But now, I get to walk back in there and watch our lives change.

I'll thank the universe every day I locked my self out of that fucking apartment.

***

I get back inside and Mo looks at me with an inquisitive look.

"Everything okay, Quinn?"

"Better than okay, Mo."

"Oh ya, anything to do with that phone call?"

"Yes, Mr. Nosy, it did. How would you feel about being our full-time engineer?" I ask him.

"I'd say that sounds like a good time to me."

He's been in the booth two out of the three times we've rented this studio before and he seems to really get the band's sound. I've never had to repeat myself to him and I love that.

Not as much can be said about the band, though. While my title is Manager, it should just be Mother. You would never know by their cohesive sound that each member of Compass is a vastly different personality from the next. That's where the mothering comes in.

I cater to each one of my "children" in their own special way. Noah is the easiest because he's done everything I've said since I booked them their first gig. It probably also helps that I let him see my boobs.

Maxwell Williams is our drummer. Think skater meets muscle head. His brown hair is cut tight to his head, and he has tattoos covering him from the chin down.

I don't know that I've ever seen him smile. He is always the serious one but by design, also very committed. He shows up to every practice and rehearsal thirty minutes early and heads straight for his kit, practicing show tricks with his sticks. The ladies eat that shit up.

In contrast to Max, there's our lead guitarist, Samuel Denton. Tall, dark and handsome, he stands at six feet tall. He has deemed himself the "ladies man" which makes you want to hate him, but somehow the ladies do seem to flock to him. He likes the attention more than any of them.

Samuel's brother, Harvey, is the rhythm guitarist. They look almost exactly alike, except Sam's hair is bleached.

Harvey is my most challenging child. I can't get too mad at him though, he's the only one of us with an actual child.

He and his wife, Trisha, had a baby six months ago. Ever since, he's been late for every practice and even missed a show once. I want to be mad, but it's nice to know loving fathers still exist.

Last but not least is our bass guitarist, Veronica Cook. She's the cool girl who doesn't know she's cool.

Roni and I have gotten really close since she joined the band last spring. It's nice to have another girl around. She's really given the band their cherry on top. The songs started sounding fuller, smoother.

Each song we've made since she joined has hit over 10,000 streams on Spotify. Her pink pixie cut and the tight clothes have also helped boost our male audience.

What they don't realize is she's more interested in Havery's wife than any of them.

I'm watching them finish this take of our next single, "N.S.E.W". It stands for, you guessed it, North South East West.

Sam and Roni wrote it one night after, and I quote, *"an exceptionally well rolled blunt"*.

"Get it, because we're called Compass." Sam said as if that was enough of a reason to record it.

On occasion, I like to join their sessions. Noah's not much of a smoker, he's more of a drinker. Sometimes he gets a little too tipsy, and it takes me back to when I was a kid standing in the kitchen looking at my dad.

Not that Noah's ever been nearly that messy, the smell of whiskey just does something to me I guess.

"Hey, how was that?" I hear Noah ask through the speakers.

I grab Mo's arm and drag him out of his chair and into the recording room with me.

"That sounded great." I say, walking in. Noah takes off his headset and walks over to me.

"Really? Because it looked to me like you were taking a phone call and drifting off to somewhere in that head of yours." He says playfully as he pulls me in for a hug.

"I was listening! I'll have you know it was a *band official* phone call that you're going to be really glad I answered."

"Oh yeah, and why is that?" He asks.

"Because Compass just signed their first record deal, Noah."

"What the fuck did she just say?" Asks Max, standing up from his drum set.

"She said record deal, right? She said fucking record deal!?" Roni chimes in, asking the room frantically.

"I did in fact say, *record deal.*"

The next fifteen seconds are filled with screaming, laughter and tears of joy. We're all in a group hug when I realize someone is missing.

"Harvey, come here, dude." I say.

I look across the room to see Harvey looking down at his guitar like it might bite him. He looks up to me and I think I see tears in his eyes.

"I can't do it." He says.

"What?" Max asks.

"I said, I can't do it. Emma is only six months old. Trisha has to be home to take care of her because we can't afford daycare. The gigs we play on the weekend are for nice extra cash but I can't risk my family's future on the chance that this might pan out. My job at the firm is really good and I don't want to risk giving it up if we fail."

"Have a little faith dude." Says Noah. He sounds like he just watched his dog get run over by a car.

"I just can't, okay. I barely see my family between practices, Sally's and my forty hour work week as it is."

He puts his guitar in his case and before anyone can grab him he's walking towards the door. Before he's fully out of the booth, he turns back like he might be second guessing his decision.

"I'm sorry, I really hope it works out for you guys."

Then, he's gone.

The room that was just filled with hope and happiness is now silent and still. No one says anything.

We all just look at one another until finally Noah says, "Well this is fucking terrible."

"Way to be the optimistic band leader you truly are, Noah." Max snaps at him.

"At least I'm still standing here." Noah says louder.

"He has a family to take care of, dude, we don't know what that's like." Sam tries to defend Harvey.

"Fuck him man." Noah shoves Sam's shoulder.

"Hey!" I yell. "Can the men stop acting like juveniles and get it together? We've been given an incredible opportunity to change our lives here. Are you going to use the first seconds of it going at each other, or, are we going to get our shit in order and do what obviously needs to be done."

"Oh and what would that be?" Asks Noah.

"We replace him." I say.

K. Nies

***

"NEXT!" Sam yells.

"Do you have to be so dramatic about it?" I ask, rubbing my sore ears.

I see Max roll his eyes and Roni looks like she's about to fall asleep.

"How many are left?" Noah asks like he can't take anymore.

We only have a week between signing and when our official recording sessions start. We've spent every day this week trying to rework songs without Harvey but nothing sounds quite the same.

"Three more, we can make it through three more, guys." I say.

"Fine, but if these three people don't work out, I say we need to just move on without filling Harvey's spot. We need to start recording, you saw that contract we have thirty days until January 14th."

"Yes but the label liked what they heard, that's what we need to sound like. We can't drop an instrument. Have I ever steered you wrong?"

"No." He presses a gentle kiss to my forehead.

We sit through two more excruciating auditions and I hear my stomach rumble. I'm counting the minutes until we can blow this popsicle stand and get chicken & waffles at Sun

Our Song

Diner. I look down at my call sheet and say the name of our final victim.

"Lincoln Archer."

Chapter 4
December 2023 - Lincoln

My hands are so sweaty I'm worried I might drop the pick when I start playing. I've been auditioning for anyone looking for a guitarist since the day I got here. Five grueling weeks of rejection and dwindling funds.

When I left Flagstaff for Nashville, I knew it would be expensive. I thought getting a guitar gig would be much easier though.

I saw a lot of postings online for bands, studio guitarists and even a few music teaching positions. I figured I could just go to a few auditions or interviews and I would get a spot.

Maybe it was naïve of me to think it would be that easy with my criminal record.

I've kept working remotely as an online banking support technician through the move. It's better to be safe than sorry and let's face it, this is my sixth audition for a band alone since I got here.

Why should this one turn out any different?

Our Song

I enter the room and see six strangers staring back at me. They look like they're about to fall asleep or walk out.

I heard the guy who was in here before me and I would probably want to tap out after hearing that too.

"Lincoln Archer." A blonde-haired woman wearing a Mötley Crüe t-shirt says smiling. She has perfect teeth.

"That's me, nice to meet you, I'm Lincoln." I stammer.

"Nice to meet you too, Lincoln. How long have you been playing?" She asks.

"Since I was nineteen."

"And how old are you now?"

"Twenty-one."

"Oh great, a child." Says a man wearing a suit of tattoos.

"Hey, I'm twenty-one Max, am I a child?" Straight Teeth questions him.

I like her, she's fiery.

"You're the exception. You're a seventy year old woman trapped inside a twenty-one year old. Who doesn't drink, reads books and goes to bed at 9p.m.?" He asks her.

Me, I reply in my head.

"Sorry we're not thirty and decomposing like you." She says.

I laugh and it seems to get only her attention. She gives me a warm look.

Some people you just know are nice people the second you meet them, she seems like one of those people. I'm grateful she's not letting them judge me before I've even played.

"Sorry about him, he's a neanderthal. Please, play for us." She sits back crossing her legs.

I take out my guitar and put it over my shoulders. I adjust my strap, plug into the amp then grab my pick. I have been auditioning with "Thunderstruck" by ACDC but I change my plan at the last second.

I'm going to play to my audience and to the one person in this room who seems hopeful I won't totally bomb. It's been a while since I've played it but something tells me to say *"Fuck it"* and to do it anyways.

Here goes nothing.

I start playing "Shout at the Devil" by Mötley Crüe.

I keep my eyes on the floor the whole time. I'm afraid if I look up and see that they hate it, I'll miss a chord. The music comes back to me and I fall into the rhythm. I let the song take me and before I know it, it's over.

I take a deep breath before looking up. When I finally do, everyone is smiling.

Holy shit, I can't believe I just did that.

I'm hoping it wasn't a total mistake when I see them form a small huddle and start to whisper. I think I hear someone say *"We can do it without him."*

Finally, a guy with blonde hair dismisses their private chat and looks over at me. His jaw is tight, and he looks kind of mad.

I've never known my guitar playing to insight anger but there's a first time for everything, I suppose. But then, his mouth forms a small grin.

"Welcome to the band."

Our Song

***

After the man I now know as, Noah, told me I was in the band they got right to the point. He told me that the band had just signed a record deal and needed to replace one of their guitarists at the last minute.

The band manager, Quinn, told me they had thirty days to write eight more songs and completely record fourteen. The album is going to be called, *Invisible Horizon.*

I found their flier at one of the Broadway music spots seeking an "experienced guitarist and quick learner."

I'm sure they left the bit about the pre-existing record deal and tour to avoid everyone and their mother from auditioning.

They wanted someone talented and committed to the music. I'm grateful they think I can fit that role. It's insane how one song can change your life.

A week has passed, and they weren't kidding about getting down to business. I went home and quit my job that night. The next morning I showed up to the studio and did my best to do exactly what they needed me to do.

I don't feel like I have enough of a standing here to contend with anyone yet so I'm happy playing the chords exactly as they're given to me. I've mostly kept to myself too.

From getting to know everybody it seems there are clear dynamics within the band. Roni and Sam seem to do a lot of the writing and take a lot of "cigarette breaks" behind the studio.

Noah seems to want the final say on everything. He mostly cares about being the front man and hearing himself sing. I notice that he and Sam often compete to be the center of attention.

Max sticks to himself but when he disagrees with something he says so and no one seems to fight him.

Quinn is the true mastermind of this show, even if Noah presents himself as their leader. He wears the pants, but she picked them out, bought them, ironed them and then *let* Noah put them on.

I see how she keeps everyone in line and taken care of. I've concluded that my first impression of her was accurate.

If I didn't know any better, I'd say Noah has a crush on Quinn. He always seems to be talking to her, and she always seems to be laughing at something he says. But, she doesn't seem to look at him quite the same way he looks at her. I don't see why she'd be interested in someone like that anyway. His energy is a contrast to hers.

I'm here to play guitar though, I need to remind myself that's the most important thing. I didn't move here for friends, girls or drama. I moved here to do the thing that saved me, music.

When I look at the people surrounding me in the studio, I reflect on my path that led me here.

I was left at a fire station when I was seven. Usually, people only do that with babies but evidently that was my mothers best attempt to keep me safe.

That's what I tell myself at least.

I've tried to make peace with it over the years. I don't really even remember my parents anymore which makes it easier.

Our Song

I don't know if I got my height and black hair from my dad or if I got my love of music and blue eyes from my mom.

I have scars but nobody to remind me how I got them.

When I was older, maybe eleven, I overheard my case worker talking to one of my many foster parents. She told her that they tried to find my mom after she abandoned me.

Apparently, they looked at the fire station's camera and all they saw was a woman wearing a baseball cap walking me up to the front doors. She pointed at them and when I started walking where she directed me, she ran the other way.

The only information I could give them was that my name was Lincoln Archer, apparently that wasn't enough.

The messed up part of me wants to watch that surveillance tape myself. Maybe I wouldn't be so broken about it all if I could see her face when she did it.

Maybe there was a look of regret in her eyes or maybe she turned around for a brief second. Maybe it wasn't simply because I was unlovable.

I was bounced between foster homes for years. People only wanted to adopt babies, not a seven year old with abandonment issues.

I smoked weed for the first time when I was thirteen. I was in the woods with some other kids from my foster home and they said it was fun. Nothing was fun there, so it didn't take much convincing to try it.

That proved to be a recurring thought process for me in my youth.

The night of my fourteenth birthday my fosterer at the time, Robert, called me downstairs. When I walked into the kitchen, he was holding an old beat up acoustic guitar.

"I overheard you talking to one of the other boys about wanting to learn how to play music. I saw it at a garage sale and thought of you." He said.

I was so grateful, I was in instant tears. It was the first time I was excited for something and I saw a future where things weren't so bad. I remember looking down at the guitar, excited to have something so amazing to call my own.

That's when I felt Robert's hand grab my butt.

I didn't move because how are you supposed to process someone you thought was taking care of you, breaching your trust and violating you?

How can you be frozen like ice when your skin feels like molten lava?

He squeezed and then moved his hand around my front side and did the same thing, and then more. I remained motionless and when he was done, he patted me on the shoulder like I had done a good job by staying silent.

I couldn't tell if it happened fast or slow. He walked out of the kitchen and up stairs like nothing happened when he decided he was finished with me.

I was stuck in the moment though, like someone stuck a pin in me, just standing alone in the kitchen.

Still staring at the guitar, I cried. What was my most prized possession thirty seconds ago quickly felt like a prize for my complacency.

I started having night terrors and didn't want to sleep anymore after that.

The next weekend I went out to the woods and smashed that guitar. Then, I tried cocaine for the first time.

Our Song

When I turned fifteen, I was moved to a different home. I think I was too old for Robert by then.

Instead of being touched behind closed doors I was hit in open rooms. The psychical abuse didn't bother me as much, which is a really fucked realization to have at fifteen.

When I was sixteen I learned about the validation of self inflicted pain.

When I was seventeen, I had sex for the first time. It was nice to like the person taking off your clothes. I also tried Ecstasy, Molly and Acid for the first time, then, a lot of more times.

When I was eighteen, I went to jail for armed robbery and got my first tattoo, in that order. It's a small bird on the inside of my left bicep done by my cell mate, Marco.

To me, it symbolized that if I wanted to be free, I had to fly.

I had to be above my surroundings and go somewhere that made me feel that freedom. I had to get better. I had to evolve to survive.

I haven't had a drink or touched a substance since the first day of my sentence.

When I was nineteen I was released from prison and put in a halfway house for men under twenty-one. That's where I met Jason Sidoti, the house manager.

It's odd to think the person closest to me only came into my life two years ago. Nonetheless, he's a brother to me now.

He helped me keep my head low and my mind clear. He also helped me get the job I just quit.

It paid for an untarnished guitar and lessons. Music gave me peace and I have him to thank for helping me find my way back to that.

When I turned twenty last month I had to leave the halfway house. That's when I bought my one-way plane ticket to Tennessee.

Chapter 5
February 2024 - Lincoln

January 30th, our album was released. The whole band went down to Victory Vinyls and purchased the first official copy of *Invisible Horizon* together.

I've mostly kept to myself for the last month. I've been so focused on playing well and not letting them down. The record store was the first time I felt like this could be my family.

Everyone was so proud of each other. Quinn made us all pose for a picture holding the record for the band's Instagram page.

For the cover, they went with a black-and-white picture of us sitting on the fire escape steps behind the studio that Quinn took.

She's had a phone to her ear every time I've seen her after that day. She is getting calls faster than she can return them.

Every radio station has been playing at least one song from the album. There's something for everyone, that is what makes the record so listenable and popular.

Your parents, siblings, grandparents, friends, neighbors, you name it, everyone is listening to our album.

I knew we were really gaining momentum when I went to the gas station for snacks and I heard it…*in the freaking gas station*. "Phases of the Moon", the album's lead single, was playing.

I looked down at my bird tattoo and smiled. That scared eighteen year old kid sitting in jail would be so proud of us right now.

Cities have even started reaching out to us, interested in us adding them to our stops.

The tour has been officially named the Find Yourself Tour. The label has paid for three buses that each have a picture of the band and the name of the tour across it.

We outgrew the bar and club scene overnight. Theaters and arenas want us to play for them now. Radio stations want us to come to their talk shows. The local news even interviewed us about our quick rise to fame. I didn't say a single word the whole time. I did, however, nod politely and sweat.

Let's face it though, I mostly sweat.

Jason called me after it aired and told me he was proud of me, but said I needed to look like I wanted to be there.

I thought about his words for a while. I eventually realized I'm so terrified of losing this, I don't really know how to act. It seems like things I love leave which makes me shit at making connections.

I'm scared to get too close, just to be left.

Our Song

We leave on tour tomorrow and our first stop is Miami. I've made a promise to myself that I will try to make those connections I fear so much. I've evolved before, I can do it again.

I have to.

Quinn has planned a celebratory get together at Sally's just for the band. She presented it as a chance for everyone to bond before we leave on tour.

If I didn't know any better, I'd say she was really just trying to get the band to bond with *me*.

From the very minimal small talk I've had with everyone, the band's been together for three years. Noah and Sam were working at Starbucks. Noah was reminiscing about a talent show he, Sam and Sam's brother Harvey played together, trying to convince Sam to start a real band with him.

By what I see as fate, Max was standing at the counter of that Starbucks waiting for his coffee when he overheard this discussion and asked, *"Are you guys trying to start a band?"*

Roni only joined last year with Quinn's endorsement. She's joked with me that it's nice to not be the newbie anymore. I can't say I love that for me, but I'm happy for her. She fits in with them so well and it gives me hope that I can, too.

As my Uber pulls up to Sally's, I take a deep breath. *You are good enough. You deserve to be here. You worked hard for this. You are not an imposter. You can make friends. You deserve good things.*

I've only been here a few times, but the bar is surprisingly lively for a Thursday. I've been playing the regular Saturday night show here with the band the second I learned all the songs. It was nice to get a few live show experiences before hitting the road.

The stage has transformed from when I last saw it, now housing a karaoke set up. As I focus in, I notice Quinn and Roni are up on the stage singing "Espresso" by Sabrina Carpenter. Roni can harmonize pretty well, she sings backup vocals on a few songs.

Quinn, however, is something else.

Who knew someone so small and cute could make such ear piercing noises. She's smiling though, and confident. It's incredibly sexy, even with those sounds coming from her mouth.

"Hey man, how's it going?" Sam approaches me, holding out a fist for me to bump.

"Hi, good. I didn't know they did karaoke here?" I bump his fist back. He explodes his hand, mine awkwardly falls to my side.

"Ya, every weeknight. It's a pretty good time. It also brings in the ladies." He playfully bumps my arm and nods to a group of girls looking at the songbook catalog.

"Nice, I'm going to grab a drink. Where is everyone sitting?"

"Over by the pool tables. Let me buy your first drink." He insists.

"Oh, I couldn't let you do that." I say nervously.

"Are you sure?"

"I'm sure, but I appreciate you."

"Alright, see you at the table, man." He says before walking away.

I feel bad I deflected what was obviously an act of kindness, probably to help "bond" as Quinn says. I don't know why I didn't just say I was sober.

I'm not embarrassed that I'm sober, I'm just embarrassed about mostly everything that led me to being sober.

I'm nervous about answering questions about myself. I'm a horrible liar. To my knowledge, they never ran a background check. I'm afraid if they find out about my past at this point, they might not want me in the band anymore.

Positive thoughts, Archer.

I walk to the bar and get a soda with lime before joining the band at the table. By the time I get there, Quinn and Roni have rejoined them.

"So who's excited for Miami?" Noah asks.

"I'm excited to see the ocean again. I miss it." Says Sam.

"That's so adorable." Roni replies.

"I'm excited to check out their live music scene." Says Max.

"I have to agree with Sam on the ocean thing." Quinn smiles. "What are you excited for, Lincoln?"

I freeze. What am I excited for? I know what I'm nervous about, I know what I'm scared of.

"Palm Trees." I finally spit out.

"Trees?" Asks Noah.

"Ya, trees. I don't know, I think it'll be…cool." Everyone's looking at me in a tense silence and I feel heat rising up my neck.

"I love this guy!" Sam exclaims, throwing an arm around me from where he sits to my left in the booth.

Everyone starts laughing, and the conversation continues. I don't think that went *totally* horribly. I opt to listen to most of the following banter. I nod and am attentive, but I'm afraid to say something stupid so I say nothing at all.

After my second soda and a trip to the restroom, I decide I need to take a minute alone to recharge my social battery. I slip out the back door we bring our equipment through on Saturdays.

As soon as I'm outside in the cool night air, I close my eyes and take three very slow and deep breaths.

"I don't mean to scare you…" I jump and see Quinn leaning against the building behind me. "…but you look like you might be having a bit of a personal moment, and I don't want to linger here without you knowing. If you need a minute alone, I can go back inside." She offers.

"No, sorry, I'm good. Sometimes I just…"

"Need a break from the chaos?"

"Exactly." I say, feeling relieved.

"I get it. They are a very loud mix of personalities. You'll figure them all out, eventually. It seems Sam's taken a liking to you." She says.

"Ya, everyone is very nice."

"Lying won't get you far. We all know Max is a grump, Noah's a show off, Sam is loud as fuck and Roni, well, I have nothing bad to say about Roni. Girl Code and all that stuff." She says, smiling.

I let out a small laugh. Then we proceed to stand in comfortable silence for a moment, both of us looking up at the stars.

"So, how long have you lived in Tennessee?" She asks.

"About three months."

"Wait, you just moved here?"

"Ya, I got here about a month before joining the band. I'm from Arizona. I came here for a fresh start and to be around music."

I don't know why I'm word-vomiting to her. She doesn't seem to mind though.

I didn't realize how little I've told these people about me until now. Every practice and show I arrive on time and leave as soon as we are done, so I stay out of trouble.

Have I become that antisocial?

"I know what that's like. I moved here from South Dakota when I was nineteen. It's tough leaving home and starting over, but I promise you, it's worth it." She smiles.

I find myself leaning against the wall next to her now.

"What was the hardest part of leaving home for you?" I ask, still looking up.

"Probably not seeing my mom as much as I want."

"Does she still live there?"

"Sort of. She's buried there."

"Oh my god, I'm so sorry." I look at her, but her eyes are still fixed on the stars as she snickers to herself.

"I should lead with the dead mom thing, sorry. She passed when I was thirteen, I'm still sad about it but time has desensitized me in a sense. It created a bit of a morbid sense of humor. Do your folks miss you?"

"I don't know, maybe?"

"You haven't talked to them since you moved?" She asks.

"I haven't talked to them since they dropped me off at a fire station." I say. She looks at me and continues to laugh, but when she sees I don't, her face drops and now she's the one apologizing.

"I'm so so-" Then, in surprise to myself, laughter escapes from me.

We both grow silent and make eye contact for a second before we both start laughing again, together this time.

It's contagious and we can't stop. We stand under the stars, laughing at the things that make us cry.

Our laughter only stops when we hear the back door open. We both look to our right.

"There you guys are. Come on, I'm about to do Bohemian Rhapsody and I need back up." Sam says, grabbing us both by the wrist.

I'm dragged onto the stage along with Quinn and Roni, where we all share a mic standing behind Sam, being his backup. I find myself feeling a little lighter.

If I were to pick a favorite person here, I'd say it's Quinn. The second I walked into the studio to audition, she was kind to me. She's always the first one to try to make small talk with me during practice and that moment we just had out back was the first time I've laughed in the last ninety days, maybe even longer.

If I didn't know any better, I'd think I'm developing a crush on her. I wonder if they have a fraternization policy in the band to avoid a Fleetwood Mac situation.

She really is beautiful.

My question is answered when we all step off the stage.

Our Song

I'm smiling again, watching Quinn's long blonde hair bounce off her shoulders as she steps down. It's when I am thinking about being close enough to her to smell her shampoo that I see Noah walk up to Quinn and kiss her. And she kisses him back.

Well, fuck.

***

After questioning my ability to read people Thursday night, I dusted off my shoulders and have continued on.

I'd be a liar if I said I wasn't disappointed. I experienced one of those heartbreaks you only get from someone you never even dated. Emotions are weird like that sometimes.

It's the first night of the tour and I think I'm going to die. Ten minutes before call time and my head is in the toilet. I don't know what I'm even puking out because I was too nervous to eat all day.

We were on the bus for fourteen hours yesterday. All I did was lay in my bunk and run through the chords in my head. I may have slept for fifteen minutes total since leaving Nashville.

Five minutes before call time and I'm standing on the side of the stage, peeking out at the crowd. We are playing the Miami-Dade County Auditorium to a sold-out crowd of 5,000 people and they are *loud*.

Quinn picked a different local artist to open for us at every show. I thought it was incredibly kind of her to use her opportunity to create them for others.

When The Latin Sound Machine finishes playing, the house lights go down and the crowd's screams grow into a roar.

They announce us to the stage and the audience explodes. I can hear them clear as day through my in-ear monitors.

Everyone starts walking out to the dark stage to get in position for the opening number and I…freeze.

My legs are cement and the stage is quicksand.

I can't move, weighed down by my own fears. Noah and Max looked back at me, confused.

Then, I feel someone grab my arm and pull out my left ear piece.

"Hey, are you good?" Quinn asks, looking panicked.

"I'm, I'm…."

"Look at me." I lift my head and am met with calm green eyes. "Everything you need is inside of you. Shatter every ceiling until you see stars."

Something in me switches on and I start to move.

My soul is buzzing.

One foot moves in front of the other and I walk across the stage to my position next to Sam.

"You got this dude, let's have a good time," Sam says encouragingly.

As soon as we start playing, I know everything is going to be okay.

Our Song

The crowd is loving us and we're all tuned into one another. I think it's the best we've sounded so far. The adrenaline of opening night and the desire to cling to our dreams is fueling us.

We are making magic.

Chapter 6
March 2024 - Quinn

The first month of the tour flashed before my eyes. Four stops in Florida and six stops in Texas.

I've now seen dolphins, dipped my toes in the Atlantic Ocean, gone to a rodeo and eaten the best BBQ this country has to offer. I know we're working, but I'd be lying if I said we weren't also having the time of our lives.

Everyone has grown a lot closer since we've been on the road. Closed quarters and shared bathrooms will do that to you, though. Roni, Noah and I stay on the first bus, the boys stay on the second and the drivers and stage crew on the third.

We spend every night parked at some rest stop, hanging out and playing cards in the boys' bus. Even Lincoln is starting to come out of his shell and share stories with everyone.

I've never had a real family until I met the band. I have a sense Lincoln hasn't either.

It's nice to have someone who can relate to the ugly parts of my past.

Noah is understanding, but he never had to work for much, not that it's a bad thing.

Both his parents are alive and well, plus, he has a great relationship with his brother. Their parents own a ski resort in Colorado.

Ski money must be good because when Noah and I moved in together, he informed me he would be paying for rent.

I put up a real fight about it at first. For the first three months, I paid half of everything we used together. Rent, cable, utilities and groceries. I didn't realize how much moving from a studio to a one bedroom would affect my wallet, even split halfway.

I had myself convinced that asking for help was a sign of weakness. Another great quality from dear old dad.

It was when my card declined for a $4 iced coffee that I realized maybe it's okay to accept help. To my dismay, I finally agreed to let Noah pay for the apartment.

He's the first person since my mom passed that has made me feel safe and secure. He's never made me feel like I owe him anything for his love.

It's because of his love and support that I am able to be the successful woman I am today. He has never doubted me and always encourages me. I feel like I will never be able to pay back what he gave me when he decided to love me.

The time is 5p.m., and the band is just finishing up soundcheck when I get a call from Kye, the tour manager provided to us by Rich Records.

"Hey Q, how are ya and where are ya?" He asks with his usual dramatic flare.

"Hey Kye, I'm good. We're playing Fremont Street in Vegas tonight."

"Happy to hear. Sounds like it's going to be a good show. Listen, I've got great news. The band is officially booked every weekend until the second week of August."

"Shut up!"

"No, you shut up!" He laughs.

"I love you. Do you know how amazing you are?"

"Of course I do. I'll send you a new calendar in your email. I've got to run, but let me know if the band needs anything. Talk later."

"*Byeee, Kyeee.*" I exaggerate the rhyme.

"Loser." He laughs again and then I hear a click.

I look up to see Noah approaching me. He's wearing a sleeveless tank and my favorite gray sweatpants.

"What are you smiling about over here?" He asks, kissing the top of my head.

"Kye just called. We're booked until August." I smile, excited to see his reaction, but I don't see anything but the room spinning as Noah picks me up in a hug and swings me around in his arms.

"I'm so in love with you, Quinn Finch. You are my dream girl."

"I love you too Noah Taylor. You *are* my dream." I say when he finally puts me down.

He has one hand on my hip and the other caressing my cheek. He kisses me slowly and softly. My arms make their way around his neck. My fingers weave through his hair and I feel the hand that was on my hip reaching towards my backside.

"Marry me." He whispers against my lips.

"What?" I say, pulling out of his grasp.

He quickly grabs my hand, trying to get me back into his arms.

"Marry me, Quinn."

"You don't mean that. You're high on excitement, you're not thinking rationally." I counter.

"I'm thinking perfectly fine. You are the best thing that ever happened to me. My life has never had a purpose until you gave it one. We are meant to take the world by storm together."

"We don't have time for a wedding, Noah. We're booked until August and we need to be available to start writing a new album as soon as we're done if they sign us for another. We can't slow down for anything."

I don't know if I'm trying to convince Noah, or myself, that this isn't a good idea.

We've been together for two years and I am truly in love with him. I suppose marriage is the next natural step for people in our position, but we aren't *normal* people.

He's a famous rock star and I'm a famous band manager.

Do we really have the time or space to enjoy those intimacies right now?

"Then let's do it tonight. We're in Vegas, for fuck's sake. I couldn't imagine something more perfect and on-brand for us. My life has been a whirlwind since you walked into it, Quinn. You gambled on me once. I'm begging you to do it again." He looks at me with soft eyes.

"You did not just make a gambling joke about our undecided Vegas nuptials." I laugh.

"I did, and you love it. Please, make me the happiest man alive and I will promise to love and protect you until the day I die." He's still holding my hand but now he gets down on one knee.

"Quinn Finch, will you marry me?" He asks again, this time more formally.

The room is silent and everyone stops to watch us. It's obvious what's happening and everyone seems to have a mixed reaction.

Roni is jumping up and down, trying her best to be quiet. I think she's starting to cry too. Max is rolling his eyes at us. No doubt for taking away from rehearsal time. Sam is giving me two thumbs up and Lincoln is just staring, looking as shocked as I feel.

"Yes." It's out of my mouth before I can overthink it.

This is the right thing to do. I love him and he loves me.

***

After saying "Yes" to Noah, he stood up and kissed me. Then he tossed me over his shoulder and walked us directly to the bus. Then…he asked the driver politely to take us to the Las Vegas Marriage License Bureau, and we filled out the paperwork.

Our Song

Not what I was expecting, but, I suppose not everything in life can be a sexy scene, like in the books I enjoy reading.

Apparently, he really was thinking about asking me to marry him before I got that call from Kye and did the research on Vegas marriage laws. It makes me feel better knowing it wasn't as spur of the moment as I thought.

$102 and two signatures later, we had a marriage license. We made it back to the venue in just under an hour.

I love how accessible Vegas is. I also love being able to get cheese fries at 1a.m. I could stay here forever.

I secretly thought about "losing" our marriage license between the office and the chapel, but I'm convinced that was just my flight response talking.

I stared down at the certificate the whole drive back to the venue. It's tattooed on my mind now.

Clark County, Nevada
License of Marriage

Groom: Noah Austin Taylor
Bride: Quinn Elizabeth Finch
Date of Marriage: March 15th 2024
Date of Application: March 15th 2024
Application ID Number: 11112023

The show just ended at 1st Street Stage and we're all walking down to The Little Neon Chapel.

It's about a five minute walk from the venue and my thoughts are racing.

I think my biggest fear is ending up like my parents. Obviously it wasn't anyone's fault my mother got sick, and something like that was unavoidable.

I'm afraid of what happens if I do find the greatest love of my life and then lose them. Not even necessarily from dying.

I'm terrified to be so entirely soul-crushed from losing someone I love, that I can't function without liquor or chemical assistance.

I'm scared that I will lose myself if I give myself to someone else.

I run out of time to list my fears internally when I see the giant neon sign come into view.

Fitting.

"You ready for this, Quinny?" Roni asks, linking her arm to mine.

"I am equally prepared *and* unprepared for this."

"Well, you have about sixty seconds to figure that out. Why do you think you're unprepared?"

"Flat out?" I ask her.

This is something we've started to say or ask each other before absolutely word-dumping in the most raw and honest way possible.

"Flatter than my chest in eighth grade, shoot." She jokes.

"I'm scared of creating generational trauma by getting married. What if it doesn't work out? What if we grow to hate each other? I don't want to lose my best friend."

"Okay first, I know we're currently attending your pity party, but don't ever call anyone your best friend again, unless you're talking about me, of course. Second, do you want the truth, or should I bring out the cake?"

"You're such a *great* friend. I can always count on you to be so gentle." I say sarcastically. "But I guess my choice is the truth."

"Too bad, it was Red Velvet." She giggles. "You are an amazing person and you deserve good things to happen to you. Don't go putting new salt in old wounds. Noah loves you hard, man. He's really sweet and you seem happy together. One marriage is not all marriages. You're in control of every choice you make and even if you make a bad one, the next one always has a chance to be good."

"I feel like I haven't done anything to deserv-'' I begin to say, but she cuts me off.

"You deserve good things because you exist and that is enough." She says as we stop in front of the doors.

We both look at each other and smile. She really is the closest thing I have to a best friend right now. I didn't realize that before.

The boys are a few paces behind us, literally distracted by the pretty twinkling lights.

Ah, *men*, so simple sometimes.

"If you want to run, Quinn, I've got my sneakers on. Just say the word. But, as someone who wants to see you win in life, I think you should allow yourself the opportunity to see that you are *more* than deserving of love."

"Thank you, Roni. I love you." I hug her.

"I love you too." She says as the guys approach.

"Woah, I thought we were attending Noah and Q's wedding, not Roni and Q's," Sam jokes.

"Stop imagining us making out, freak." Roni laughs, bumping his shoulder.

"I wasn't imagining you making out *for your information*. I was imagining you taking off Quinn's-"

"I think this conversation is over!" Noah interjects. "Can I marry this woman now?" He asks.

He opens the front door and we all walk into the chapel. It's surprisingly church-like, neon lights and indoor graffiti aside. I called earlier and made an appointment for 11:45p.m.

They offer a surprising amount of packages ranging from $100-$1,000. I went right in the middle with the "Neon Sweethearts Package".

It includes music, a veil, up to six guests and any choice of character themed ministers.

They had your classic Elvis, then a couple more interesting options like Michael Jackson and Jesus Christ, they even had Death.

I went with what was clearly the best option. Lucky for me, Noah was too busy getting ready for the show. He said I could pick what I wanted and he would be happy with whatever I decided on. He was just happy to marry me.

Challenge accepted, Noah Taylor.

I'm now grinning ear to ear, knowing what is about to happen.

Once we are done filling out the remaining paperwork, we all walk into the chapel as a group. I stop halfway up the aisle and Noah looks at me.

Our Song

"I should probably go out there and come back in when the music starts, like a real wedding." I say.

"This *is* a real wedding, Quinn."

"I know that." I smile and start walking back the way I came.

When I turn to shut the doors and wait for the music to start, I see Roni is behind me.

"What are you doing?" I ask her.

"Walking you down the aisle." She smiles.

I feel tears start to threaten my eyes. I'm never this emotional, but today has given me whiplash.

"Let's do this thing." I smile, taking her hand in mine.

Not a minute after the doors shut do I hear my entrance song start to play. "Walk This Way" by Aerosmith is surprisingly beautiful on the piano. Roni starts laughing next to me.

"Only you." She's shaking her head when she opens the door for us.

Noah is standing at the end of the aisle waiting for me. He's smiling at me like it's the best day of his life. It gives me those butterflies you get on first dates. Like this is the "first day" for us all over again. But this is a different kind of first day. This is the first day of the rest of our lives.

Roni and I start walking and I am already regretting wearing these white high heels. I never wear heels, it usually only takes five minutes before I feel my heart beating in the souls of my feet and I'm done.

I sent one of our drivers, Celine, out to Walmart during the show when I realized I didn't have anything to wear.

Celine did exceptionally well given the way Noah is looking at me right now. I should tip her an extra fifty dollars when we're back on the bus.

I usually opt for black converse, black leggings and some type of band t-shirt. Definitely not flowy sundresses like the white one I'm wearing right now.

But Noah says he likes me in heels, so here I am. Walking down the aisle on my wedding day like a newborn gazelle.

I see Sam, Max and Lincoln all standing in the first row together, turned toward me and smiling. Sam is standing in the middle with his arms around the two of them. I feel Roni squeeze my hand tight.

I want to cry again. This time, I know for sure it's not because I'm scared or worried.

I'm excited, I'm in love. I feel empowered. I have earned this life, these friends and this family.

I make it to the front and Roni lets go of me before taking a seat next to the boys. Noah takes my hands in his and smiles at me.

"How are you feeling?" He asks in a whisper.

"Happy." I truly mean it, as I whisper back.

"Where's the minister?"

"Just wait for it." I smile.

I finish speaking just as the music cuts out and the lights in the chapel go low.

Suddenly, intense music starts playing and the wall behind us is lit up with a signal.

More specifically, The Bat Signal.

Our Song

The lights slowly come back up as a man in a full Batman suit somersaults down the aisle to the front of the room.

"This is what you picked!?" Noah exclaims.

"You said anything." I reply as we both start laughing.

I look over at the band and they're all laughing, too. Then, the lights come on and Batman coughs to clear his throat, taking a position behind Noah and I.

The band sits and we all quietly wait to hear just how good this Batman really is.

"Hello, friends, family and *citizens of Gotham*." He says, really emphasizing the Batman quote.

I choke down another laugh.

He sounds like 2005, *Batman Begins*, Christian Bale. But, he looks like *Batman VS. Superman*, Batman, Ben Affleck.

I can't believe I only paid $500 bucks for this.

"We have gathered here today to bring two people together in holy matrimony. Love is beautiful, but love can also be hard. *I know pain*, and with love sometimes comes pain. But what makes love work is *failing and getting back up*. Showing up for your person no matter the obstacle, time and time again.

"You either die a hero or live long enough to see yourself become the villain. So be a hero to your partner. Save them, cherish them and protect them.

"Do you, Noah, take Quinn to be your lawfully wedded wife?" He finally asks Noah.

Noah takes a minute to answer because his mouth is literally hanging open. I can't tell if he's regretting his words or having as much of a blast as I am.

This is gold.

"I absolutely do take Quinn Elizabeth Finch to be my lawfully wedded wife." He says, before placing a small kiss on the top of my left hand.

Then he lets go of it and slides a *fucking ring* out of his pocket. He puts it on my ring finger and now I'm the one in shock. It fits perfectly.

"Where did you get this, when did you…" I run out of words and find myself, maybe for the first time ever, speechless.

"I have my ways. I love you and *my wife* deserves a ring."

I'm melting where I stand.

I'm not confident that I can even feel my legs anymore. Is this real life? I could be wrong, but I think Batman just wiped away a tear.

I look down at the ring, a beautiful infinity silver band with a diamond in the middle shaped like a heart. I'm appreciating its sparkle when my vision goes blurry from more of my tears.

Noah wipes my cheeks as I turn my head to look over at Roni. She's smiling so big I can see her molars. Lincoln and Sam are still laughing together about the Bat-Minister.

Max is…*holy shit*, Maxwell Williams, "badass drummer of Compass" is bawling *like a baby*. Full-blown sprinklers. The kind where you need to use your shirt as a tissue. True shoulder shaking sobs.

When I stare at him a minute too long, everyone, Batman included, follows my eye line and sees I'm looking at Max.

We all grow silent for a minute before he realizes and looks at us.

"Fuck you guys, I love, love. Okay." He says, wiping away tears.

"Awww, Maxi-Pad, you sap," Sam says, pulling him into a side hug.

"Quinn," I hear Batman continue. "Do you take Noah to be your lawfully wedded husband?"

"I do." I say.

"*I am vengeance, I am the night, I am Batman!* I now pronounce you husband and wife."

Noah and I kiss each other with smiles still on our faces. Then his tongue finds its way in my mouth and as I'm about to lean in I hear, "*Batman and Robin Will Never Die*, and neither will your love!" Then the band and I watch in awe as Batman somersaults back down the aisle.

"What's next, Wife?" Noah asks.

"New Mexico, Husband."

Chapter 7
April 2024 - Lincoln

I'm shaking as I try not to throw up. My eyes are squeezed shut, and I can't convince myself to look over the edge.

When Quinn decided as Band Manager that we had to do one tourist activity together as a band in every city we performed in, I thought it was a great idea.

We have the extra cash now and it's cool to get to experience the cities we're playing in.

That was before this woman put me on a *fucking hot air ballon*.

The six of us and a pilot, or whatever you call this hell operator's title, are just casually standing in a basket 2,000 feet above the safe, solid ground of New Mexico.

I open my eyes and see everyone is all smiles. I, on the other hand, am clenching the side of the basket as if that will offer any type of stability to my uneasy stomach.

"Lincoln, are you doing alright?" Sam asks.

"Ask me again when we're on the ground." I smile lightly, trying not to look as terrified and nauseous as I actually am.

"You're doing great, sweetie!" Roni grabs my hand in a comforting gesture.

I look to my left and see Noah kissing Quinn, the sun's setting light peaks out between their lips. I want to hate Noah, but I can't.

Something in me just doesn't get a good vibe from him, but he's not a bad guy aside from the fact that we are just two different types of people *and* he married the only girl to ever make my heart beat. Not to be dramatic or anything.

He always wants to be the center of attention and occasionally gets loud when he drinks, but he makes Quinn happy and that's all I want for her.

If I was in this position a year ago, I might've been drunk right now. I'm proud of myself.

It's been surprisingly easy to keep myself distracted on the road. I've managed to keep my head clear and myself clean. Everyone besides Quinn drinks. It doesn't bother me like it did that first night we all hung out at Sally's. The temptations have mostly passed, but I still noticed every drink poured.

No one has out right asked me if I'm sober, but they *have* stopped asking if I want a beer. I appreciate the unspoken understanding we all have now.

I don't know if they can tell I don't partake because I'm in recovery after driving my life directly into the ground, or if they think I'm like Quinn and just don't like the taste.

Either way, the pressure of being asked if I want a drink is off and it's made things easier. I've grown a lot closer to everyone, but I'll tell them when I'm ready.

Maybe I'll tell Sam first. We seem to always be the last two people awake on our bus and never fail to have good conversations. He's been calling me his "replacement brother" for the tour and I'd be lying if I said it didn't make me feel good.

The success of the band has also proven to be a great distraction for my sobriety. The album has hit number twelve on the "Billboard Top 100" and four of our songs are in "The Top 25".

"Phases Of The Moon" at number six, "Heartbeats" at number twelve, "Catastrophe" at number seventeen, and "Saturday at Sally's" at number twenty-four.

According to what the label told Quinn yesterday, we have sold 250,000 copies of our record in the last nine weeks. Variety Magazine has even named us the *"ones to watch in 2024."*

We're steadily playing every Friday, Saturday and Sunday night. Sometimes, the occasional Thursday or Monday too. Supply, demand and all that.

The pattern has been two weeks in each state and then we're onto the next. We're selling out bigger venues at quicker speeds, too. Quinn's goal is to have us play almost all fifty states by the end of the year.

I love that I finally get to travel. Before moving to Nashville, I had never left the state of Arizona.

It's a crazy feeling when your dreams are no longer dreams, just memories of moments you actually lived.

"Oh fuck!" I hear Roni say next to me.

Our Song

I look to my left, where she's staring at Max vomiting over the side of the basket.

At least I wasn't the first.

Watching him puke is the final push my body needed to empty the contents of my own stomach. I take to the other side of the basket and bend over it, watching my lunch rain down on Albuquerque.

"I hope there aren't any people standing in the line of fire." Sam says, laughing.

"I think we need to land this, Sir." Quinn says to the pilot, looking like she might also vomit if she has to continue watching us.

"This was a great idea, Q-Tip! Let's do this again. No, I know! We should go skydiving next!" Sam says to her, in his lovingly sarcastic fashion.

"Fuck off, Denton." She fires back as she rolls her eyes.

"*We are family. I got all my sisters with me,*" Roni starts singing.

"Seriously, Roni?" Quinn snaps.

"*Get up everybody and sing,*" I try to sing through a shaky breath, lifting myself back over the side of the basket.

"Fuck yeah!" Roni says. Noah and Sam are laughing together now. Max still has his head over the edge.

"How am I responsible for you people?" Quinn scoffs, as we finally start to descend.

***

It's our last night playing Sandia Amphitheater. We've played three sold-out shows here this week.

We're on the last chorus of our closing song, "Deep End". I approach the edge of the stage and look down at the front row. I squint my eyes because I think I'm seeing things. When I look closer, I realize I'm not.

There's a beautiful girl wearing nothing but a black bra and denim shorts in the front row. She's holding up a sign that says "*I want to marry Lincoln Archer*." I can feel myself blushing .

Sam walks over to me, sees the same sign I do, and starts laughing.

Noah hits his final note, and the audience is screaming. I can feel the stage vibrating beneath my feet from the crowd jumping, demanding more. My skin feels electric.

We all make our way to the center of the stage where Noah is. In routine, we take a bow together arm in arm under the spotlight before the stage lights go down.

I'm never going to get sick of this feeling.

When we all get back to the buses, Roni and the guys decide to go to Cake Nightclub in the city. Ever since Vegas, Quinn has loosened up a bit and lets everyone be responsible for their own curfew. Before that, we all had strict orders to be back on the bus by midnight.

I can't tell if the loosening of reins is because she finally trusts we can all handle "tour life" or because she's done trying to wrangle us.

Our Song

Either way, I'm not disappointed because it leaves nights like this one, when it's just me and Quinn hanging back on the bus.

I go out with them sometimes, same with Quinn, but as someone who is not drunk, it can get exhausting being around drunk people. She gets that.

I also like to avoid hanging out at clubs specifically. That's where the pills are.

One might think Noah would be suspicious or weirded out that I hang out alone with his wife, but he doesn't look at me as a threat in the slightest. I try not to think about that too much.

While I think I'm closest to Sam, Quinn is the easiest to talk to. There's something about her calmness that makes me feel safe enough to say anything to her.

"Just you and me?" Quinn asks, walking into my bus holding her pink Snuggie.

Sam likes to refer to our bus as "The Bro Dome." For whatever reason, Max laughs like a small child every time Sam says it.

"Just you and me," I confirm. "The usual?"

"Yes please!" She says, taking up her spot on the recliner.

"Two Shirley Temples, coming right up!" I say as I get to work.

"The show went great tonight. The crowd was wild."

"Yeah, I know, it's kind of crazy how fast we're blowing up. There was a woman in the front row proposing to me tonight." I laugh, pouring Ginger Ale into two cups of ice.

"Oh my God, did you say yes?" She grins.

"Of course, we're running off to Vegas next weekend."

"Okay Link, don't knock it until you try it." She snickers.

I smile so hard my face hurts. I've never had a nickname before. I know that probably sounds like a stupid thing to get excited about.

It's something so personable and intimate it makes you feel like someone really cares about you. Like they're so excited to tell you something, they shorten your name to get the words out quicker.

"Touché." I say as I pass her a cup before taking my seat on the couch next to her.

"Any idea when they're going to be back?" She asks.

"Not a clue. I think Sam said some girl invited them there, so if I know Sam, at least last call."

Quinn made *many rules* at the beginning of the tour. Another rule is keeping safe spaces. With everyone's security and privacy in mind, no one was allowed on the buses unless they were band members or crew.

No one has had issues with that given we're all so driven to just play music and work hard. Now that we know we're doing well, everyone's a little more relaxed with things, but that rule remains.

"Can I ask you a question without offending you?" She asks, looking at me curiously.

"Depends." I reply.

"Why don't you drink? If you don't want to answer, I totally understand. I just noticed, you hang back a lot, and you know…don't ever drink. I want you to feel safe to tell me stuff and know you have friends here. I'm good at keeping things to myself, too."

"I appreciate that. I really do think I consider everyone here a friend. Especially you."

I think she blushes, but then she turns her head and starts looking out one of the busses windows.

"You never answered my question." She says to the glass.

"You noticed that?"

"I did, like I said, if you don't feel comfortable…"

"No, I do. I just…don't know where to start. I feel like my actions need context, so I don't seem like a bad person." I say.

"You're one of the kindest people. How could you think that about yourself?" She asks, turning back to me with a serious look on her face.

I drop my head and stare at the floor, afraid to look her in the eyes. I take a moment, thinking of what I'm about to admit to her.

"You don't know who I was before I moved to Nashville. Let's just say drinking…and other things…inhibited me from making good choices. So much so that I don't smoke, drink or do drugs anymore. I've been clean and sober for almost three years. I've only recently realized I'm really proud of myself for that." I feel like I've run out of air by the time I get it all out.

My head is still down when I see her purple manicured hand squeeze my knee.

"Thank you for telling me that, Lincoln." Her voice is soft and quiet, treating my truth with care.

I wish she'd call me Link again.

I dare to look up at her, and when I do, I feel a single tear fall down my right cheek. I jump back and sit up straight, quickly wiping it away. I know it's too late, though. She definitely saw that. She sits back in the recliner.

Her hand is gone now and I miss it.

Now that she's practically seen me cry, I wonder if she thinks I'm weak and that I'm not going to make it. Maybe she's thinking about auditioning a new guitarist right this second. I can't get a read on the thoughts behind her expression.

"You must think I'm so lame, crying like this," I say quietly.

"Feelings are normal Link. Only serial killers don't cry. It's good to know I haven't been hanging around the hash-slinging-slasher or whatever."

"SpongeBob, really?" I ask, a light laugh escaping me.

I love hearing her say it, *Link*.

"I know, I'm a delight. Bikini Bottom villains aside, I hope you don't feel embarrassed. Sometimes you just need to let it out. We can only keep so much in.

"I learned a while ago, you can hold onto something for a long time, but after a while, you have to realize it might be weighing you down and holding you back.

"Eventually you need to decide. Is *this thing* I'm dragging with me through life really worth it? Does *this thing* define who I am right now?

"It seems like this particular *thing* was who you were, not who you are. Yesterday doesn't matter when we're living today and we have tomorrow." She says.

"That should be a lyric." I think out loud.

"It is."

"By who?"

"Me." She says. I think she looks nervous now.

"You write?"

"I do. I used to do it all the time, but these days I don't really have time, running the band and all."

"You should make time for that. I'd love to hear a song sometime." I say, happy this conversation is moving away from me. Even happier she's sharing a new piece of herself with me.

"It was just one line. I don't really share what I write. I used to want to write songs, but being the manager, it's consuming. It's just a hobby at this point. My songs were never any good."

"Don't diminish yourself like that. Plus, if I have to be vulnerable in this friendship, so do you. I want to hear one sometime."

"Fine…sometime." She agrees.

I feel my heart doing that *stupid* beating thing again.

Chapter 8
April 2024 - Quinn

After New Mexico, the band did three nights at Coors Field in Denver, followed by two nights at The DCU Center in Aspen. Colorado was beautiful. Our first off day there was the last day of their ski season. I made us all go snow tubing.

I think it was the first one of my planned outings that everyone smiled and got along. It's nice when the children don't fight.

I tried to enjoy every last second of time before this morning, when our buses crossed the state line into South Dakota.

I never would've thought to book a stop in my hometown of Kimball. It's not exactly well known.

That was until my fifth grade music teacher, Mrs.Ford, reached out to me. Through an email, she expressed that the music program was suffering here and that the town didn't have money in their budget to keep it running. She heard that I was managing a successful band and thought I could help.

Our Song

I didn't think twice about my personal shit and told her we would come, free of charge, for one Monday night show.

This two-hour concert will hopefully raise enough money to keep the town's school music programs around for at least the next few years. I'm grateful for the power I wield and will use it wisely.

The band didn't question me when I told them we needed to play a charity concert. Everyone was down to help a good cause and trusted me enough to decide that this was.

One of the local farmers opened his field up for the town to host us. I believe she said they're having the band play on an eighteen wheeler flatbed in place of a stage. Very *"small town"* style.

While I'm happy about all those things, it's hard to ignore the other side of my feelings. It's been two years since I've been home or seen my dad.

We exchange thirty to ninety second phone calls on major holidays and birthdays. Except my last birthday…when he forgot to call me.

I often wonder if I am a bad daughter for walking away from him. For not doing more to help him. It wasn't for lack of trying, though. I did try…for *years.*

I had to walk away for myself. A child should never have to parent their parents, and that's exactly what was happening between us.

I don't know that he even misses me. If he does, he's never said it. It seems clear from the few phone calls he does answer that he's been drinking more since I left home.

I called him last week and left a voicemail on his answering machine telling him about the show and that I would leave two tickets for him at the front gate.

I don't know if he's going to show up tonight, but I have this stupid glimmer of hope he will.

***

The lights go down and the band is running off the stage. Everyone is all smiles, except me, but I try my best to hide it.

I went down to the front gate midway through their set to see if my dad grabbed the tickets I left.

They were still there.

The band heads straight to "The Bro Dome" bus to unwind while they wait for the field to clear out. The plan was for the whole band and myself to go down to my favorite townee spot, The Crazy Horse, later. I can't seem to move on from my own disappointment.

I knew it was likely he wouldn't show. I suppose any amount of hope, even a small one, is enough to hurt you when it's wasted.

Before I can think better of it or to tell anyone where I'm going, I stray from our group heading towards the buses. I start walking out of the field and down the street with the traffic of people leaving the concert.

It's less than two miles to my dad's house from here. The twenty minute walk does nothing but piss me off more.

Our Song

I am his only daughter. He was supposed to take care of me and protect me. But he gave up. Despite me trying and loving him, I needed him!

I'm shouting to no one inside my head.

He couldn't even show up for me one night? It's been over two years since he's seen his child and he can't even be bothered to show up two miles down the road?

The light from his front porch comes into view when I turn down the dirt driveway. His beat up GMC pickup is parked in front of the garage door.

He's home.

I grab the key under the doormat and let myself in. Everything looks the same as the day I left. The only difference is this place no longer feels like my home.

I don't know if it's the time and distance or the realization that this hasn't been a real home since my mom died eight years ago. Regardless, it feels like a fever dream I don't belong in.

I can hear the sound of the TV coming from the living room, reruns of *The Sopranos,* are playing on the screen. I can see the back of his head sticking up from the top of the recliner, still slowly balding. The table next to him is littered with empty whiskey glasses and bottles.

I cough, trying to announce my presence subtly, but he doesn't hear me over the TV.

"Dad." It's barely a whisper from my lips, "Dad. It's Quinn." I say louder this time.

I see him reach for the remote and wait as he pauses the TV.

"Quinn?" He says confused, getting up from his seat.

"Hi Dad, I'm home." I say, involuntary tears pooling in my eyes.

I barely recognize the man standing in front of me. My father feels just as much a stranger to me as the house did when I first walked in.

"You're back. How was school?" He asks.

"What?" I ask, confused.

"How was school today, Quinn?" He stumbles towards where I'm standing in the doorway of the living room.

I hear the clanking of cans clashing on the floor by his feet. He does his best to step around them, but it makes him lose what little balance he has.

I think he's about to fall over when he catches himself on a wall at the last minute. He stands up straight and I notice how dry and dull his skin looks. His eyes are bordered by dark caves that look like they might succumb to a landslide.

"How old do you think I am, Dad?" I ask in horror.

"Well…you just turned sixteen last week…wh-" He hiccups, "Why do I have to tell you how old you are? You're old enough to remember your age…" He's incoherent as he pulls me into an unwanted hug.

He smells like tobacco and his best friend, Jim. The odor feels like poison in my lungs. I start to cry, unsure of what to feel.

Sad, hurt, angry, devastated.

"Dad, I'm twenty-one," I say, pulling out of his reach and taking a step back.

"What…Why are you saying that, Quinn?"

"How much have you had to drink today?" I ask him. His eyes are bloodshot, struggling to stay completely open as he slurs his words.

"I just had one drink with my dinner."

"Dad, it's eleven-thirty at night. How many drinks have you had today? Are you doing this every day?" I get a little louder with each weighted question.

"I'm...I just lost track." He says, rubbing his eyes, leaning against the wall that just caught him. He can't even stand up by himself.

"Why are you like this?" I yell, "Why can't you be a *fucking father*? Why do you choose the liquor over me?"

"I don't, I-" He stammers.

"STOP LYING TO ME!" I don't even sound like myself anymore.

My throat feels tight and shaky. When I try to yell more words, none come out.

I want to scream but it feels like blankets of my sadness are smothering out the flames of my anger. I take a deep breath and I push through.

"Since the day we buried Mom, you've been nothing but a *disappointment*. She died, but I still needed *you*!"

"I lost my wife." He sounds like he wants to cry, finally participating in the same conversation as me.

"Has it ever occurred to you that I lost my mother *and* my father that day? I had to raise myself because you couldn't. I had to be strong for you *for years*! It was never enough, though.

"*I* was never enough for you to be sober, *I* was never enough for you to love me, *I* was never enough for you to just show up and be *my father!*"

"That's not how.-" He starts to say, but I cut him off again.

These last two years of half assed phone calls have made me curious of what it would be like to have a real conversation with him again. Not just the fake niceties we've been exchanging.

I guess I'm getting my answer, *a fucking Oppenheimer.*

"That's not, what?" I ask, even though I was the one who cut him off, "That's not how it was, *or* is it just not how you remember it? News flash, "*Dad*"." I say, actually doing air quotes around his title, "How do you expect to remember anything when you're consistently drowning your feelings in a bottle?"

We both stand in silence, staring at each other.

Designer and design.

Neither one of us moves, we just breathe in the musty air of this house.

It's a twisted standoff, straight faces and all. I clear my throat and decide that I need to end this visit.

"Thanks a lot for showing up tonight. I was really looking forward to you seeing how much better my life is now that you're no longer in it.

"I don't know why I thought it would make me feel good to see you show up for me, maybe even show you're proud of me. I'm realizing now, nothing I do will ever be good enough for you. The only way I could get you to love me is if I were Mom and I'm not."

I turn around and start walking for the front door. I'm begging in my head for him to stop me and apologize.

"Quinn…" He finally says.

I turn around, expecting for his expression to match the defeated tone of his voice, but there's nothing but anger there now.

"You will never be *half* the woman your mother was." He spits out like venom.

It feels like I was shot through my chest.

I'm going to be an open wound for the rest of my life.

I don't even know what to say to him, but I need to say it quickly. He doesn't deserve to see me cry more, or to see all the ways he affects me.

I say the first thing that comes to mind before turning around and slamming the door shut behind me.

"I hate you!"

Chapter 9
April 2024 - Lincoln

I'm laying in the tall grass of the field we just performed on. The owner was nice enough to let our buses park here for the night.

The charity show was such a great crowd, I'm still coming down from the adrenaline and they cleared out about two hours ago.

Everyone coming together for a good cause gave a different energy to it all. We were just there to play and have fun. It didn't feel transactional and rehearsed.

Now that I can dream bigger, I know I want to explore philanthropy in my time between albums.

If we get signed for more, of course.

I don't need much to be happy and I want to help kids like me.

This show inspired my first step. Like most bands, we have merch tables set up at every show. The t-shirt with just a big picture of me and my guitar has been selling out at every stop for whatever reason.

I asked Quinn to donate my portion of the merch profits for this month of tour stops to the Kimball Public Schools music program, anonymously.

I'm not paying for rent currently and everything I own is on this bus. I figured it was a good way to start.

I looked for her after the show to find out how much she raised, but I couldn't find her. The band went back to one of the buses for a drink.

As soon as the rest of the crowd left twenty minutes ago, they called an Uber to some bar Quinn mentioned at soundcheck.

I opted to hang back and just enjoy the quiet countryside. We're always playing in big cities. This view feels like a vacation. I'm almost drifting off into a peaceful sleep under the stars when I hear someone walking towards me.

I sit up and see Quinn walking through the grass towards the buses.

"Quinn, are you alright?" I stand up, accidentally scaring her.

"Holy shit, Link." She jumps back.

"Sorry, I didn't mean to scare you. Are you okay?"

"Ya, I'm good. Where's Noah?" She asks.

"He went with the band into town."

"Did he ask anyone where I was?" She's starting to look more angry than scared…is she also upset?

"I don't know. The band said they were going to that bar and I said I was hanging back. Maybe he did ask someone…"

"Don't lie to make me feel better." She says plopping down on the grass, where I was just laying.

"I'm not lying, but I do want to make you feel better. You seem…agitated."

I lay back down on the grass next to her. This reminds me of the night before we left for tour, looking at the stars together behind Sally's.

"What do you think about Noah?" She asks me.

This feels like a trap. What should I say?

"He's nice. I'm glad I get to work with him." I respond, trying to sound respectful and polite.

"Do you think he's been drinking more than he was before the tour? I know you didn't know him for more than a month before we left…"

"Hard to say. I guess I don't pay too close attention to people's drinking."

That was a lie.

I count every drink everyone gets to have.

Where is she going with this?

"Do you think he is drinking more?" I ask her.

"I don't know. I can't tell, but he's felt absent lately. I don't know if it's the drinking, the tour or maybe he's just outgrowing me." Her words are quiet. Like she doesn't want to admit that to anyone else.

I turn on my side to face her and she does the same thing.

"Does Noah's drinking bother *you*, because that is the only answer that matters." I say.

"I don't want to talk about sad things anymore." She changes the subject.

I know better than to test my limits and try to push her into talking about something she's clearly not ready to.

"Tell me something happy, then." I counter.

"What do you mean?" She laughs a little, and it makes me feel better. I hate to see her look sad.

"Just tell me anything that has ever made you happy. Just one thing."

"Hmmmm, that's kind of hard. Give me a second." She says, as she rolls onto her back again, looking back up at the stars. I follow her lead.

"Take your time, Win." I say, testing the nickname I decided I needed to give her in exchange for mine. I look over and see the corner of her mouth turn up. I think she likes it, but if she doesn't, she doesn't say so.

"Writing, I guess. It makes me happy."

"Why?" I ask her.

Quinn and I have spent a lot of nights alone, when everyone else goes out drinking, but it never really comes up. Now that I'm thinking about it, Quinn hasn't brought up her writing since New Mexico.

I still want to hear that song she promised me, but I have faith she'll show me when she's ready.

"It's a release, sometimes an escape. Do you ever look around and wonder what your life would be like if you could make choices, knowing their outcome?"

"I think everyone does." I reply.

"Well, song writing lets me write about choices *and* pick their outcomes. I get to go somewhere else, and be someone else."

"I can understand that, but, for what it's worth," I turn back on my side and prop my head up on my arm to look down at her. "I like *exactly* who you are."

She looks over to me and smiles. Under the moonlight, I notice dried streaks of black tears on her cheeks.

"Were you crying?" I ask, wearing a look of concern.

"It's your turn." She says.

"What?"

"Tell me something that makes you happy, Link."

"Tell me why you were crying first." I dare to push, still trying to sound gentle in my tone.

It's eating at me that something made her cry and I don't know what to do to fix it. I feel protective and I need to know who did this to her.

"Let's just look at the stars." She says, ending our conversation and looking back up at the sky.

"Okay, Win."

***

I wake up next morning to find the buses have rolled out of the field and are stopped at a rest-stop Gas Station/McDonalds combo on the side of the highway.

Most of the crew is grabbing breakfast before fueling up and heading out for a day of driving. Everyone on my bus is still sleeping when I get up for a coffee.

Our Song

I walk into the McDonald's entrance and see Quinn sitting by herself at a table against the front window. Her headphones are on and she's typing on her laptop. I really don't like how things ended last night.

We left a lot of things unsaid and just laid in silence until she finally went to bed. Then, I did the same.

I wish she felt like she could tell me things. I had a hard time sleeping, my brain fixed on what caused those tears.

I don't bother her and walk to the front counter to order my coffee. When I wait, I think more about last night. Maybe I should've just kept the conversation going and ignored what I saw.

I should have at least told her something that made me happy instead of pushing. Maybe the conversation would've naturally continued and then she might have opened up to me.

Why did I have to press her?

I grab a napkin and borrow a pen from the cashier, then write down my answer. I don't know if she'll even remember our conversation from last night. I want to give her a sign I'm here for her without being overbearing again. I want her to feel better and not so alone.

Before I can decide against it, I'm walking towards the door with my coffee. I place the napkin, writing side facing down, on her table. We have a brief moment of eye contact before I walk away, back towards the bus.

When I get out to the parking lot, I look over my shoulder and through the window to try and catch her reaction. She's smiling, looking down at the napkin where I wrote *"You."*

Chapter 10
May 2024 - Quinn

Of all the places I thought I would visit in New Jersey, the Atlantic City Police Department was definitely not one of them.

I'm sitting in a private room waiting for an officer to come tell me why the hell I'm probably bailing out every member of Compass at one o'clock in the goddamn morning.

I got a panicked call from Roni that they were *arrested* as my phone died. Apparently, I forgot to plug it in before I went to sleep. I didn't think twice before driving one of the buses over here.

The officer who brought me into this room was nice but also very unassuming, giving no hint of what exactly happened.

He just sat me down, placed a folder on the table and said someone would be right with me. That was *twenty minutes* ago. I'm half convinced they've forgotten about me.

Our Song

Twenty minutes, it turns out, is as long as it takes for me to decide to *also* break the law and peek at what's inside the ominous folder. I've justified that it's mostly likely information I'm going to get from the band, anyway.

I double check the door is still shut and slide the folder towards me. I lift it open enough to read it, but also just enough that I could still close it without anyone noticing the second I hear the door open.

Atlantic City Police Department
County of Atlantic, Department of Law
Onsite Report Summary

Officer: John Nolan, Badge Number:1996
Bodycam Audio Transcriber: Dexter Weston, Clerk ID:978

Call: Disturbance called from residence at 1095 Chandler Boulevard at approximately 12:20a.m. May 9th.
Officer John Nolan reported to the scene and began taking statements.

OFFICER NOLAN: One at a time, I'm going to need to hear exactly what happened. (GROUP BEGINS YELLING AT ONCE, UNABLE TO TRANSCRIBE AT THIS TIME) I said, one at a time!

VERONICA COOK: It's not even a big deal, dude. This prick deserves worse.

SAMUEL DENTON: Roni, stop. This is my fault. The guy that lives here is a prick, though.

LINCOLN ARCHER: Just tell him what happened Sam, this guy isn't seriously going to press charges.

SAMUEL DENTON: You see, Officer Nolan, it was really supposed to just be an innocent prank. I didn't know it would lead to this.

NOAH TAYLOR: Tell him about eighth grade, then he'll understand.

SAMUEL DENTON: Yes, eighth grade! Have you ever had a bully, sir? A true, shove you in your locker, monster. Because I have and he lives here. It started at the beginning of that year. He would take my lunch money, small stuff like that. Then it turned into me doing his homework or getting my head dunked into the toilets.

OFFICER NOLAN: Is this going somewhere?

Our Song

NOAH TAYLOR: Let him finish, dude!

LINCOLN ARCHER: Don't yell at a cop, Noah!

SAMUEL DENTON: Both of you, shut up! Yes, this is going somewhere. You see, it was almost our Formal Dance, the one before going off to highschool. And I was working up the nerve to ask out this girl, Dixie Swanson, a total babe on the track team. Somehow Evan Bulger, the asshole who lives here, my bully, found out when I planned on asking her to the dance. So Evan and a bunch of the guys from the basketball team got together and…

VERONICA COOK: They "Carried" him!

OFFICER NOLAN: They picked him up?

VERONICA COOK: No! Like the movie with the pig's blood being dumped on the girl, Carrie, at a prom.

OFFICER NOLAN: They dumped blood on you?

SAMUEL DENTON: I wish. I think that would have been less embarrassing, still gross, but less embarrassing. You know those big orange Gatorade cooler dispensers sports teams have? Well, they decided to take one and hide it in their locker room. Every day leading up to Friday, when I was going to ask Dixie out, they all...filled it.

So when school let out, and I started to head to the track field to find Dixie, they followed me. I had no idea. She looked up at me as I approached her. She looked so pretty that day. I was about fifteen feet away from her when out of nowhere the basketball team, with Evan as their leader, stormed me and dumped the cooler full of...urine...over my head before running away and laughing.

The thing that made this particularly awful wasn't just that it happened in front of Dixie, but that it happened in front of almost the entire school.

There were a lot of sports teams practicing on the field and a bunch of students just hanging out on the bleachers. Each one of them got a front row ticket to the worst day of my life.

After that they called me Smelly Sammy. They joked that I could never get the gross smell off of me. Kids wouldn't sit with me at lunch anymore, people would leave soap and deodorant in my locker, some even sprayed me with Febreze when I

walked down the hall. Obviously, Dixie wouldn't go to the formal with Smelly Sammy. The torment only stopped when my family moved to
Nashville that June because my dad got transferred. A fucking miracle.

OFFICER NOLAN: While all that does seem exceptionally cruel, I'm still not seeing how this connects to why I have all of you detained in zip ties on the curbside of his residence.

VERONICA COOK: Revenge! (SUSPECT HICCUPS)

SAMUEL DENTON: I know this might sound crazy, but we're all in a band and we're on tour. When I found out that one of our stops was in my hometown, Atlantic City, I thought it might be funny to get some harmless, but totally deserved…retribution.

OFFICER NOLAN: Retribution?

VERONICA COOK: He means revenge!

NOAH TAYLOR: Roni, stop talking!

SAMUEL DENTON: Roni's right, it's revenge. But here's the thing, I didn't know it was going to turn out like this. I figured it would be harmless. A dozen or two eggs, some rolls of toilet paper and a good time, you know?
The plan was for me to meet up with the rest of the band after getting drinks with some of my hometown friends. I had found out through social media Evan still lived here, so I texted everyone the address and time. I also told them to bring some eggs.

OFFICER NOLAN: But you weren't throwing eggs when I got here?

SAMUEL DENTON: No, I wasn't. I was running late. I got...distracted...by a woman at the bar as I was leaving to meet up with everyone. I can't pass up a beautiful woman officer. I lost track of time. One thing led to the next and we're in the back of her car making out in the parking lot of the bar.

OFFICER NOLAN: I'm going to need you to explain this a little quicker.

LINCOLN ARCHER: I think I can take over this piece. We all got here at twelve, just like Sam told us, only Sam didn't show. We waited for about fifteen minutes and after he didn't come and he wasn't answering his phone, we decided to go through with it…for the sake of our friend.

VERONICA COOK: We threw the eggs right at that fucker's door!

LINCOLN ARCHER: Yes…We did. Which I'm assuming is when Evan heard us and called you guys before coming out to yell at us himself.
We were about to run down the driveway and leave when a car started to pull up the drive and our exit was blocked. Then the car stopped, and a woman got out of the driver's side, and then…Sam got out of the passenger side.

MAXWELL WILLIAMS: He was about to fuck his mom, dude!

(SUSPECTS WILLIAMS AND COOK BOTH LAUGH SEVERAL MOMENTS)

(SUSPECTS TAYLOR, ARCHER AND DENTON BEGIN TO LAUGH AS WELL, SMALL WORDS ARE

EXCHANGED, UNABLE TO TRANSCRIBE OVER AT
THIS TIME)

SAMUEL DENTON: I didn't know it was his
mom, I swear! I just thought the universe
was helping me out tonight.

VERONICA COOK: Helping you fuck his mom!
(HICCUPS)

OFFICER NOLAN: So you folks decided to egg
this man's house without the man he
wronged even there. Then this man (POINTS
AT SUSPECT DENTON) pulled into the
driveway with Mrs. Bulger without
knowledge of who she was?

SAMUEL DENTON: Yes, Sir.

OFFICER NOLAN: Jesus Christ.

I shut the folder when I hear the door knob start to turn.
An officer wearing the name tag, "Nolan," walks in and takes a
seat.

"Hi, I'm officer John Nolan. You must be their
manager, Quinn Finch?" He extends his hand.

"Yes, nice to meet you." I shake his hand in return.

"I know Veronica called you. I assume you were looped in?"

"Yes." I say.

Not *technically* a lie, his folder did loop me in. I feel the need to play defense on behalf of the band. Being confident and knowledgeable might help.

"While Evan requested everyone be arrested at the scene, Mrs. Bulger seemed very understanding. She didn't want to press charges.

"We felt that given the disorientation of the members, we should put them in the drunk tank to sober up and have someone come get them."

"I'm sorry. Did you say they were all drunk?" I immediately panic, thinking about Link caving into peer pressure.

"Well, the one kid, Lincoln, said he was sober but what twenty-one year old rock star isn't drinking with his buddies." I breathe a sigh of relief and hold back a small laugh before he continues.

"I brought them back here to sober up and catch a ride home. However, they have officially been trespassed from the property on Chandler. Here's a copy of that paperwork." He slides some legal papers over to me that were tucked in the back of that folder.

"So, does this mean they're free to go?" I ask.

"Yes ma'am, just need you to sign this and I can bring them out to the front waiting area."

I sign whatever he hands me without reading it or thinking twice. I just want to get out of this room and make sure everyone is okay.

Once I'm done with the forms, he gets up and escorts me back to the front lobby. I only wait about a minute before everyone comes walking out of the door next to the front desk.

"Quinny!" Roni runs to me and hugs me tight. "I knew you'd come save us." I hug her back and decide to deal with my drunk children when they're sober in the morning.

"Come on, everyone, one of the buses is parked out front. Let's get some rest. We have a show tomorrow." I say.

Once I get everyone moving out the front door, I stop and grab Link's hand.

"Are you okay?" I ask, still worried the officer may have been right.

"I'm good, Win." He smiles at me and I know he's sober.

My heart feels warm. Ninety percent from the relief of knowing he's sober and ten percent because that damn nickname gives me a feeling I can't explain.

Chapter 11
May 2024 - Lincoln

I'm sitting in a chair in the green room assigned to us on the set of *Good Morning America.*

Quinn booked us the Monday morning, 9a.m. spot for an interview followed by a broadcasted four song performance in Central Park.

We've sold another 100,000 records this month and we're playing two nights at Madison Square Garden this weekend. We haven't sold out yet but everyone's hopeful after this morning's performance that we will.

Things on the road have been pretty calm. Prison really brought me closer to the band, even if we were only in their intoxication cell waiting to get picked up like kids from the principal's office.

When Quinn got us and her first reaction was to make sure I was okay, my heart committed to her.

I'm going to be one of those sad dudes that never moves on from the one he can't have. I just know it.

Since I slipped Quinn that note, we've kept things pretty casual and surface level in conversations.

She did, however, slip me a napkin-note this morning with my coffee that had *"Good Luck"* written in purple pen with a smiley face drawn underneath it.

My heart melted.

I appreciate that she replicated the same vessel by writing in on a napkin. The purple ink is a very Quinn touch. I tucked it in the hidden pocket inside my guitar case where it will live forever.

I'm thinking about the next napkin-note I'll write to her when a PA knocks on the door to call us to set.

They have us all sit in tall chairs, Noah and Sam centered in the two front ones. Roni, Max and I take the three seats behind them. I appreciate moments like this when Sam and Noah fight for attention. I'm not great with words, so letting them lead these things is easy.

The lights turn on us and a guy with a giant headset starts the countdown before the "Live" light above the cameras goes green.

"Good Morning America, I'm Robin Roberts and I am joined today by the band Compass."

"Thanks for having us, Robin." Noah says, making sure he's the first one to speak.

"So tell me, what has it been like for you guys? It's been exactly four months since your debut record, *Invisible Horizon* came out and you guys have already sold 300,000 copies of the album. That's pretty incredible."

"Yes, we've *all* worked so hard, *each* one of us," Sam says.

I can see him on one of the monitors facing us that he's grinning from ear to ear, looking right into the camera.

"I love to hear that. I'm sure it takes a village. What has been the best part about touring so far?"

"We work with some pretty amazing people," Roni says, "One of them being our manager, Quinn. She has us go on small adventures in each city as a band doing tourist things. It's a lot of fun."

"That sounds incredible. What's your favorite thing you've done so far?" Robin is clearly asking Roni, but of course Noah has to take back some of the focus.

"Well, *my wife* Quinn, our manager," he says, like he's taking credit for her, "she is such a good planner. We all had a great time in New Mexico on a hot-air balloon. Isn't that right, Max?" Noah laughs.

I can't tell if he's trying to be funny or just a dick. I'm distracted, trying to decipher his tone when I hear my name and panic because that's all I heard.

"What?" I ask.

"I said, what's it like being the youngest member of a rising band, Lincoln?" Robin asks, *apparently*, for the second time.

No one ever asks me things, *shit.* I'm panicking and I'm certain it shows.

I guess the good part about being the youngest is that most people assume I don't have a lot to say. Or, that I don't have enough life experience to be interesting yet.

If they only knew.

"It's awesome. I'm living my dream and I'm honored to do it alongside such great people." I can feel the sweat rolling down my back.

I see Quinn smiling near one of the cameras, throwing a double thumbs-up at me.

I take a relieving breath and look at myself on the monitor to make sure I'm not smiling too much now, except it's not my giant grin at Quinn I notice first. It's Noah's face and he looks *mad.*

Of course he's mad. Someone asked me a direct question and not him. I feel sorry for his need to be in the light like this. I think it speaks to his childhood. From what Quinn's told me his parents are rich in money, not love.

"What is your favorite song to play?" Robin asks the group.

"Let It Ride!" Sam answers, taking all the camera's attention again.

The rest of the interview goes smoothly in the sense that I'm not called upon to speak again. Noah also seems a bit more relaxed now that he got more air time.

We have about thirty minutes to make it to the stage. Everyone is getting their makeup touched up in the hallway before we walk out the side door and take a quick ride to the set up in Central Park.

I notice Quinn and Noah lingering a few feet behind us, arguing. He looks pissed and his hands are moving around sharply as he speaks to her. Whatever they're talking about, he's angry, and she seems unbothered.

I wonder if they do this frequently based on how unphased she seems by his behavior. I don't know what it's like on their bus, but I have noticed Roni sleep on ours a few times.

Our Song

I always assumed it was to give them privacy for…activities.

I'm curious now if it's ever because they fight. Roni is such a loyal friend to Quinn she'd never tell.

Noah walks back towards us and I turn to make it less obvious I was just watching them. I can't help but notice the sadness in Quinn's eyes, she looks so tired.

Noah brushes past me to get to the door and be the first to walk outside.

"Hey, you okay?" I ask Quinn as she approaches.

"Yeah, it's nothing."

"Okay." I say, learning my lesson not to push. We stand next to each other in silence for a moment.

"Sometimes I wonder what it would be like to be normal again." She says.

"Sounds boring." I respond, which pulls a laugh from her.

The door is opening, and the band begins walking out. Once Noah has cleared the exit I turn to Quinn and hug her tight.

"You're an amazing person." I say into her hair. It smells like strawberries.

She hugs me back even tighter. Letting her go feels like cutting off a piece of myself.

"Thank you." She says before I walk out the door.

***

Performing in Central Park on GMA will definitely be one of the biggest highlights of this tour for me. We played "Phases of the Moon", "Catastrophe", "Embark" and "Red Light."

By Wednesday, both of our shows at Madison Square Garden had sold out.

"Phases of the Moon" took the number three spot on the "Billboard's Top 100" that morning.

We just finished our second show at Madison Square Garden and I have an overwhelming sense of accomplishment. I'm on cloud nine and even said yes when Sam asked if I wanted to go to a club called Mission with everyone after the show.

I haven't been in a club since it was illegal for me to be in a club. Something about being underage and doing things you're not supposed to do gave me an addictive dose of adrenaline. Evidently, playing a sold out arena gives me that same natural high. I'm confident that I can handle being here though, I feel invincible.

Mission is like every club I've ever been to. Giant bars on both sides, a huge dance floor in the middle and a DJ set up in the back. By the time we get through the doors, the place is packed. Quinn managed to reserve us a booth in the VIP section. "Our name is starting to mean something." She said on the way over here.

I bob my head to the music and watch as Roni and Quinn dance it out on the floor. Sam, Noah, Max and I are all seated together in a round booth upholstered in tufted green velvet.

Our Song

There's a few groupies and crew members hanging around us, mostly talking to the other guys. My attention is too focused on making sure no one is bothering the girls when they dance.

I know Roni could probably unalive someone given the proper motivation but, it makes me feel better knowing myself they're safe.

Noah's busy talking up the redhead sitting on Sam's left leg. Sam's occupied talking to the brunette on his right leg.

Max is asking one of the crew members about the logistics of a lifted drum kit.

The night continues smoothly. I make small talk and people-watch while I sip down sodas with lime. It's almost 1a.m. when I decide I'm going to Uber back to the buses.

Clubs are open late in NYC and I have a feeling everyone will be here until close at 3a.m. Before I send a ride request, I decide to hit the men's room.

When I open the door, I see Sam and Noah bent over the sinks. They quickly turn to face me, trying to cover up whatever they're doing.

"I told you to watch the door, dude." Sam says to Noah, he sounds annoyed.

"Relax, it's just Lincoln. He's not going to say anything. *Right, Lincoln?*" He asks, taking a step towards me.

That's when I see what they are trying to hide. Three perfectly formed lines of cocaine laid out on the black marble countertop.

That's enough for each of us, suggests the cursed voice in my head.

"I didn't see anything," I say, before turning around and walking out of the bathroom as fast as I can. My pulse is racing from the fight within me, to not turn around.

I'm racing out of the club, weaving between people dancing. I accidentally bump shoulders with a few as I'm zooming out.

I try to apologize quickly and keep moving. I find a side door that leads me into a dark alley lined with dumpsters.

I step out and turn right when I see a street light illuminating the main road at the end and start walking towards it. I need to get the fuck away from this place.

Now.

Part of what has made being sober easy is not being directly exposed to substances. The drinking is obviously always there, but for me it's less enticing and far less addictive than the drugs ever were. I had no idea they did cocaine.

When did that start?

Seeing the coke right in front of me like that…The moment I saw it my first thought was to do it, *not run.*

That realization crushes me.

I no longer feel confident in myself. It's easy to assume you're going to say no if anyone ever offers you drugs again, until it happens or almost happens, I suppose. They didn't have to ask though. I instantly knew I wanted it.

I can't stop replaying that sixty second interaction. If I stood there long enough for them to ask if I wanted a bump, I would've said yes.

I might have even asked them for one if they took too long to offer. Recognizing that makes me feel weak.

"Link, wait up!" I hear Quinn's voice in the distance behind me.

I turn and see her running down the alley. She stops me in front of one of the dumpsters.

"Where are you going?" She asks. It's hard to see her face in this light, but I think she looks worried.

"Back to the bus."

"Are you okay?"

"I'm good."

"You're clearly not good. Don't lie to me." She pleads.

I'm so frustrated with myself and about the last five minutes. That's how I justify being a dick to her.

"Why should I tell you? You never tell me anything?"

"It's complicated." She says.

"Are we real friends or not, Quinn? You say we can talk about anything, but the second we start to talk about hard things, you say nothing. We used to have *real* conversations, but ever since that night in South Dakota you've shut me out. Why should I tell you anything?" I immediately regret my words.

"You're right. Ask me anything and I'll answer, but then you have to tell me what's wrong. Deal?" She proposes.

It bothers me that she's not phased by my demeanor. I feel dirty for speaking like that to her.

"Fine. What were you and Noah arguing about before we performed at GMA?" I ask her.

I see her shoulders shift and she walks us further away from the door as if someone might hear us. We're nearly to the corner of the building, just before the streetlights, when she leans against the brick wall.

"We were fighting about you." She says.

"Yeah, I figured."

"How so?"

"It was pretty obvious. Noah was pissed they asked me a direct question and not him during the interview. I don't know why he needs to be the center of attention at all times."

"You think you know everything, don't you?"

"Was that not why?" I ask, confused.

"No." She shakes her head.

"Then why? What did I do?"

"It's nothing you did. It's what *I* did. Noah wasn't a huge fan of me giving you a smile and thumbs up after you answered that question. He's just sensitive sometimes." She says, brushing it off.

I'm actually shocked. Was he seriously mad about that?

"But you're our manager. Your job is to encourage us and be supportive."

"That's not how he sees it. He said, '*Other people saw, and that makes me seem like a fool, seeing my girl smiling at another guy like that on national television.*'

"Over a smile? You were behind the camera. Who could even see you?" I ask her.

"Yes, I know. Now it's your turn. What's wrong?"

I'm still processing what she just told me, so I take a minute before answering.

I thought Noah was just jealous that I took up too much of his spotlight. He was mad at Quinn for *smiling* at me?

I can't help but feel bad for her, then I feel a little guilty.

I wonder if it wasn't just her smile that made him mad. I wonder if he noticed how I smiled back at her with my heart on my sleeve.

"I walked into the bathroom. I saw some people doing coke, and it was very…tempting."

I opt out of telling her exactly *who* I saw doing the coke. I'm not sure about her stance on drugs, but based on Sam's reaction to me catching them, I'd say she'd be pretty upset.

While I don't particularly care if she were to get mad at Noah about it, I care about Sam and, as his friend, I chose not to disclose names. That's not the important part of why I'm a wreck right now.

"Did you…" She trails off.

"No, I ran away, like a scared little kid. That's what you've caught me in the act of doing, running away like a child."

"I'm proud of you." She says, grabbing my hand.

"My first thought was to ask for a line, Win." I squeeze my hand tight around hers.

"But you didn't, and that's what matters. You're strong."

"Thanks." I say, half accepting her words.

I truly believe, she believes, I'm strong. I'm not, though. I feel like a fraud.

"I need to get back to the bus. Do you want to catch a ride with me?" I ask her.

"I probably shouldn't, Noah's still…" She gets quiet.

"Don't worry about it. I'll see you in the morning." I let go of her hand.

Instinctively, I want to hug her, but I don't allow myself the reward that would be smelling her shampoo again.

I walk away and don't look back.

Chapter 12
June 2024 - Quinn

Kye called me on the bus ride to Boston last night and let me know that the band's tour has been extended to November. When I called a band meeting this morning, everyone was thrilled with the news.

What's more exciting is that the label has agreed to pay for hotel rooms in cities we play more than one night in.

"We get to sleep in real beds!" I said ecstatically.

"We get to use real plumbing?!" Sam asked with the same level of enthusiasm.

It's been almost six months since the record's release and we have officially hit Gold Status with 500,000 copies sold. I think our spot on GMA really helped.

I'm working to get the band more air time. Hopefully more exposure like that will sell even more records and keep our momentum going.

Looking for more TV opportunities has also allowed me to stay busy in our down time between shows. I can't help but notice things between Noah and I seem to get more tense as our success rises. I think it's just a lot of stress for both of us.

I try to keep myself as collected as possible when we argue. He has a lot of pressure on him and I understand that. Letting him just get it all out is the best option. He'll yell or say whatever he needs to, then once he's calmed down, we're fine.

That night with my dad in South Dakota, Noah and I had our first real fight as a married couple. I was pissed he didn't look for me or call me before going out to the bar. When he rolled back in around 2a.m. I was still awake on the bus, waiting to give him a piece of my mind.

Roni went and slept with the guys while Noah and I screamed at each other until we ran out of energy. He slept on the couch and I apologized to him the next morning.

I had convinced myself that I started it and was really just upset because of everything else going on with my dad. It wasn't actually *that* big of a big deal he went to a bar without checking in with me.

Noah said he forgave me and outside of our normal bickering we were pretty calm. That was until New Jersey. On the way out of the police station that night, Noah saw me hang back and briefly talk to Link.

When we got back on our bus, he asked what our "secret conversation" was about.

I said it was nothing, because Link still hasn't told anyone else he's sober yet and it is definitely not my place to share that. That's when he accused me of being unfaithful.

I finally felt myself starting to get mad, breaking free of the chains of numbness I've binded myself to. Part of me also wanted to laugh, but I knew that would only piss him off more.

Instead, I took a deep breath and told him I've always been faithful and that I was sorry if I gave him that indication.

I learned in that particular fight that he cooled down quicker when I didn't fight him back at all.

Plus, if I'm being completely honest, I do have a small, near non-existent feeling for Link.

I keep telling myself that it's because I see the same hurt in him that I have and that's why he makes me feel less alone. Of course, feeling seen makes you feel good. But that doesn't qualify as a reason to step out on my marriage.

Noah's the love of my life. Sometimes, he struggles to process his emotions and Link just happens to deeply understand mine.

It's no one's fault.

I've also noticed Noah is more frequently agitated when he drinks heavily, but I haven't quite figured out how to unpack that yet, or if I even want to.

Finally, we had our spat at GMA, but I think that was the easiest one yet. I just bit my tongue and by the time he got off stage, everything was fine. In fact, everything's been fine since then. I know it was only last week, but still, things are really good right now.

We've had a great week and the entire band is in high spirits this morning. We have two sold-out shows at the TD Garden in Boston this weekend.

I'm currently making us all go on something called a "Duck Tour". We all just got on this bus-boat looking vehicle *thing* that's supposedly able to drive on land *and* water.

My skepticism was enough to purchase us tickets.

When I called to make the reservation, I tried my new trick of name dropping and like magic, they were able to secure an entire boat for the band and crew, for free…in exchange for a mention on our Instagram account. So *pretty much* free.

I'm not entirely sure why there are so many ducks in Boston or why they're so popular that they get their own tour, but I guess I'm about to find out.

"Welcome ladies and gentlemen! My names Tony and I'll be *yah* tour guide." Tony says with an exceptionally thick accent.

I thought the movies were just dramatic, but this guy sounds like Mark Walhberg.

"We *ah gonnah* drive through this city's best streets and *rivahs* today. Now, as I'm sure you already know, this is the TD *Gahden…*"

Tony continues on telling us about the rich history of Boston and all the sites as we pass them. I'm only half listening to his spiel, too busy enjoying this perfect day of sunshine.

This "amphibious landing vehicle", as Tony called it, has a roof but no glass where the windows or windshields should be so it's completely open. Inside are school bus style bench seats.

The warm breeze and bustling city has a certain charm that, when mixed together, almost feels cozy.

That is until I hear someone lay on their horn behind us and yell several profanities before speeding past us.

"That's just Mikey." Tony says like that is an informative explanation, then goes right back to telling us about Faneuil Hall.

Our Song

We see sites like The State House, New England Aquarium, Quincy Market and a very tall building called Prudential Tower.

After about thirty minutes of sightseeing landmarks, we approach a boat ramp tucked under the Zakim Bridge.

"No fucking way this thing swims." Says Sam.

"They wouldn't be in business if it didn't float, Sam," Replies Noah.

"Who knows, maybe Quinny just signed us up for some scam where they lure us out to the water and rob us before making us swim back to shore." Roni chimes in.

"Okay, you're watching *way* too much Dateline." I say, laughing at Roni's thought process.

"What are *you* laughing about?" Sam says, looking at Max.

Max's laughs are rare, so I'm confused about why he's laughing now. This is definitely *not* funny enough to warrant a laugh from him.

I look around to see what I missed, but all I'm met with are other confused looks.

"Because…" Max can't even get the next word out before he laughs loudly again. His whole body is shaking in the seat.

Now he has the attention of the whole crew and Tony.

"What's going on?" Tony asks into his microphone.

"I finally realized what I want to be when I grow up." Max manages to get out, still in hysterics.

"What?" Roni asks.

"A *conDUCKtor*." He finally says, falling onto his side, laughing in the bench seat.

There's a pause while everyone debates if that's the funniest or lamest joke they've ever heard. A sudden eruption of laughter pierces the silence as the boat starts to roll into the Charles River.

Tony does his best to recover from the best joke I think he's ever heard in his career, then continues the tour.

"We're floating!" Sam exclaims in relief.

I snag a few cellphone pictures of the sites from where I sit next to Noah. His arm is around me and I lean back into his chest.

"I love you." I say.

"You too, Quinn." He says, placing a small peck on my cheek before he goes back to listening to Tony.

I try to take a few good candid photos of the band sitting in the boat for that Instagram post. I snap a quick selfie with Noah. Then I get a good one of Roni and Sam laughing at either something Tony said or how Tony said something.

I attempt to get one of Max smiling, but the chances of that happening twice in the same day are slim.

I turn around and see Link by himself at the back of the boat, looking out the window. He seems at peace, sitting in a stoic pose with his arms crossed against his chest. He looks like he should be a painting in a museum.

I lift my phone and get a quick photo of him. It's a little blurry from the small waves under the boat, so I try to snap another, but when I do, Link looks over and notices what I'm doing.

He's aware I take care of our social media, so he knows I'm not just being a creep by taking photos of him. I half expect him to look annoyed at me for interrupting his quiet moment.

That's when he laughs and sticks his middle finger up at me. I laugh and snap a picture.

"Post that one." He mouths to me.

I roll my eyes and slide back down in the seat before I get myself into trouble.

***

It's Saturday night, and the band is towards the end of their set. I've been busy doing some meetings for our upcoming west coast shows, so that means I've been in California time all day. I'm excited I get to see at least a little of their performance.

The crowd is loud, and the stage is shaking from everyone's excitement. I look out and see Max dripping sweat, drumming out his soul.

Roni and Sam are leaning on each other, back to back, playing their guitars. Link's head is tilted back with his eyes closed completely in the zone. Noah is walking around the stage with the mic, singing to sections of the audience.

He comes close to where I am, on stage left, when I notice it.

Noah's not wearing his wedding ring…again.

About three stops ago, I noticed more and more frequently Noah wasn't wearing his ring when he's on stage.

It didn't bother me at first. He has enough to remember before performing a two-hour concert. I explained it away easily. He was just being forgetful.

Then last week, when he didn't wear it again, *and* went out of his way to walk down to the barricade to sign a girl's chest, I was a little annoyed.

I haven't said a word because he's a rock star and I know that this is all part of his stage persona. I'm confident that he would never try to hurt me, but I don't think it's healthy for me to hold in these particular feelings. Lord knows Noah doesn't hold in any of his.

When the band finishes their set, Noah and I head up to our room in the CitizenM Hotel. It's conveniently attached to the arena, so it only takes us a few minutes to get to the elevator.

Everyone else headed straight to a place literally called The Greatest Bar. I asked Noah to come back upstairs with me before going out.

I get the impression he thinks we're going back to the room for something much more exciting when he sticks his hand up my dress the second we're alone.

It's tempting to give in, just say forget it and let his plans take over mine.

I'm saved when the elevator door opens to our floor. I walk ahead of him, trying to keep a bit of a distance between us until we get to the door, in case he distracts me again.

I swipe the room's key card and before I can decide how I'm going to start this conversation, I see Noah walk to the mini bar next to our bed and pour a drink.

I realize I need to start talking before the liquor takes over or we might just end up yelling at each other all night.

"Can we talk?" I ask, sheepishly.

"Well, that doesn't sound good." He says, taking a seat on the end of the bed.

I choose to stand in front of him, leaning against the dresser. I need to be face to face with him for this discussion. I think if I look him in the eyes, I'll be able to tell if he's lying to me.

"It's not bad. It's really just a question I guess…I've noticed lately…"

I have a hard time getting the words out. He's looking at me with an intense stare, only breaking it to sip his drink.

"Why didn't you wear your ring on stage tonight?" I finally ask.

"Must've forgotten." He says nonchalantly.

"Well, I thought that too, but tonight isn't the first night I've noticed you didn't wear it." I say calmly.

The last thing I need is for Noah to think I'm attacking him. I just want to ask if it's intentional and express my discomfort with it. Even if it's as simple as he's forgetful and just needs to be more mindful, I'm confident we can talk this out like adults.

"What are you talking about?" He asks, visibly frustrated.

"I noticed the last few stops you've forgotten to wear your ring a handful of times." I explain.

"So what, you think I'm doing it for the ladies? Because *newsflash* Quinn, I could fuck anyone I want. I'm *famous,* but I don't." He snaps.

Ouch…

"Okay, woah. There's no reason to say uncalled for shit and get mad. I'm just trying to get on the same page so we can move forward."

"*The same page?* So what, I don't wear my ring sometimes. It's not the end of the world, it's a ring." He shouts.

"Yes, it's a ring, but it means something to me. To *me*, it's important. I'd just feel better if you would wear it, that's all."

"Maybe you should work on being less insecure so I don't have to worry about fucking jewelry." He yells at me, standing up from the bed.

I can smell the liquor on him and it's *strong*.

When did he really start drinking today?

"Why are you being so cruel?" I can feel tears burning my eyes as I ask.

"I'm not cruel, Quinn, you're being dramatic."

"You're the one being dramatic!" I yell at him, my frustration near boiling over.

"It's a fucking ring, Quinn, get over yourself." He barks as he turns to walk away from me.

Now I'm pissed.

I grab his arm and start to pull it to turn him around and scream back like I deserve to.

That's when I feel the impact.

My face is stinging like someone just threaded a million needles through my skin.

I hear ringing in my left ear. I raise my hand and my face, but it's numb to my touch.

Did he just slap me?

Our Song

I feel tears rolling down my face, but I'm silent. Noah is silent. He looks confused, like he wasn't the one who just hit me.

His stare moves down at his shaking hand and the realization of what he just did seems to hit him like a freight train.

He steps forward to reach for me, but I back up.

"I'm *so* sorry, Quinn.." He whispers.

He tries to step towards me again, but I take another, much larger, step back.

Out of his reach.

Then another.

"Quinn, I didn't…I didn't mean to…" He has tears in his eyes now.

I'm speechless. I don't know if there's a combination of words that could properly convey how *not okay* I am right now.

My hand is still on my face when I turn to my right and see my reflection. The body length mirror hung on the wall is filled with the image of a woman I don't recognize.

I look weak and pathetic.

Black mascara is running down my face, my left cheek red like it's sunburned.

The tears sting my skin as they fall. I turn towards the door because I can't bear to look at myself like this and I certainly can't look back at him.

I grab my purse off the wall hook and walk out of our room.

As soon as the door shuts behind me, I start sprinting down the hall. I don't think Noah would chase me, but I need to get out of this place and *fast*.

I run past the elevators and take the stairs down. Thankfully we're only on the seventh floor but I'm still winded by the time I make it down to the main level. I take a few deep breaths before I open the door.

I make myself walk slowly through the lobby and out to the street, trying not to make a scene. I turn left without a clue of where I'm going, but I keep moving.

There's people everywhere I look.

I pace quickly, brushing by everyone until I see a side street that looks less busy than the one I'm on, so I turn down it.

There are a few little shops that are closed at this hour, an ATM stop and a small bar called "Valenti's".

Looking through the window, I see they have some sort of live music, so I walk in. It's loud and packed, the perfect place to hide from my life.

I walk up to the bar and take the last open seat. The bartender comes over to me with a smile.

"What can I get, *yah*?" She asks.

"Give me a whiskey, double."

Chapter 13
June 2024 - Lincoln

"I win, bitches!" Roni yells at me and Sam.

We're all playing Skee-Ball in the back of The Greatest Bar. I think all bars should have stuff like this. It makes the space enjoyable for people like me who don't drink.

"Fuck off, you cheated!" Sam fires at Roni.

"How?" She looks like she might swing.

"I don't know, witchcraft?"

"You're just a fragile boy, Sammy. It's not your fault that you weren't hugged enough as a kid." She jokes.

"Okay you two, let's go back to our table. There's other people waiting to play." I say in an attempt to de-escalate the situation.

"Fine, but we're having a rematch before we leave." Sam says.

"You're on." Roni agrees.

We make our way back to where Max is sitting at our booth and start talking about the show. Playing at TD Garden was insane. There's such good energy in this city.

I'm having a great night up until I see Noah walk in. He looks distraught. I can't tell if he's angry or upset. I don't know that I've ever seen him be the latter.

"Sam, can you come to the bathroom with me?" Noah asks him when he approaches, not acknowledging anyone else at the table.

"Uh, sure?" Sam says cautiously.

Noah turns and starts a fast-paced walk to the men's bathroom.

"Come with me," Sam says.

I expect him to be saying it to Max or Roni, but when I look up he's staring back at me.

"Why me?" I ask.

"Because Max is emotionally unavailable and Roni has a vagina." He says.

"But he only asked for you." I argue.

"Yeah and he seems sad and Sad Noah is *a lot*. So please don't make me console him alone."

"Fine."

Against my better judgment, I get up.

I follow Sam into the bathroom where Noah is already waiting, leaning against the counter.

"What is *he* doing here?" Noah asks when he sees me enter behind Sam.

"Moral support Noah, we're not the enemy. What's wrong?" Sam asks him directly.

"I'm just having a bad night." He says, looking at the tile floor.

It's when he says this I realize Quinn wasn't with him when he got here. If I had to guess they got into one of the fights they think no one notices.

I hope she's okay.

"Well, maybe you could be a little more specific and we could figure out the best way to help you." Sam says gently.

"I…I…I need a line. Do you have anything?" Noah asks Sam.

I've thought about the club night in New York every day since it happened. I wondered if it was a one-time thing or if it was a fresh habit, picked up in our new lifestyle.

I started to question if there have been drugs around me the whole time and I somehow wasn't noticing.

Fuck me.

I need to get out of here *now*. I can't leave without looking like an unsupportive dick, though. I don't need to make him hate me more than he already does.

But, I also can't relapse and still be a successful musician.

"I think it's better if I give you two some privacy." I try to say as politely as I can as I unlock the door and leave.

I don't linger long enough to see their faces, but I'm sure after a few drinks they'll forget this even happened.

I'm about to walk back to the table, where I see Roni and Max laughing about something on Roni's phone, but I stop.

I don't think I can be around Noah and Sam, knowing that they're doing that right now.

They'll make it look too fun.

I leave without thinking twice. I calmly walk outside, unlike the first time I was around it when I all but ran in a full sprint.

Maybe not actually seeing it makes it easier to walk away this time.

The night is warm and humid when I exit the bar. The foot traffic in the city is lighter this time of night. I contemplate going to my room, but I can't just sit at the hotel. I need to be distracted. I need to do something.

I walk further down the road to find anything to keep me busy. It's only 12:30a.m. so places are still open for at least another two hours. There has to be something to do.

I take a few turns down the side streets when I hear the clashing of symbols and a roar of applause. I follow the noise to find a little dive bar with live music.

Perfect.

The moment I open the door, the AC feels like a kiss of relief on my skin. The band on stage appears to be doing covers of eighties rock.

I hear them start to play "Highway Star" by Deep Purple when I take a seat at the bar.

The temptation to drink is nonexistent when I have a craving for something much stronger. I order a soda with lime from the bartender and turn around to watch the band.

They're absolutely killing it and the crowd loves them. It reminds me of when we played at Sally's back in Nashville. I smile at the memory as I turn to take a sip of my drink.

That's when I see Quinn at the other end of the bar.

She doesn't see me, though.

Her focus is fixed on the band, but it doesn't look like she's actually watching them.

She looks sad.

Our Song

I can see it in the way her shoulders are sagged and her eyes are a little puffy, like she's been crying.

I immediately devise a plan to make her smile. I wave over the bartender and borrow a pen. I write on a bar napkin and ask her to deliver it to Quinn.

She smiles at me with a small amount of pity. I think she's under the impression I wrote down my phone number.

Quinn's clearly out of my league, so I can understand her train of thought.

The bartender gives Quinn the napkin anyway and I watch her read it, then look up at the bartender with confusion. Then the bartender points to me.

Quinn's frown shifts into an infectious smile that makes my heart feel like it's on fire. I grab my drink and move across the room, taking a seat next to her on the other side.

"Seriously? 'If you were a booger, I'd pick you first'. Where did you learn that one, the third grade?" She laughs, reading my napkin-note back to me.

"I thought it would make you smile. Seems like lame jokes make you laugh." I say.

Now that I'm closer to her, I notice something's not right here.

I can smell whiskey and I think it's coming from Quinn. I look down at the bar and my suspicions are confirmed when I see a short glass with a sip of brown liquor left in it.

Quinn follows my eyeline and sees what I noticed.

"It's been a rough night." She states before swigging back the rest of her drink.

Her words aren't exactly slurred, but she doesn't sound like herself either. I want to ask how many she's had, but that's definitely rude.

"When did you get here?" I ask instead.

"About three drinks ago." She replies, answering my true question.

"Are you okay, Win?"

"I love that, by the way, *Win*. Noah never calls me anything but Quinn. It feels like I'm just playing a character sometimes. Have you ever felt like that?" She asks me, definitely feeling the liquor.

"I do get that. What do you say we go for a walk by the water? It's really nice out." I suggest.

It's my best attempt to indirectly persuade her to stop drinking, so she doesn't get sick in the morning. I'm also being a little selfish because I want her company before she gets any more buzzed and calls it a night.

"I love water. Let's go to the water." Her eyes light up.

***

It takes us about ten minutes to walk the three blocks to Lovejoy Wharf. It's tucked right under the Zakim Bridge. I found it last night on a walk when I couldn't sleep.

There's a small footpath that leads us to an empty boat dock where we get comfortable. I sit and crisscross my legs.

Quinn kicks her shoes off and takes a seat at the edge, putting her feet in the water. Then she lets out a big sigh.

"This is nice." She says.

"It is. Do you want to talk about why you had your first drink in the seven months since I've known you?" I ask.

She takes a few minutes to answer. Thinking hard if she wants to let me in or not.

"Tell me something sad, Link." She says, dodging my question while she looks out at the water.

"What? Don't you want to hear something happy?"

"No Link, I'm sad right now. I don't want to talk about *why* I'm sad. But, I also don't want to talk about happy things. I just don't want to feel alone in my sadness right now, so please tell me something sad. Just be sad with me for a little." Her voice is barely a whisper when she says the last sentence.

I can understand being so upset you just need to sit in it before you can properly process it. I wonder how bad that fight must've been with Noah.

"Hmmmm, how sad?" I ask her.

"Sad with a capital S." A small giggle escapes her.

I think hard. I have plenty of chapters of my life that I could tell her. I've never really talked about the things that have happened to me in great detail.

I told Jason the most, but even in our conversations I never knew how much I should admit to him, so I never went too deep.

I'm scared that if people saw every part of me, they wouldn't want me anymore.

"Are you absolutely sure?"

"Yes Link, I'm sure."

"Promise you won't hate me." I'm nervous now.

"How could I ever hate you?" She turns her body to face mine and grabs my hand in hers.

"You don't know Lincoln Archer, you know *Link*. The person I am now." I try to explain to her.

"Nothing you say could ever make me hate you, Lincoln Archer. I promise." She squeezes my hand before letting it go and putting her feet back in the water.

"Okay…" I'm struggling with where to start.

"Take your time." She smiles, reassuring me.

"I was arrested when I was eighteen for armed robbery. I was tight with this kid, Eric. We rented rooms in the same house and ours were across from each other. We became pretty close the first few months I lived there.

"We'd hang out and play video games or he'd sneak me into bars with him. He was five years older than me and I sort of looked up to him. I thought he was really cool. What I didn't find out until much later was that he sold heroin, not just to me, but most of Flagstaff.

"I started to notice Eric being more ballsy after a while. Doing things that could land him harder time. The night I found out he was also illegally dealing firearms, I decided I needed to say something. I cared about him like family. I told him it was too risky and that someone could get hurt. He told me everything was going to be fine.

"That 4th of July, Eric and I stopped at a Gas & Go for some ice on our way to a party. I was driving because Eric had a little too much to drink during our pregame. We went into the store and he said he was going to look at snacks, so I went to grab the ice from the coolers.

"I got two bags and made my way back to where Eric was. When I turned down the aisle, I nearly dropped the ice. He was being held at gunpoint by the store owner.

"Apparently, Eric was so intoxicated he forgot it's not okay to steal and was caught by the owner trying to fill his backpack with Skittles and Takis.

"The owner was pointing his gun at Eric, yelling at him to empty his bag. One thing about Eric was, he didn't let anyone yell at him. Instead of emptying his backpack, he pulled his own gun from his waistband and proceeded to point it at the owner.

"The stand off lasted seconds, but it felt like hours. I was off to the side of Eric, begging him to put everything back. He told me to mind my own business. Which, if you ask me, is a pretty ridiculous thing to say to someone you just put in the middle of a shoot out.

"The owner finally lost his patience and said Eric had until the count of three to drop his weapon. When he counted "One," Eric didn't flinch. When he counted "Two", Eric took a deep breath in. As he counted "Three," there were two loud bangs, followed by a thud.
"The first bang was Eric shooting the owner in his arm. The second bang was the owner shooting back. The thud was Eric's body hitting the floor from the impact of a gunshot wound between his eyes."

"Link…I'm *so* sorry." Quinn turns and holds my hand again. I squeeze hers this time before I continue speaking.

"The owner made me get on my knees in front of Eric's dead body when he called the cops and waited for them. For five minutes, I slowly felt my jeans soak with the blood from my friend's head while being held at gunpoint.

"I was arrested for accessory to armed robbery and given one year in prison. When I was there, I got my life together and I truly changed. That's when I decided to be sober and I haven't done anything since. I wake up, stay clean and play music. That's all I can do."

Quinn has tears rolling down her face. I reach forward to wipe one away, but she jerks back and does it herself.

"Sorry." I apologize.

"No, you're fine. I'm sorry. I'm just…a mess right now. That's awful, Link." She looks more sad than when this conversation started.

"I know. I told you I wasn't a good person." I say.

"What are you talking about? You didn't do anything wrong besides have shit choices in friends. You were at the wrong place at the wrong time. I can understand feeling so isolated in the world that you hold on to someone who is toxic just for the sake of not being alone."

Quinn has such a good way with words. She makes me feel seen and heard for the first time in my life.

She feels like the *right* person, but I'm at the *wrong* time.

I'm too late.

***

Quinn and I made our way back up to our rooms around 2a.m. It's killing me not knowing exactly what had her so upset.

I swear before she got off the elevator she looked like she wanted to tell me something, but she stopped herself.

All I can do is move at her speed and on her terms, hoping one day she figures out she can fully trust me.

When I open my door, I see Sam sitting on his bed scrolling on this phone.

"What's up dude? Where did you go tonight?" He asks.

"I went for a walk."

"Until 2a.m.? I was worried about you."

I don't know if it's how safe Quinn made me feel tonight or the fact that I broke a theoretical dam, but I can't hold it all in anymore. I sit at the foot of Sam's bed.

"Sam, can I tell you something?" I ask.

"Of course." He puts his phone down, giving me his full attention.

"I'm…sober. From alcohol, but mostly drugs. I haven't told anyone besides Quinn because I'm afraid of being judged or being asked questions I don't know how to answer yet without looking like a bad guy. So…yeah, I'm sober." I feel a small weight lifted off my chest.

"Shit dude…that's why you ran out of the bathroom?"

"It is." I confirm.

"I'm so sorry man, I won't put you in that position ever again. I feel like an asshole. It's just something Noah and I do once in a while, you know…Well, I guess you don't know…Fuck, that didn't come out right…" Sam stumbles over his words.

"It's fine. Just promise this stays between us for now. I'll tell everyone else when I'm ready, okay?"

"I got your back man, I meant it when I said you're my replacement brother. Maybe the replacement part is a joke, but I mean the other part. You're my brother now, Lincoln."

Chapter 14
July 2024 - Quinn

Holy hell, it is hot outside. It's only the first week of July, but it feels like the dead of summer. I can feel small beads of sweat roll down my back as Noah and I walk through Times Square.

After our shows in Boston, we did two in Rhode Island and four in Pennsylvania. Currently, we're back in New York because Compass has been nominated for "Rookie of the Year" at the Listener's Choice Awards.

I doubt we're going to win, but being nominated alone is an honor. I'm honestly just excited for them just to say our name on TV. Although, getting caught in the background of a panning camera or two wouldn't hurt either.

We hit 750,000 records sold on July 1st. My goal for the entire year to hit Platinum with 1,000,000 sold is feeling *very* realistic.

Aside from the band's progress the last three weeks, Noah and I have made a lot of progress as well.

That night in Boston was…*horrible.* I'm forever grateful I bumped into Link.

Or more like, Link bumped into me in a dive bar on the edge of wasted. Either way, I'm glad. We hung out talking and trying to forget our problems.

I feel a little guilty for asking Link to tell me something sad that night. I knew about him not having parents and growing up in the system, but to know he has witnessed so much too, it makes me see him more clearly.

Knowing that he has experienced so much pain, I can't help but keep an extra closer eye on him now.

Sure, there's worry from my standpoint as his manager to keep him in line, but it's because I care about him as a person the most. I value our friendship and I'm honored he's opened up to me.

Since that talk about the robbery, he's expanded on a few other areas of his upbringing. Most of which are stories of when he was using and the crazy things that he and his friends would do. "Sounds like you were in a rock and roll band." I joked.

That got a good laugh from him.

The hardest thing about my friendship with Link is Noah. And the hardest thing about my marriage with Noah is Link.

I find myself relentlessly reliving through *that* fight with Noah. It's a flashback in a film scene stuck on repeat, playing in my mind every day.

When I got back to the hotel, after hanging out with Link at the wharf, Noah was waiting for me.

The moment I opened the door, he got up from the couch and apologized for slapping me…without actually acknowledging that he slapped me.

When he started to walk towards me, I took a step backward and he froze.

"I'm not going to hurt your feelings ever again…Quinn, I am *so* sorry. From the center of my soul, I will never do anything to upset you. I would never…I don't know where that came from."

"It comes from liquor and jealousy." I replied to him bluntly.

Seeing him so apologetic made me feel like a mixed bag. I felt scared that this wasn't going to be the last time. I also felt relieved that he was promising it would never happen again.

How can he really know that it was the last time? And how can I?

His words were right, but I still felt sick. Not in the literal sense, but like a part of me hadn't come back from that night in Boston.

A piece of me had broken off somewhere. Like a lost earring, you don't notice until you go to take it off at the end of the day but it's gone.

"How can I know you won't hurt me again, Noah?" I asked him.

"I don't know, Quinn, but *I know* I won't. I will work my hardest every day to prove that to you. *I know* I need to gain back your trust but, I swear on my life, I will. Just please give me a chance, baby." He said.

I hated the warmth I got from him saying it, *baby.* It's the rarity that made it feel so special.

I'm not some lovesick girl who can't get her priorities straight. I'm not so stupid that I don't realize the weight of what happened.

I'm a woman in a marriage trying my best to mean my vows and honor the commitments I made.

Noah has helped me through some of my darkest times. I felt I owed it to him to help him through his.

That's the promise I made, as sick as it sounds. I forgave him but I did not excuse him.

We've been attending couples' counseling once a week via Zoom with a therapist from Nashville. The plan is to continue therapy until I decide otherwise, so I made sure to pick one from home so we can eventually have in person sessions.

I agreed not to tell the therapist about the slap. It's very clear Noah is ashamed of it and that gives me hope he won't do it again, so I don't find it necessary to talk about…yet.

The hope that he knows what he did was wrong keeps me holding on.

Aside from talking about Noah's *"uncontrollable anger"* in therapy, we've also discussed his liquor consumption, our lack of communication, and our lack of alone time.

The last one is why Noah and I are currently walking down 7th Avenue in ninety-three degree heat. We opted for a private sightseeing adventure together through the city before the awards show tomorrow night.

Our Song

It's nice having one-on-one time with him. I kind of forgot what it was like. We haven't had any since the tour started six months ago.

We got lunch earlier and took a Big Bus Tour so I could take pictures with my polaroid. It's been a nice day with him.

Therapy's made me realize that maybe I have been a little absent in our marriage too, which might be why Noah feels so insecure at times.

I work a lot and I know I can be so narrowly focused sometimes. We both have work to do. We're not broken, we're just, works-in-progress.

***

"I'm going to fucking throw up, is that Taylor Swift?" Roni asks across our large, round table.

"We're nominees here, not fans." I remind her.

"Yeah, but it's fucking *Taylor Swift*."

"Okay, fine, you have a point." I cave as we laugh together, trying to catch a glimpse of where she's seated at one of the front tables.

Where she's an A-List star, we are for sure D-List at best. We're nominated with several other artists who all have at least 100,000 units on us.

Our saving grace is that "Phases Of The Moon" finally took the number one spot last week on "Billboard's Top 100".

I think we all know our chances are slim, so we're just here for a good time. It's been surreal seeing people who've only lived on our screens sitting in the same room with us.

I just drank water poured from the same pitcher as Madonna, for Christ's sake. I could die with a happy and fulfilled life now.

Link returns to the table from the bathroom and I notice as he sticks a napkin in my purse when Roni is distracted.

She's craning her neck, drooling over Beyonce from ten tables away. We exchange a smile and I push it down further into my bag. I make a mental note to look at it later.

Max, Sam and Noah come jogging up to the table as the lights start to dim, indicating we're about to go live again. Noah sits down next to me as Jimmy Fallon takes the stage.

"Welcome back everybody! I'm honored to announce the presenter for our next award, Rookie of the Year! Please make some noise for a previous winner himself, Post Malone!"

The room erupts with cheers and Post Malone walks out from the right side of the stage, a bright spot of yellow light following him in his green suit.

The two exchange a quick hug before Jimmy hands him a large black envelope.

"Listen up," I turn around to get the attention of our table quickly, "Remember to smile and clap the whole time. They might pan to our table during the ten seconds of screen time our name gets. Let's look happy and be good sports." I say to everyone.

"We get it. No one likes sore losers. Thanks, Q-Tip." Sam says sarcastically.

I look back to the stage and watch as the background screen changes to various pictures of album covers as Post reads each nominee's name. It's then followed by a live pan to them sitting in the audience.

Just like I thought.

"Smile everyone!" I say, still looking ahead at the stage from my seat.

"Scythe's" he says into the mic. The screen shows a live feed of the all women rock group smiling and clapping before he reads the next name.

"Compass." He says and my stomach flips.

I'm going to throw up. I see the camera man rounding our table out of the corner of my eye. I'm too occupied checking the screen to see what everyone else in the world can see right now to look over at him, though.

The camera pans past Sam first and he gives a cheesy wave right into the camera. Not horrible, but not what we discussed.

Roni's in frame next and she decides to take Sam's lead by looking right into the camera and she sticks out her tongue and gives a "rock on" sign with her left hand.

Does nobody listen to me?

Then, the camera hits Link and I swear the crowd gets a little louder. He waves as it smoothly pans over to Max, who is staring up at the big monitor behind the stage, clapping with a straight face. When he sees himself on the screen, I notice he has a small smirk, like he was just star-struck by himself.

Finally, it gets to Noah and I see my right arm in the side of the frame. He smiles into the camera and as he goes to blow a kiss into it, but the feed cuts out to the next band Post says into the mic.

Noah doesn't notice his screen time get cut short, but I do, and a small laugh escapes me.

I look at the rest of the table to see Max and Link also laughing, I assume for the same reason. We say nothing and watch Noah smile and lean back in his chair.

"I hope you enjoyed our ten seconds of screen time, boys." Noah says as he takes a drink from his beer. He agreed not to drink hard liquor until after the show.

Progress.

"And, the winner is…" Post says finally, opening the envelope, "Oh damn, I love these guys, Compass!"

I don't move. Nobody at our table moves for at least five seconds. I know logically the room is loud, but I don't hear it. I see everyone clapping from the surrounding tables. They're all staring at us, but I can't hear them.

I exchange looks with everyone at our table. We're all silently verifying this is real life. Noah finally breaks the silence when he shoots up from his chair.

"Holy shit, we fucking won!" He yells, as everyone else stands up at the table cheering and hugging each other.

Noah is the first to start the band's walk up to the stage to claim the big golden ear shaped statue they call the Listeners Choice Award.

Sam, Roni and Max all follow behind, but I remain standing at the table. As Link starts to pass me, he grabs my hand to pull me up with them.

"You're in this band too, Win." He says, looking back at me.

I hesitate, but I can't say no to him with the way he's looking at me right now. I stop fighting and walk on my own, releasing his hand.

Our Song

We all make it up to the stage and I watch Noah take the award from Post. Sam and Max shake his hand. Then, Post leans in and gives Roni and I each a hug.

I'm never washing this dress again.

Noah walks up to the podium and starts a very unrehearsed speech. No one planned for this outcome. I'm a very big believer in always having a plan, but I hadn't even considered us winning.

We won.

"Thank you everyone who voted for us." Noah begins confidently speaking into the mic, "Thank you to our fans who have been with us since Nashville and the ones we've picked up along the way. Thank you to everyone who has come out and seen us on tour. Thank you to Grant Madison and the whole team at Rich Records. Thank you to our Tour Manager, Kye Stewart.

"Thank you to our Band Manager and my wife, Quinn Finch." Noah points back at me and the spotlight shines brighter on me.

The band starts clapping and hugging me on the stage. They're a couple of assholes, but they're *my* assholes.

"We are so honored to have won this award and we look forward to earning more. Thank you, New York!" He finishes as he holds up the award to the crowd like it's baby Simba and he is Mufasa.

I feel numb as we all walk off the stage wearing smiles and head back to our table.

Jimmy announces another presenter to the stage, but I don't hear who was called or what award is next. I'm so consumed by the adrenaline of this win. No one else exists in this room but us.

***

Everyone's probably at Corniela's Bar by now. When the show was done filming, we all agreed to go out and celebrate together.

I decided to take a shower and change into something more comfortable first, so I took an Uber back to the hotel.

I'm wrapping myself in a fluffy hotel towel when I hear my cell phone ring. It strikes me as odd because it's 11p.m. and everyone I know who would call me would be in bed by this hour. Anyone in the band would have just sent a text.

I grab my phone and see a number I don't recognize across my screen. When I look closer, I notice the area code, "605".

That's home.

It has to be my dad. Who else from South Dakota would have my personal number these days? It's not a birthday or holiday, so I'm willing to bet he needs money.

Maybe his phone got shut off, and that's why he's calling from a random number. Maybe that's also why I haven't heard from him since I told him that I hated him back in April.

"Hello?" I answer.

"Hi. Is this Quinn Finch?" I don't recognize the woman's voice asking who is asking.

Now I'm leaning towards the possibility of him being arrested and needing bail money.

It's happened twice before.

"Yes, it is. Is this about my father? What did he do now?" I ask, assumingly.

"He died."

***

I finally managed to get myself dressed. I'm sitting on the floor next to the bed, staring at my cell phone. I don't know what to do with myself.

I want to pretend nothing has happened, but I don't know how. I could sit here until Noah comes back, but I don't want to ruin his night. That also leaves too much time for me to sit here and over think things.

I know I said I hated my father, but I didn't, really.

I was mad.

I was hurt.

I feel the tears fill my eyes again and I grab for another tissue, but the box is empty.

Am I a hypocrite for crying right now?

That's what I'm asking myself when I remember I have more kleenex in my purse. I get up and grab my bag from the table near the door.

I fish around for the packet but instead pull out Link's napkin-note from earlier. I forgot it was in there.

I unfold the white napkin to find black ink written in Link's hand writing.

"You look beautiful tonight."

I laugh.

I laugh again and pick up my cell.

I click the phone icon and dial. The phone's ringing and I'm still laughing.

"Hello?"

"Hey. Why is it quiet?" I ask, confused why I don't hear bar music in the background.

"Because I'm in my room at the hotel. I started to head to the bar, but decided I wanted to change first. I don't get why everyone else wanted to stay dressed up to go to a bar. It's uncomfortable."

"Meet me on the roof." I say it quickly before I hang up.

The Hilton NYC has an exclusive rooftop pool and patio for hotel guests to use. The pool closed at 10p.m. so at this hour not many people should be up there.

I put on my black moccasin slippers and slide the room key into my pocket. I leave my room and head to the elevator.

When I enter, I'm greeted by my reflection in the mirrored panels lining the elevator.

I look…rough.

I'm wearing black leggings with small thunderbolts and a Boston band tee. My hair is still wet and I have no makeup on.

What a mess.

When the elevator doors open to the roof, I step out into the warm night air. The breeze offers a small relief as I take in a deep breath. There's only one couple up here and they're sitting on a couch on the left side of the roof. I turn right to give them privacy.

Our Song

I look over the edge at the city lights and think of everyone living their lives right now.

Why couldn't I be one of them? Would my life be easier?

Before I can have more spiraling thoughts, I hear footsteps and turn around.

"Hey." Link says.

Chapter 15
July 2024 - Lincoln

"Hey." she says back to me.

"Are you okay?" I ask her.

I know that's a dumb question the second she turns around to face me. Her eyes are red and puffy. She's definitely been crying.

When I look closer, I notice she's in her pajamas and her hair is wet.

One thing I've learned about Quinn is that no matter the chaos going on around her, she is always put together, or at least makes herself appear that way. *This* Quinn, the one standing in front of me, is *not* okay.

I don't think it's possible for her to look bad, but I know her and can tell that whatever happened is heavily affecting her.

"I don't know." She responds to my question before turning back and looking over the edge.

I take a place standing next to her and lean against the railing, looking down at the drop.

"It's okay not to know." I reply, giving her the space and time to say whatever she's comfortable telling me.

"I don't know how to feel. I want to be angry or upset, maybe even mad. I definitely should be sad…but right now, I can't tell if I'm feeling everything or nothing at all." She says, staring straight ahead.

I want to guess it's Noah being himself, but I try my best not to assume. Instead, we stand in silence for a few minutes when I try to craft the best response.

The New York City skyline is breathtaking at night. Every building lit up across the horizon looks like stars fallen from the sky.

Behind each shine, a person is living their life. Unaware of how beautiful just flipping on their light switch might be to someone looking on from a distance.

"Do you want me to tell you something sad?" I finally offer.

I know she doesn't want to hear something happy. What person going through something as heavy as Quinn seems to be would want to hear anything positive. Happiness can feel like twenty-four grit sandpaper against your soul when you're occupied by sadness.

"Link…I can't ask you to do that. Just because I'm sad and can't articulate my emotions like an adult doesn't mean I can pull you into the undertow with me. When I asked you last time…that was wrong…I shouldn't have…"

"You did nothing wrong. I wanted to tell you about the robbery. If I didn't then, I wouldn't have eventually. I could've told you something small sad, like having my favorite book stolen or getting bullied. But I want you to know my truth…you're my best friend, Win." I admit shyly.

That gets her attention. She turns to look at me. Her eyes roll over me like she's reading the back of a book, deciding if she should buy it.

"If I wasn't convinced Roni would pop out of nowhere and ax-murder both of us, I'd say you might be my best friend, too." She smiles and then looks back out to the city.

"So as your *'secret'* best friend, let me tell you something sad."

"Fine." She agrees, not breaking eye contact with the skyline.

I don't know where to pick from since every day before I joined this band was its own genre of sadness. Quinn already knows about my firehouse abandonment, so I start at my first foster home and move forward from there. I feel like context is important and will ease her into my trauma, as if trauma is a thing to be eased into.

When I finally get to the part I was dreading, the *real* sad part about getting my first guitar, I hesitate.

I've never told anyone what happened to me until now. I push through it anyway.

"Oh my God, Link…Did you tell anyone?" She asks, turning to face me again.

I look to meet her stare and see the tears harboring in the corners of her eyes. It makes me want to hold her and tell her it's okay.

I'm okay now.

"No. I know it sounds messed up, but Robert's house was nice. A lot of the homes I was tossed into before weren't always nice. There are a lot of people out there just fostering for the money. Some people viewed me as a paycheck, like my existence was transactional. And I felt that way for a while…"

"I'm so sorry you had to live through that and that you had to hold on to it alone for so long. It's never okay for anyone to touch anyone in a harmful way."

I notice she gets louder towards the end of her statement. I try my best to hide the curiosity in my expression, but I know I'm failing by the way she's looking back at me.

"Don't be sorry, broken pieces can make beautiful art when you put them back together, like stained glass windows. They're just painted broken glass melted together, but when the light shines through, they're beautiful." I say.

"What if it feels like your broken pieces make something ugly? Like they don't fit back the way they did before. Something so far from art that you can't bring yourself to look at it?" She asks. This time, a single tear escapes her right eye.

"You just need to find the right light. Besides, I think your pieces are beautiful."

As I say the words, I reach next to me and grab her hand. We stay like that for a moment, frozen. Then she lets go and leans her backside against the rail again.

She takes a few deep breaths. It's clear to me that whatever she is trying to figure out how to say is hard for her.

I join her in looking up at the sky, not saying anything.

"Noah slapped me." She says too casually to the stars.

White hot anger pumps through my body. I push myself off the railing and take a step back, locking eyes with her.

"He *what?*" I ask her, like I didn't hear her perfectly the first time.

"It's not a big deal…" She looks down to face me now.

"Are you okay? Is he in the room?" I ask quickly.

I turn to walk for the elevators before I even have time to think about what I'll do when I see that *piece of shit.* I *knew* there was something about him.

"Link, wait!"

"What?" I say, turning around.

"It happened in Boston." She says like it's a good enough reason to *still* not hit him right now.

"Why didn't you say anything? You could've told me." I walk back to her, leaving no more than six inches between us.

"It…it wasn't a big deal. It was one time. It hasn't happened since. I'm fine." She replies.

It sounds so rehearsed. Like she's spent time telling herself that in the mirror.

"It *is* a big deal." I argue.

"Please don't be mad at me." She chokes the words out through tears.

Fuck.

She's not the one I should be mad at right now.

"I'm sorry, Win. I just…I care about you." I say, pulling her into a hug.

Her arms lightly wrap around my waist, but I pull her in tighter, cradling her head in my hand against my chest. I smell her strawberry shampoo as I feel her grip me a little tighter, her small frame shaking in my hold.

I reach down to her face to try to wipe away some of her tears, but she steps back.

Still holding onto me, but we're face to face now. My left hand gently holds her face, making her look up at me.

I take a deep breath and stroke my thumb down her soft cheek.

"I could never be mad at you for anything. My anger was misdirected and I'm sorry. You deserve better than that from me, and you certainly deserve better from him. You are so special, Quinn Finch, and you should be treated like the rarity you are."

I'm questioning if I crossed the line when she runs right across it as her mouth crashes into mine.

Her lips are full and warm and she tastes like cinnamon.

My body burns cool with the sensation of fevered heat between us. I caress her face with both hands as her tongue finds its way to mine.

My body feels awoken from a long slumber.

That's when she lets go of me and steps back. My hands drop to my sides, lost without her in them.

"I can't…I shouldn't have…I have to go." She stammers, turning and running to the exit, opting for the stairs past the elevator.

I don't follow her because if she's running away from me, she doesn't want to be chased.

That's the moment I realize this will be a secret and I will be a regret.

Chapter 16
July 2024 - Quinn

I'm a selfish person and a cheating wife.

It's been two days since I've spoken to Link. I can't look at myself in the mirror, nevermind approach a conversation with him about everything that happened between us on that rooftop in NYC.

There seems to be some unspoken silence agreement between us right now. After I fled from the roof, and debatably the best kiss of my existence, he texted me.

Lincoln: I'm sorry.

It killed me to know he blamed himself for my reaction, but I couldn't bring myself to respond. Truthfully, I wanted to kiss him long before I actually gave in.

I've been denying myself to think about what I realized that night in Boston.

Our Song

Lincoln Archer *sees* me.

After I knew what it felt like to be held in his arms and that he tasted like peppermint, I couldn't risk any more contact.

I'm married to Noah and even though things are hard lately doesn't mean they're completely irrevocable.

I have a theory that if I continue with the silence between Link and I, he'll see me for the horrible person I am and hate me.

That would be best for him, *hating me.*

Call it the coward's way out.

The thought of him looking at me with hatred breaks my soul. It's a twisted fate I've chosen, but I can't lie to him either, and that's exactly what I would have to do if we spoke.

I'd lie and tell him it meant nothing. That I regretted it and I don't want it to happen again, *and again.*

I can't say those things to him despite whispering them to myself like manifestations every day since. Willing myself to feel that way.

The only fucked up saving grace lately is that death requires a lot of planning and attention. Call it unhealthy if you want, but I've kept my fathers passing to myself for the time being. I wasn't ready to talk about the night it happened with Link or Noah.

When Noah got back from that bar, he was happy and drunk, still amped about winning that award. I pretended to be tired and went to bed once I knew he was back and safe.

I couldn't bring myself to ruin the night of the only two *living* men in my life.

Ignorance is bliss.

According to the conversation with the woman who called me about my father's death, there wasn't exactly a body to bury.

He drove his pickup into an oak tree on his own property at roughly eighty miles per hour. My best guess is he was on his way home from the bar.

Thankfully, he only killed himself.

I guess you could say I'm in the anger stage right now. I skipped denial because I've spent the last decade of my life planning for this type of call.

I've hired a service to go in and pack and donate his belongings from the house. Once they've cleared it out, I have a realtor lined up to sell it and then I can close that chapter.

One less worry.

I loved my dad, even when he was in shambles. His death has made me realize that when someone is so lost to their own carnaging vices, you grieve them long before they're dead.

Maybe I've skipped all phases of grief and gone right to acceptance.

For now, I'm keeping it packed away in a folder in my email.

We don't have any family or close friends to notify, so cleaning up the traces of him is all I have left.

I thought about having everything put in a storage unit to go through eventually, but I fear eventually would never come. I'd just end up paying its rent until I'm dead and someone else has to get rid of it all.

I'll tell people when I'm ready.

Our Song

The two days that have followed my silent grief over my father *and* Link, we've spent on the buses driving to Pittsburgh to shoot a music video for "Phases Of The Moon".

My phone has been blowing up, responding to calls and emails from everyone prepping the sets. The escape of getting lost in my work reminds me why I love this job so much and why it's so important I keep it.

It makes me feel valuable.

The music video was a suggestion from the label after our nomination, before we won it. Grant said it would be good to show a refined story of the band for new listeners to really understand them.

The band all voted to shoot a video for "Phases Of The Moon" because it was our lead single and an anthem for growth and success. It has a good story behind it and it will resonate with a larger audience.

I feel the bus come to a stop as I send the last email to the junk removal company.

We're here.

Besides not speaking to Link for the last two days, I haven't seen him either.

The bus has stopped a couple times for a few radio show appearances, but I've refused to get off. Hiding my avoidance under my work load, responding to emails, calls and zoom meetings. The band's media training is strong so I justified missing the interviews.

No one's batted an eye. Noah hasn't said a word of my behavior being out of character. I'm playing the part well. I hope I can keep up the facade all day.

All of our sets have been built in an empty house that's currently for rent. We paid the realtor for a few days to use the property. Our first scenes of the music video start in the garage.

The First Phase.

The band empties from the buses and heads right into the house to find hair and makeup. We're going for a more youthful look to start.

This phase represents the beginning of the band when they were just practicing in a garage. Finding themselves and their sound.

The morning flies by as I check in with the people on set that the label hired.

I'm standing around with other crew members in the driveway when I hear the director, Marsha, yell into her megaphone.

"Okay people, everyone, please find your marks and let's get this thing started."

One by one, the band members empty out of the house and take their places like this is any other night in an arena.

The last member to come out is Link. The second he steps out, our eyes meet. I feel like a sniper emptied a round in my chest.

The most painful part is how brief it is.

It's over before I can really try to get a read on him. His face is flat, not showing a hint of emotion. In fact, now that I look around, everyone's a little *off.*

A countdown starts, and the band plays. They'll layer over the audio from the studio so it's clean in the video.

Our Song

The band insisted on playing it live for shooting scenes instead of pretending to play over a track so the camera captures more authenticity.

After they play through the first verse of the song for the ninth time, the director finally calls "cut", satisfied enough to move onto the next scene.

The Second Phase.

The band heads back into the house to change and get touch ups while the rest of the crew move all the equipment and instruments to the backyard where the next phase is being filmed.

I run up to catch the door behind Roni, heading in last, after getting caught up flirting with one of the set designers in the garage.

"Hey, Roni, wait up!" I get to the door right before she shuts it behind her.

"Hey." She turns to me.

"Is everything okay with everyone?" I ask.

"Oh, you know, just the men being boys. Bickering over bullshit. They'll be fine once they hit the craft tables and get some carrot sticks and juice boxes." She laughs, easing my worries in the slightest.

"What are they arguing about?" I try not to seem like I want to know as bad as I actually do.

"Literally so stupid, Noah accused Lincoln of giving him a dirty look when they were with wardrobe. Then Lincoln said that he was being "self centered as usual", which made Sam laugh.

"That really pissed Noah off, so then he made a comment to Lincoln about him being a sad puppy or something. Max yelled at them all to shut up before it got any further and they listened to the big beefcake. Like I said, they'll be fine."

"Okay, let me know if anything else happens. I'm going to see if I can help with anything outside."

"You got it Quinny." She smiles before walking away.

I head out back to see the craft tent swarmed by about twenty extras the label also provided for the last two scenes.

This second phase represents when the band was playing weddings and backyard birthdays before they booked actual gigs.

There's a small stage set up with an early version of the band's logo hanging up on a tarp behind it. A big compass with shattered glass.

I head over to the crowded tent and reach for a water bottle just as another hand reaches into the same cooler.

I look up and am met with Link's blank stare. He grabs a water bottle and stands there like he's waiting for something.

If I had to guess, he's letting me decide if we're speaking or not.

I open my mouth but nothing comes out, instead I just grab a water bottle and walk towards the camera setup.

Nothing I say will make anything better for either of us.

The band shoots the backyard scenes, recording the first chorus and second verse in just under two hours.

Marsha's yelling in her megaphone to break for a sixty minute lunch before we head to the basement for the last shots.

The Third Phase.

Our Song

One thing that made this location a particularly good place to shoot was the finished basement that included a small bar and stage, like the one at Sally's back in Nashville.

I sent the set designers pictures of the band performing there, and they truly did it justice. It feels like a miniature version of home.

The band's tour footage, showing them singing "Phases Of The Moon" in concert will be edited in to create the last chorus of the song.

The Final Phase.

I'm feeling nostalgic when Noah comes up behind me and pulls me in for a hug.

"Hey." He says pressing a soft kiss to my head.

"Hi, is everything okay with you guys? Roni mentioned arguing?" I ask.

"Everything's fine. Lincoln was grilling me, and when I called him out then, I was told *I was crazy*. But you know what I realized? He's just a sad little puppy. He follows you and Sam around like he's lost. I can't believe I was ever threatened by him. I'm sure he's just jealous of me. He's kind of *pathetic*."

"Noah!" I quickly pull out of his grip.

I'm angry and I ready myself to defend Link, but then think better of it.

This suffocating feeling is going to be the end of me.

God, Noah can be such an ass.

"What?" He looks angry and confused, but mostly angry.

"Nothing, it's just not nice to talk about our friend like that." I recover.

"He may be *your* friend, but he's my *coworker*." He replies hastily before walking over to the stage set up.

The bridge is being recorded in this last scene, so all the extras have changed out of backyard BBQ attire to night club wear.

The director calls for places and I see Link come down the stairs in a sleeveless Aerosmith shirt and ripped jeans.

The "bad boy" look wardrobe gave him has me checking the location of my jaw.

Link looks through me.

He doesn't make eye contact, as if it might be too painful to look directly at me. That or he's looking past me, like I don't exist.

Exactly like I wanted, right?

So why does that hurt so badly?

I hear the music start by the time my thoughts catch up to me. I stick around for the next hour until I hear Marsha yell "cut" one final time.

I casually bolt up the stairs to head back to the bus.

I've accomplished everything I needed to and the tension, which seems to be unique to me, is overwhelming.

I make it out on the front lawn when I hear him.

"Quinn…" Link says.

He's not yelling, he's speaking level and cool. The opposite of how him just speaking my name out loud makes me feel.

If I felt like I was being crushed before, this must be what it feels like when you finally burst from the pressure.

I turn to face him. Taking a deep breath and trying my best to match his even tone.

"Yes?" I ask, playing it professional and cordial.

"Please talk to me." He steps closer to me, sounding somber.

"I can't Link…I…I don't want to lie to you." I say. That prompts a perplexed look from him.

"Then don't…please just say anything to me."

"It can't happen again." I say.

"I understand." He says in a tone I recognize.

It's the one that tells me he's already grieved the idea of us. My confirmation does nothing to lessen the hurt he's wearing.

"I'm sorry." I whisper.

"For what?" He steps even closer to me.

"That I hurt you."

"You didn't hurt me, Win…you revived me." His expression softens, and he looks like he wants to reach for me, but doesn't.

"It can't happen again." I repeat, unsure how to think new thoughts over the painful swarm of hornets in my stomach.

"You said that," we stand in a long silence before he continues, "Just answer one question for me, please…and we'll never talk about it again. We can go back to normal and I'll bring none of this up to a soul."

"Okay." I hesitate.

"Do you regret it?" He asks, hope gleaming off the riptides in his eyes.

"Yes." I lie.

Fuck.

Chapter 17
August 2024 - Lincoln

I don't know if I'll be able to have kids after sitting on this saddle for the last hour. Horseback riding is not meant for male anatomy and I will die on that hill.

The smell of the droppings from Max's horse in front of me have me truly kicking myself for not bailing on this side quest Quinn planned for Arizona.

I was so close, too.

The last two weeks have been...*trying* to say the least.

As I promised Quinn at the music video shoot, I've gone back to acting normal. Or at least as normal as I could be after she told me she regretted me.

I talk to her as if nothing happened now.

Through all our stops in Ohio and Illinois, we've slowly become less stiff around each other, but it's not what we were.

We have empty conversations, void of any real emotions. Not telling each other sad things, happy things or our darkest secrets anymore.

Our Song

Everything is surface level. A skewed faux friendship. Quinn's been idle since NYC but no one else seems to know her enough to notice, but I do. I know there are things she's not telling us. I can tell by the way she hesitates before every sentence she speaks.

My best guess is that she probably doesn't want to be my friend at all. Her life would be easier if I left the band and she could go back to how it was before I ruined it.

My chest aches every time I have to see Noah holding or kissing Quinn. He doesn't deserve her, and she deserves better than either of us.

While I've never been supported by so many good people in my life, I've also never felt so alone.

It's bizarre how those two realities can run concurrently.

That's why I thought a day to myself to walk the trails would be a relaxing escape. Unfortunately, Sam is persistent.

"Grand Canyon horseback riding, man!" he yelled at me this morning, convincing me at the last minute that if I bailed, he would never forgive me.

As the people pleaser that I am, I *literally* saddled up.

Now my southern region is sweaty and sore and *oh my God*, why does Max's horse keep doing that?

Seriously, what do they feed them?

Being from Arizona, you'd think I would have a western bone in my body. I appreciate the scenery and sun, but there's a reason I moved to a city like Nashville.

It had similar charms to Arizona, however, it was full of life and soul. Not empty voids and canyons.

The orange marbling on the walls beside us is breathtaking, though. Years of weathering, erosion, and life all contributed to these beautiful canyons.

As we come out the other side of one, our tour guide stops us in front of a dusty wooden shack with a horseshoe on the door.

We watch as he hops off and ties his reins to a bike rack next to the structure, signaling us to dismount and do the same.

"Alrighty y'all, this here is the halfway mark before we turn around and go back to the other side of the canyon. We're gonna break to stretch our legs." Our tour guide Bobby Jo says in a true cowboy accent, before casually lighting a cigarette.

"Um, the website mentioned a scenic picnic on the trail?" Quinn chimes in, pulling out her phone to double check the booking.

"Apologies dear!' He says, opening one of the bags strapped to his horse before he starts pulling out warm water bottles and crushed granola bars.

"If the food was in your bags, what's the shack for?" Sam asks Bobby Jo.

"That's an outhouse. Which, speaking of…" he trails off before taking a few brisk strides in its direction "nature calls!" he finishes, disappearing behind the wooden door.

"He is not seriously about to…"

Quinn is cut off by the echoing sound of a steady stream. We all collectively shift ten feet away from the outhouse, snickering amongst ourselves.

"Is this real life?" Roni asks the group, laughing loudly.

Our Song

"This was specifically described as a *luxury* horseback ride through Arizona's greatest scenic vistas!" Quinn says, with that cute frustrated look she gets when things don't go exactly how she planned them.

"Relax." Noah says, wrapping his arm around her.

I swear I see a small flinch from her before his hand takes a position on her shoulder.

"Come on Q-Tip, this is a once in a lifetime opportunity to go to the bathroom in the desert! Well worth the money!" Sam eggs her on jokingly.

"Yeah, I'm going to have to pass." She says, finally laughing.

"The seat is hot if anyone else wants to give her a turn." Bobby Jo says as he returns to the group while still tightening his belt buckle.

"You know, I think we're all ready to get back on the trails." Roni says.

"You got it, pretty lady. Saddle up folks!" He yells as if we aren't standing right next to him.

Roni has a look of disgust on her face. Out of everything she's witnessed today, being called "pretty lady" seems to be the most wretched to her.

We quickly mount our horses and start on the trail that leads back to the ranch.

Just as we start moving, I smell it, *again*.

"Why does my horse keep shitting?" Max yells, finally fed up with his horse and its odor.

"Oh, that just means Clara likes you!" Bobby Jo shouts from the front of the group.

"Awwwww! *Max and Clara, sitting in a tree, S-H-I-T-T-I-N-G!*" I hear Sam sing from behind me.

***

We're playing two sold-out shows at Celebrity Theatre in Phoenix tonight and tomorrow night.

Playing in my home state is giving me a contagious adrenaline rush. I feel a semblance of happiness for the first time in weeks.

Jason is even driving down from Flagstaff for tomorrow night's show. I've been feeling so lost and alone lately, it will be comforting to see the closest person I have to family.

"Two minutes!" yells one of the PAs.

The theater is set up like a circus. It's a giant circle of rising staggered seats surrounding a circular stage.

When our tour manager, Kye, found out it was a round stage, he made arrangements to set up a rotating platform on top of it so we wouldn't have to cut off any seats for obstructed views.

We'll be spinning in a circle surrounded by screaming fans when we play our set.

Everyone's pretty excited about it besides Max, who's worried about motion sickness of all things.

The lights go down and we walk up a ramp leading to the platform hidden in the darkness. One of the sound technicians starts playing an extended intro of our opening song, "Embark".

The crowd is up from their seats and cheering as we all take our places on stage.

Our Song

The crew placed fluorescent yellow taped squares on the stage floor for each of us.

With the size and rotation of the stage, we've been *encouraged* not to venture too far away from our marks.

I'm sure a lawsuit involving one of us falling onto a fan is probably the last thing Quinn wants to do paperwork for.

Sam's fingers start moving as the recording fades out and his guitar takes over the amp.

"Are you ready, Phoenix?" Noah yells into his microphone.

The room is full of chanting as I start strumming my guitar. Max kicks in on drums and another flood of screams fills the theater when Noah starts singing.

Then, just as the first chorus starts, a small pyro spark on each side of the stage goes off and the platform starts spinning.

Everyone on the floor loses it. The chanting sea of fans are singing the words back at Noah.

I notice a group of girls wearing shirts with my face on it scream extra loud every time I rotate past them.

The song ends and we take a brief moment to all soak in the cheers.

It's intoxicating.

"Welcome to the Find Yourself Tour Arizona!" Noah greets the crowd before continuing his welcome speech.

Sam and I switch out our guitars as Roni grabs a quick drink of water.

"As you might notice tonight, we have an extra special set up…" everyone cheers, cutting Noah off, "We're so excited to be here with you tonight. Now, as some of you may have heard, we have a little song called "Phases Of The Moon" that's been number one for five weeks now!" The applause grows louder.

"We're so excited to share with you that tonight, at midnight, our official music video for "Phases Of The Moon" will be released! Sing along if you know it!" He finishes.

I can barely hear the counting in my ear piece over the chaos unfolding. Max starts the opening percussion and again I find myself lost in the music.

***

I'm the last band member to leave the venue. Everyone went out to a bar in the city right after the show ended.

I don't want to risk running into anyone I knew from *before* and have to potentially talk about things I don't want to talk about.

The last thing I need is for Max or Roni to look at me differently or for Noah to have any more ammunition against me.

Our tour buses are parked in a private lot about four blocks away, so I decide to enjoy the warm summer night and walk to them.

I've been staying on the buses instead of my room at one of the label provided hotels so I can play my guitar when I can't sleep…which seems to be every night lately.

It's almost midnight when I approach "The Bro Dome".

Our Song

As I near the door, I notice the figure of a person I don't recognize leaning against it.

My presence doesn't seem to get their attention as I approach. When I'm about ten feet away, I see it's a woman scrolling on her phone.

I feel a bit relieved, realizing it's probably just a fan looking for an autograph or hook up. Every few cities, we have fans that find the buses and stake them out, hoping for a private hangout on a rock stars tour bus.

I could text one of the crew to help me escort her away, but she looks harmless. I'm sure I can sign whatever she wants and send her on her way.

"Can I help you?" I ask softly.

The woman jumps in fright and grabs to her chest.

"Holy shit, you scared me…which I'm sure is weird for me to say since I'm the one leaning against your bus right now…in the middle of the night." She says.

When she steps closer, her features are better illuminated under the light cast by a parking lamp near the bus.

She's older than our typical female fan, maybe in her late thirties. She has short brown hair and bangs cut across her forehead.

Her eyes are pale and she has deep laugh-lines around her mouth.

"Sorry. Uh, can I offer you an autograph or something?" I say, trying to be kind to this seemingly frantic stranger.

"No…no. I, um…" She laughs nervously.

"Are you okay?" I ask her, starting to worry that I should've texted someone.

"I'm fine totally…I just didn't expect…we'll I mean, I've seen you on TV and online. It's just different seeing you in person. I never imagined you'd be so…" She stops again.

"I get it, but I'm just a regular person though. Speaking of which, a regular person needs sleep," I joke, lightly, "So, maybe I could sign whatever you want or take a picture with you so I could get some sleep if that's alright." I say gently.

"I don't want…I don't need an autograph…I…." She stammers.

Her eyes stare at me intently as I reach to pull my phone out of my back pocket to call for help.

"I'm your mother, Lincoln."

Chapter 18
August 2024 - Lincoln

I'm sitting on a bench in Encanto Park wondering if I'm an idiot. I agreed to meet *her* here this morning at nine. I've been here since seven.

Our conversation ended pretty quickly last night. I barely got a word out.

After the woman, whose name I still don't know, told me she was my mother, she handed me a piece of paper with her number on it. Then she asked me to meet her here in Encanto Park in the morning before she walked away to give me space to think about it.

I stood in the parking lot for an eternity processing what happened.

I watched the spot she disappeared from, wondering if this was a joke. The kind with a hidden TV camera crew in a bush somewhere.

But when the night remained quiet and there was no sign of anyone else, I finally got on the bus, making sure to lock the door behind me.

I tried to sleep, but I just tossed and turned, wondering if this could be true.

Could she really know I was her son? And if I really am, what does she want from me?

She abandoned me when I was seven.

What does this mean for my future? Do I have more family out there? Does she know who and where my father is?

The questions kept me awake until my body finally shut down around 2a.m.

After three short hours, I woke up and decided I needed to do something other than lay in bed and mentally drain myself.

I ran to the park; I ran around the park, and then I ran around it again.

Now I'm sitting on a bench at its entrance, trying not to look as anxious as I feel.

It's five minutes past nine when I see a silver sedan pull up and the woman from last night get out of the back seat. The car pulls away when she finds me on the bench.

As she approaches, I hear the thump of my heart picking up in my ears. My mouth is dry as I stand to greet her.

"Hi." She says first.

I can see her more clearly in the light of day. Under the cover of night, she seemed more youthful. In the harsh sun, her freckles are darker, her skin looks drier. She has to be at least forty years old.

In the observation of her features, I find myself looking for pieces of me. She has my nose or more accurately, I guess, I have hers.

Weird.

"Hi, how are you?" I ask her, standing up from the bench.

"I'm good. I'm really glad you came. Do you want to grab a cup of coffee?" She motions towards the cart next to the Encanto Park welcome sign.

"Sure. That would be nice." I agree, following her lead.

We stand in line behind two other people, silently waiting for our coffee. I notice she stands about a foot shorter than me.

It's hard not to make it obvious that I'm staring at her.

She, on the other hand, seems calm and oblivious to my presence. Much more composed than the frantic bundle of nerves she was last night. This seems like any other day for her.

I catch her smiling at a German Shepherd playing fetch with its owner on the lawn nearby.

"You wanted a pug so bad when you were little. Every day, from the time you were four until about six, you asked for a pug. You told me you were going to name him Buddy and that you guys were going to be best friends." She giggles, reminiscing.

"I don't remember that." I reply quickly, coldness lacing my response.

I feel my body tense and every nerve ending is on fire.

I'm haunted by a memory I don't even remember.

I close my eyes and picture myself as a little kid, begging for a puppy. It feels familiar, but it could just be my mind playing tricks on me. I still don't know that this woman is for sure my mother, but I intend to find out.

Call time for soundcheck isn't until 4p.m. and I plan on getting answers, even if it takes all day.

When I was waiting on the bench, I sent two texts before silencing my phone.

One to Jason confirming the details for tonight's show and where to pick up his backstage pass. The second, to Sam saying I was visiting hometown friends for the day so no one would be looking for me.

"What can I get you folks?" The man behind the cart asks us.

I snap back to reality and order my coffee. The woman, *my mother*, goes to grab money from her wallet but I stop her and pull out a twenty dollar bill from my pocket, handing it to the man.

"Keep the change." I say before walking towards one of the picnic tables next to the pond that borders the park.

We take seats sitting opposite of each other. For a while, we take turns staring at each other when the other pretends to look off into the distance, all while we sip our coffees.

"There was a lake near our old house that you used to love swimming in." She says, looking out at the water.

Her need to bring up memories that are clearly hers alone is starting to make me agitated.

"Why are you here…? Why now?" I ask, looking her in the eyes now.

She puts down her cup and awkwardly adjusts herself in the seat.

"Because I missed you. Because-"

"You miss me?!" I cut her off, now I'm seeing red.

"Yes, I do-"

"No! You can stop talking now. You don't get to tell me you miss me. How do I even know you're my mother?" I ask her accusingly.

I notice my voice is raised when the people playing chess at the next table over, stop what they're doing and stare at us. She doesn't seem to notice, though.

"Because I know you have a scar on your left knee in the shape of a heart. It's from when you fell off your bike. You were about six and still had your training wheels on.

"Some of the older kids in the neighborhood were making fun of you, I guess. You made me take them off when I got home from work.

"Then you made yourself learn how to ride a bike without them that night, and you did. Just a few bumps and scrapes along the way. The one on your knee being the only permanent one."

She's right about the scar. There's a strange look of pride on her face.

Why does it make me feel good?

"I don't even know what to call you." Is the only thing I can think to say.

"Whatever you want, Mom, Mother, Asshole, Horrible Bitch, Nancy."

"Nancy?" I repeat back as a question.

"Yeah, that's my name, Nancy Hale." She says.

Nancy Hale.

I say her name about 100 more times in my mind.

My mother, Nancy.

"But my last name is Archer." I argue.

"Your *middle* name is Archer, your *last* name is Hale."

"I can't even imagine how many questions you probably have. I know you have no reason to trust me but you already know my sickest secret." Nancy says.

"What's that?" I ask.

"Abandoning you, Link."

The moment the name leaves her mouth, I snap again.

"Don't call me that. I'm Lincoln to you." I state aggressively.

I don't care if things aren't great with Quinn and I right now. Only *she* gets to call me that. Hell, if Quinn didn't hate me right now, I probably would've called her last night. Maybe she would've talked me out of this.

My hands start to hurt from the white knuckled grip I have on the wooden picnic seat.

"Okay, *Lincoln*." Nancy acknowledges my request before she continues, "The worst thing I ever did was leave you at that fire station. I was young, I was scared…" I see tears well in her eyes and I have to look away to avoid growing compassion for her. I cut her off before she can say more.

"I was *young!* I was *scared!* Does that mean anything to you?" I say, looking at the ducks swimming in the water instead of the regret streaming down her face.

"I know, but you deserved better. I thought anyone could give you a greater life than me. I truly thought you had a better shot without me. And look at you, I was right. You're a big rock star now."

"*You* don't get to take credit for *my* success. I worked for everything I have. I built my life from nothing! I am who I am, not because of you, but *despite* you." I shoot back, this time staring at her cold blue eyes.

She should cry...she should feel bad...right?

"You're completely right. That wasn't okay for me to say. I wasn't trying to take credit for you. I know it might not mean anything to you, but I've spent the last fifteen years getting better.

"I'm not perfect, but I'm fixing myself every day. I think I'm finally a version of myself that might deserve a relationship with you. I was going to look for you eventually, soon in fact.

"But then, back in May, I turned on Good Morning America and they had on this new and upcoming band called Compass. They were playing a live show in Central Park. I loved the sound. It reminded me of some of the stuff I listened to in my twenties.

"When the camera panned to you...I thought my heart stopped. You didn't look up in the camera, you were too focused on playing your guitar, but I just knew. You're my son.

"I did a little more research and found out you were from Flagstaff. When I noticed you didn't speak about your family in interviews, it just confirmed the gut feeling I had.

"I saw online you guys had a tour stop planned for Phoenix. I knew this would be my only chance to try to get in contact with you. The show was already sold-out, so I figured out where the bands park their buses when they play Celebrity Theater.

"I was hoping I'd bump into someone who would at least give you my number. When it hit 11p.m. last night, I realized that you guys were probably posted up in some fancy hotel but I was determined to wait until the morning if I had to, just to give someone my number to pass along to you…then you showed up, out of nowhere in the middle of the night.

"When I saw you in person, it was like every maternal feeling I've buried as punishment for being undeserving resurfaced. I just wanted to hug you and apologize. I saw you were nervous and reaching for your phone, so I decided to just give you my number and asked you to meet me here, putting the ball in your court before you got too freaked out, then I left.

"I don't want to force you to talk to me. I don't want to force a relationship with you. All I'm asking is for you to give me the day. Let me show you who I am, then you can make a final decision if you hate me…please."

I take my time responding. A few minutes go by, filled with the sounds of birds chirping and people talking in hushed tones at the surrounding tables.

"Fine, but this doesn't promise anything past spending the day with you." I establish.

"Deal." she says with a smile

***

To my surprise, the day flies by. When I stopped looking at Nancy as my "abandoning mother" and tried to see her as a person, it got easier, bit by bit.

After coffee, she rented us a paddle boat to ride along the water through the park. The pedaling proved to be a good distraction when conversations would grow silent.

It was also nice to focus on something when trying to get through tougher discussions.

It's always easier to say hard things to people when you're not looking at them.

On our excursion, she told me more about her past. She was sixteen when she had me. My father was her old boss from a

pizza shop she worked at back then. When he found out she was pregnant, he paid her off to…get rid of me…and to never speak to him, *or his wife*, again.

She took the money and bought a car for us to live in when she worked, making deliveries for a different shop.

It was our first home before she got a permanent spot in a women's shelter once she had me.

After our paddle boat ride, we grabbed sandwiches from a food truck in the parking lot and sat by the water again, this time on the grass by the edge.

That's when she told me about Brad. She started dating him when I was about three. They got an apartment together and for a while, I guess things were normal.

Brad had a good construction job and my mother started her own nanny service. The only stipulation to clients was that she could bring me with her.

She was smart and driven. I started to get lost in her stories, wondering how any of it ended the way it did.

About two years into their relationship, Brad fell off a ladder at work one day. He hurt his back pretty badly and had to get surgery.

He was out on leave for six months when he healed. The doctor prescribed him OxyContin and several other pills for pain.

For months, the doctor had filled prescription after prescription when Brad complained of pain still. Nancy told me she suspected the pain was fake after a while.

Then she told me that one day I asked her about my real dad, and she felt pain, so she took one of Brad's pills.

The next day, another.

They spent the next two years fighting over how to split Brad's prescriptions.

That was until Brad's doctor was disbarred for malpractice.

Brad's new doctor took him off the OxyContin and made him go to a methadone clinic to come off of all his medications. He was angry and my mother was left without a source for her fix.

The street value of pills was high, but heroin was cheap and strong.

So that's what they did.

It wasn't long before things blew up. Brad didn't go to the clinic because he couldn't pass their drug tests, which resulted in the loss of his workers' compensation checks.

Shortly after that, my mother showed up doped out to a house one day and that was enough for word to spread and for her to lose all her business.

Without a source of income, savings dwindled. Utilities slowly got shut off. Vehicles were repossessed. The inevitable sped up by the prioritization of drugs over things like food and heat.

One night, Brad got a little too greedy with his dose and didn't wake up. When Nancy came to and found his dead body, she freaked out. That's when she put on my coat and walked us down the road to the fire station.

She told me that when she walked away from the fire station, she decided to get sober and went back to the house to collect every trace of us. Then, she called a cab, leaving Brad's body to be found by someone else.

She spent her last $100 to get a one-way bus ticket from Flagstaff to Phoenix and a motel room for the night.

The next night, she started working on the streets with a few of the women she met at the motel. She worked enough in one night to pay weekly rent at the motel and feed herself.

Twenty-four hours later, she relapsed for the first of many times, feeding her habits.

Eventually she was able to afford to switch to waitressing, when she stopped using, which is what she's still currently doing. She said hasn't used heroin in five years and that she wouldn't have been able to get clean without me as her motivation.

We're currently sitting in an Uber, on the way to her place. She said she had some photos of me she wanted to give me so I figured I'd Uber to the theater for soundcheck from there.

I can't believe I'm even thinking about it but, I might almost *like* my mother.

What she did was horrible, and I don't know if I could ever fully let go of that.

But now, with context, I understand it.

Just a little, I get how someone might feel like a black hole who's pulling everyone into their darkness.

When the driver pulls up to the Divine Pine Motel, I'm a little taken aback. I guess I didn't realize she was still living at the motel. I think she can read it in my expression when I look at her.

"It's just me, so the rent is cheaper for just a room." She says, smiling as she gets out.

I follow her to door number fourteen on the bottom level. When she opens it I'm met with the stale smell of cigarette smoke. It's tidy for the most part. A few piles of clutter on the table near the kitchenette and some laundry on the armchair next to the small couch adjacent to the bed.

"Have a seat on the couch. I know I have those pictures somewhere." Nancy says.

I take a seat and watch her rifle through a few bags and boxes throughout the room. When she finds them, she takes a seat on the bed across from me, on the other side of the coffee table, and hands me the photos.

I leaf through about twenty pictures. There's a few of Nancy when she was young, one of her pregnant with me, and a few others with me as a baby.

There's one photo of me blowing out candles at a fourth birthday party I don't remember having.

The next, a picture of me dressed as Mickey Mouse for a Halloween I don't remember either.

Despite the absence of my memories, I have to admit, my mother and I looked happy.

My focus is taken from the photos when I see Nancy shift on the bed and a little packet of white powder falls out of her pocket onto the floor. I look down at the bag for a long moment before she scoops it up.

"It's just coke, sorry. Sometimes I need it to get through my late shifts. You must get that. Do you want some?" She asks, casually.

In all her confessions, I've revealed nothing about myself.

"I thought you said you were clean…" I say, feeling the urge to cry.

"Yes, I've been clean from heroin for five years. A little coke never hurt anybody." She states.

I'm trying to process what I just witnessed when she changes the subject quickly.

"So I was thinking maybe the next time you have down time from the tour you could come stay with me, or maybe I can even come to you in Nashville. I've never left Arizona before."

She's smiling at me like she didn't just destroy the image of her that I spent the day painting.

I don't respond, so she continues.

"It would be easier for you to visit me if I had a bigger place, though. I know we're just starting our relationship again, but maybe you could float me a few bucks for a place for you to stay when you come visit me. You're a famous rock star now, I'm sure it will be a drop in the bucket for you."

"Are you asking me for money?" I ask her, wondering where this took a wrong turn.

"A loan really, I'll pay you back. Once I have somewhere nicer to stay, maybe closer to the city, I can get a better job waiting tables at a nicer restaurant and pay you right back. It's mostly so I can see you though. It's for you." Her tone deceptively clashes with her words.

" You're unbelievable." I say, standing from the couch.

"Link…I was jus-"

"MY NAME IS LINCOLN!" I scream at her.

I'm blinded with rage. I march out the door and slam it shut behind me.

Before I can rationalize more, I go back into the motel room.

I walk up to Nancy.

I pull the bag of coke from her pocket.

I rip it open with my teeth.

I scoop some with my bus key.

I snort it.

I hand her the bag back and flee the motel room, slamming the door behind me again knowing that this will be the last time I ever see Nancy Hale.

***

I run for about six blocks before I finally call an Uber to bring me to the hotel where I have a room I still haven't checked into.

Quinn is going to kill me for missing soundcheck but I can't show up like *this*.

I can't believe I did that.

Why did I do that?

What the fuck is wrong with me?

I feel like my body is vibrating when the paranoia kicks in. I look at my phone and ignore the missed calls from Quinn.

Our Song

She can't find out I relapsed.

I send a quick text to Jason telling him I'm caught up with something so to come backstage *after* our show instead of before. Hopefully that doesn't raise too many red flags.

I need to take a shower.

An ice-cold shower.

I need to wash off and wake up from this feeling.

I stand under the icy stream for at least a half hour. When I'm finally done, I towel off and finally look at my phone again. We go on in one hour, fuck.

Why did I do that?

There's about ten missed calls and several texts from different members of the band. I decide to respond to Sam only, via text.

Me: I'm on my way.

Sam: Where the fuck
are you?

I hit send and get dressed.

I'm coming down to a normal heart rate by the time I finally arrive at the venue. I have the Uber driver pull me around the back so I can use the private entrance.

When I get out of the car, I see Noah sitting on the back steps. He looks up at me and laughs when I approach.

"Quinn's pissed at you dude," Noah chuckles to himself, taking a large swig from a pint of vodka in his hand. I notice it's almost empty.

"Should you be drinking this much before the show?" I ask him, almost wanting him to hit me.

A sadistic way to punish myself, I suppose.

"Should you be this late to a show? Besides, Quinn can't bitch at me when she's too busy bitching at you." He says in return.

"Touche." I reply, walking past him without further argument.

I find my way to the green room where Roni and Sam are trying to calm down Quinn.

"There you are!" She rushes over to me. "Where were you?!" There's not a trace of anger on her.

She's worried…about me.

She still cares about me…

I hate myself.

Just imagine how she'll feel if she finds out you snorted cocaine.

"I got caught up with friends. My phone was on silent. I'm sorry." I lie.

I'm having a hard time deciphering if I hate myself more for relapsing or lying to the woman I…*love.*

I *love* Quinn.

I don't know why now is the time that I'm realizing that.

I'm too late.

Our Song

I'm not good enough for her anymore. Maybe I never was.

I understand now why Nancy left me as a kid. I never thought I could, but I get it now. She thought I deserved better than her, the same way I know Quinn deserves better than me.

Fuck.

"Places people, we need to move." One of the crew shouts, shuffling everyone out towards the entrance of the stage.

I notice Noah stumble inside and fall inline with the rest of us like he's been here the whole time.

We find our taped squares on the stage and before I know it, Sam starts playing.

My fingers move purely out of routine. I'm playing my part, but I can't seem to focus.

My head is aching from my racing thoughts and the crowd screaming. I almost forget where I am when the stage starts rotating. I look up to help gain my balance.

That's when I see Jason in one of the front row seats shouting and crying tears of pride and joy *for me.*

I'm about to start another inner monologue of self hatred for disappointing the man that's a brother to me as well as all the other people I love, when something else catches my attention.

I turn to my right to see Noah trip over his mic stand, lose his balance and fall off the rotating stage, right into some guy's lap.

The stage lights come up and the crowd starts booing.

I fucking *hate* Arizona.

Chapter 19
August 2024 - Quinn

Is there a full moon that I'm unaware of, because *what the hell* is going on with everyone tonight?

"He just texted me. Lincoln is on his way!" Sam exclaims, relieved.

"On his way from where?" I ask, also relieved, but mostly furious.

"I don't know, the text just says 'on my way'. Relax Q, we have forty-five minutes until call time. We're okay." Sam tries his best to reassure me.

Nothing will make me feel better until I psychically see him and know for myself he's alright.

Earlier, when Sam told me Lincoln texted him saying he was meeting up with hometown friends, I was already suspicious.

Link's told me a decent amount about his life, and I'm almost 100 percent sure he doesn't have any friends he still talks to in Arizona.

Our Song

He has Jason, but I know he mentioned to Roni he wasn't driving down until tonight.

I kept myself busy all day, staying out of his business, desperately fighting the urge to text him to check in every hour. I can't send him mixed signals like that. It's not fair.

I have to remain professional and respect his boundaries. He's an adult, and he doesn't need me babysitting him. Or at least that's what I thought, then he didn't show up for soundcheck.

He's never been late for anything as long as I've known him. I immediately wanted to call the cops because something seriously had to be wrong, but that seemed extreme.

So I caved, and I called him. I had a good reason, as his manager, for checking in on him after missing soundcheck.

But he didn't answer.

I called nine more times since the first call, all unanswered.

Sam told me he would show up and not to worry. Noah said we could do it without him. Roni told me that she was sure everything was fine. Max just rolled his eyes.

Roni and Sam are sitting next to me on a gaudy orange velvet couch in the green room when I realize Noah is missing now, too.

He was just here a minute ago.

I stare blankly at the door for twenty minutes before I finally see Link walking in.

I jump to my feet, rushing over to him, but stop myself from pulling him into me.

"There you are! Where were you?" I'm pissed but also scanning him over to make sure he's in one piece still.

"I got caught up with friends. My phone was on silent. I'm sorry." He says, avoiding eye contact.

I *know* he's lying.

There's something wrong with him, but I can't tell what.

"Places people, we need to move." One of the crew yells.

Everyone's up and walking to the stage before I can finish scolding him. For now, I'm just glad he's here.

When we turn a corner out of the back hallway, I see the back of Noah's head and think I've gone insane because he definitely wasn't just in the green room, *right?*

My head's moving a mile per second as I see *all* my children off to the stage. I turn to head to my seat in the VIP booth while I try to slow my racing thoughts.

How do I even approach Link without making it personal?

I was worried sick about him *all day*.

I thought of him holding me again, telling me everything was okay. I thought of him dead in a ditch. I thought of him kissing me. I thought about him relapsing. I thought of him smiling at me. I thought of him crying or hurt.

How do I not hug him if he's sad?

How can I know his touch and stand close enough to listen but far enough to be out of reach?

I take my seat and watch Noah start singing the opening verse. I look to his left and see Link. He's playing fine. If something is seriously wrong with him, he has no obvious tell.

Our Song

The stage starts rotating as the audience goes wild. Noah's halfway through the first chorus when I see him start to wobble.

He looks like he's reaching for his mic stand for balance but instead he trips over it, taking a dive into some fans' lap.

What the fuck!

I jump up from my seat to get over to the section where he fell off the stage.

As I'm running down, I see the house lights come up and hear the crowd start booing.

This is so bad.

What was Noah thinking? Is he *drunk?*

When I make it to the floor, I see a medic with a bag run past me. I follow him over to the front row where Noah fell.

By the time we get there, he's standing up looking completely fine.

"I have the worst balance. I'm so sorry, sir. What size shirt do you wear?" He asks the concert goer as he sees me walk up. "Quinn, can you get this kind gentleman any shirt he wants from the booth?" He asks me.

"Are you okay?" I ask, ignoring his request.

"I'm fine. I just lost my footing."

"Are you sure that's it? Did you drink anything today?" I ask at a level only we can hear.

"No, you're being ridiculous." He says before he pulls me in for a quick kiss and climbing back up on stage.

When he pulls away, my lips burn with the taste of vodka.

***

These boys, *these children*, are going to be the death of me. I can't spend too long worrying about Link's wellbeing and sobriety before I'm worrying if the alcoholic I married will ever see sobriety as an option at all.

By some miracle, Noah rebounded with speed and hopped right back on stage. He's a smooth talker and as soon as the lights were off again he got the room's energy back to max capacity.

Aside from a few unfortunate hashtags on Instagram, such as #NoseDiveNoah and #NoBalanceNoah, as well as a blurry five second video of his slip, no one seems to be looking too far into it.

Also, no scary calls from anyone at the label, but I suppose there is still time for that to happen.

This will hopefully just go down as a silly misstep of the clumsy lead singer of Compass.

The rest of the show goes smoothly, but I notice Noah stays still on stage. I also notice how tense Link is.

I keep seeing him making eye contact with a guy in the front row that I'm assuming is Jason. I fight the urge to walk over and introduce myself. I'm desperate to learn more about Link from someone that cares about him as much as I do.

When the band finishes their encore song, "Red Lights," I head back to the green room and wait patiently for everyone to get back.

Sam and Roni stroll in together, talking about an idea for the next show. Max follows, making a B-Line right for the craft table.

Then Noah walks in and pulls me in for another hug.

"What a show, right?" He says like he didn't fall off the stage.

"It definitely was. Let's go back to the hotel room tonight. We went out last night." I say.

A discussion needs to be had about what happened tonight, but this is not the place or time.

"Not even one quick beer with everyone?" He begs me in a playful manner.

"No, Noah." I say, seriously.

"Jeez, okay buzzkill. I was just trying to have fun with you. Let me change and we'll go." He says, before disappearing into the bathroom.

"Has anyone seen Lincoln?" I ask.

"He walked out the back door with some guy when we got off stage." Max says.

I look to the bathroom door and see Noah's still inside. I'm just going to go check on him quickly. I need to ask one more time that he's okay so I can sleep tonight.

I know there's an argument to be had with Noah when we get back to the hotel and I bring up the vodka I clearly tasted from his lips.

I can't do that *and* worry about Link at the same time.

When I get outside, I look both ways up and down the alley, but don't see anyone.

Did they leave already?

He was so excited to introduce the guy he calls his brother to us yesterday. I don't have time to keep looking for him though, instead I send him a text."

Me: I hope you're okay.

Short and sweet.

Just a manager checking on her guitarist, who nearly missed a show and then disappeared into the night.

Very reasonable.

"What are you doing out here? I thought you wanted to go back to the hotel?" Noah asks, holding open the back door.

"Yes, sorry. I was just getting some air. Let's go." I lie, easily.

***

"We need to talk." I start, "What really happened tonight?" I ask Noah. He's laying in bed while I sit cross-legged at the end.

"I told you, I lost my balance." He hurls back protectively.

"Right, but when you kissed me, I could taste the vodka, Noah."

"*So*, I had a shot before going on stage. It's not a big deal." He scoffs.

"But when I asked you if you had anything to drink, you said you didn't. So you lied to me?"

"I didn't lie to you. I forgot." He counters.

"If you're forgetting your drinks, *there's a problem*." I say.

My palms are sweating as I gear up for the inevitable yelling that comes next.

"I don't have a problem." Noah shouts, shooting up from the bed.

Predictable.

"No? You don't think falling off the stage from drinking too much alcohol is a problem? You could have gotten hurt, or worse, you could have hurt someone! We could have gotten sued!

"If you didn't get back up as fast as you did, we could have been canceled. We could have lost our record deal. You would have ruined everything we worked for!" I yell back, compelled to stand up, too.

"Everything *we've* worked for? This is *my* band Quinn, I *let* you be a part of it." He says, turning to the mini fridge and pulling out a nip of Tito's.

"Just because you're embarrassed doesn't mean you need to bring me down!" I snap.

He drinks it down in one gulp as he steps toward the nightstand where the trash bin is and tosses the empty bottle.

That's when my phone buzzes.

I watch him look at it lit up on the nightstand.

Then he picks it up and unlocks it.

"Why the fuck do you care if Lincoln is okay, *Win?*" He spits out the name like poison.

My body grows cold and I freeze, unable to move and unsure of how to respond. Nothing I say is going to talk him down from his anger now.

"He almost missed the show tonight. I just wanted to make sure everything was fine." I say quietly.

"Mhmm, and why the fuck is he saying '*I'm good Win, I wouldn't be without you*'?" He reads the text out loud with rage.

"You're over analyzing this." I try to convince him, "He knows we're married, Noah. You guys are in a band together. Do you really think he's going to throw away fame? Don't be stupid." I say to Noah.

My words hurt me, but it's the ones I don't say that hurt more.

Don't be stupid, Quinn, he'd never risk it all for you.
You can't risk it all for him.

"Did you just call me stupid?" Noah yells in my face, seeming to abandon the anger from seeing the text.

I take a step back

"No, I said *don't* be stupid. I didn't say you *were* stupid." I throw my hands up in a surrendering pose.

"Don't fucking play with me, Quinn." He snarls, his breath hot against my skin.

I step back until I feel my back hit the wall.

"I'm not playing with you, Noah. Stop yelling, please." I beg.

Our Song

"You want me to stop yelling, *Win?* Would that be good for you, *Win?* Do you want to be with Lincoln, *Win?*"

"Stop!" I scream.

"What's the matter, *Win?*" Noah says, grabbing my throat.

I try to reach for his hand, barely grasping onto this wrist with both my hands. I try to break free, but my attempts prove to be unsuccessful.

I try to breathe, but a choked sound comes out of me instead. I gasp and it feels like I'm breathing through a paper straw.

"I…can't…bre-" I struggle to say.

One moment it's like there's nothing but blackness behind Noah's eyes, the next someone turns a light on and he lets go of me.

He looks down at his own hand, just like he did when he slapped me.

This time, he doesn't apologize, though.

Instead, he backs up from me. I watch, still leaning against the wall, afraid to move, as he goes to the mini fridge and puts a few nips in his pocket.

He gets his coat and slips on his sneakers before walking out of the room, closing the door gently behind him.

I stand against the wall, watching the door in terror, until my legs hurt, then I slide down and sit on the floor.

I pull my knees to my chest and sob.

Then, I sob some more.

I fucking *hate* Arizona.

Chapter 20
August 2024 - Quinn

Invisible Horizon went platinum the night Noah choked me in Arizona.

Two weeks have passed since then. The band performed a few more shows around Arizona before spending this past week playing around Utah.

The music video for "Phases Of The Moon" currently has four million views on YouTube and is still holding the number one spot on the "Billboard Top 100".

Currently, we're back home in Nashville. The band is almost finished recording a new song, "Moonshine Manor" for a new Netflix movie called *Wild*. It's going to be the song they use for the trailer.

It's sort of twisted how one half of my life literally couldn't be any better and the other half is in tatters.

It's even more twisted that one can't exist without the other.

Our Song

    After the band finishes their last recording session tomorrow afternoon, our two and a half week break starts.

    The tour was originally supposed to end the last week of August, but then it got extended. The only lapse in dates being the first two and a half weeks of September.

    These next few weeks are either going to be what Noah and I need, or frankly, what kills me.

    Some time away from being "Noah The Rock Star" and just being "Noah The Person" might be good for him and healing for our relationship.

    I'm hoping the removal of high-volume stress and public exposure will make him feel and act normal again.

    I need to know he can still be *him* under the character he's spent the last seven months playing. He used to be so gentle with me, *I miss that.*

    Since the night he saw that text from Link, we've had only surface level conversation.

    The next morning I woke up with him sleeping next to me in bed, smelling of booze. I laid there for what felt like hours until he woke up. I didn't want to risk waking him. It was my attempt at trying to prolong any heated arguments or fights that could escalate to another…altercation.

    To my surprise, he got up like it was any other day. He got dressed, ate breakfast, brushed his teeth before heading down to the bus for a day of driving.

    I sat up in bed, watching in fear the whole time. I felt like I was waiting for the tornado to touchdown, but it never did. He even kissed my forehead and said goodbye to me before going to the bus, too.

    At first, I questioned if he got so drunk when he left that he forgot what happened, but he was only buzzed when held me against the wall. There was no way he didn't remember.

I saw it as I had two options.

One, I chase after him and invite the tornado in.

Or two, I play pretend as long as he does.

We've been playing pretend for two weeks now.

He never brought up the texts with Link, so I never brought up the vice grip he had on my throat. Not exactly a balanced scale, but that's the price I'm choosing to pay to have my life stay together.

I chose not to respond to Link's text and waited for an untraceable, in person, conversation at the next rest stop on our way to Utah. I told him not to text me anything other than band related things.

He pushed me to give more context and asked why I was being so cryptic. I couldn't put my personal shit on him, even if it sort of had to do with him.

He also asked me if Noah hurt me again, and yet again, I lied to him.

Who have I become lying to the two men I....care very strongly for?

These days, I am unable to clearly define lines and feelings across the board.

Not really talking to Link for the past two months has hurt me more than I care to admit. This fake friendship feels like a death sentence.

I know I have Roni and the others guys to talk to but no one to really have a discussion with. Each stolen glance between Link and me adds to the ache in my heart.

Slowly and painfully.

We're nothing but greetings and goodbyes now.

I want to tell Link every day that I miss him.

Aside from whatever unspoken bullshit that lingers in the air between us, I miss my friend at the root of it all.

I want to tell him everything I haven't been able to. I want to tell him my dad died. I want to tell him that the neon yellow shirt he bought in Phoenix is ugly as sin.

I want to tell him I cry every night in the shower. I want to tell him I wrote a song for the first time in months. I want to tell him I miss the taste of his lips and how they fit with mine.

I want to ask him if he's okay. I want to know what happened in Arizona.

I want to ask him to run away together and never look back.

I want these feelings to go away because they are too heavy for me to carry by myself.

Nothing I want matters.

What I need does, and what I need, is my relationship with Noah to go back to the way it used to be. If not for my sake, then the bands.

Noah and I need to work. We need to fix this. That's exactly what this break is going to do. I need to remember how I got here and who I did it with, even if it's hard.

Sam's staying at Harvey's, spending time with him, his wife, and their daughter. Roni's going to Florida to meet up with an 'old fling' as she referred to it. Max is volunteering at an inner city school, teaching drum lessons in his free time.

Then there is Link, who, according to Roni, is staying at the Holiday Express in Nashville until we head back on the road. I know we just stopped in Arizona, but I'm surprised he's not using the time to go back for a little longer.

There I go again, wondering things that aren't my business.

"What kind of animal is that?" Roni asks me.

"What?" I ask, confused, forgetting where I am.

"That one, over there, looks like a racoon but it's maroon." Roni says, pointing at one of the caged habitats.

Who deeply contemplates their life choices and purpose, so much so, that they forget they're standing in the middle of a zoo?

Oh yeah, me.

"It's a red panda, Roni." I finally reply.

"Are you okay?" She asks.

"Yeah, why?"

"Flat out, Quinny, tell me what's going on with you."

"I said I'm okay." I reiterate.

"I really hate when you lie to me."

"I'm not lying. I'm fine, really. I'm just tired." I say, defending the lies I can't seem to stop telling.

"If you say so, just know I'm here if you need to talk about anything." She says before pulling me in for a hug.

I lean in and squeeze hard. I can't remember the last time I had a hug like this.

I feel the smallest piece of me heal.

"Okay ladies, are you ready to feed some lemurs!" Sam comes up and joins in, making it a group hug now.

Our Song

"Yes! I'm going to steal one and teach it tricks." Roni laughs, breaking apart our huddle and walking toward a tall man in a safari hat talking to Noah.

"Hi everyone, my name is Nick and I will be helping you folks feed our ring-tailed lemurs today. Follow me." He says to our group, before walking around to the right outer side wall of the exhibit.

We all step into a sunlit cement room with cerulean painted walls. There is a giant table in the middle, taking up most of the room covered with towels.

I watch as another zoo worker brings a produce filled bucket to Nick and places it on the table in front of him. Then, leaves the room, shutting the door behind her.

"Okay folks, everyone grab a few pieces of food. I'm going to open this window and they'll come right in. They've got strong little noses on them. Let them approach you and hold the food out with open palms. Some may eat out of your hand, others may take the food and go back into the sanctuary to eat alone before returning for more. Everyone one ready?" He asks, as we all grab several fruits and vegetables from the bucket and shake our heads.

Nick wasn't kidding. Not seconds after the window is open, two large lemurs come swinging into the room. They look around cautiously before deciding our group is no threat.

"Holy shit, they're like hulked-out squirrels!" Max exclaims, arms shaking as he laughs.

The one with orange eyes was about to approach Max's strawberry filled hand but as he starts cackling, turns and makes a B-Line for Link's romaine lettuce.

We stand silently, arms out and filled with food, watching in awe as three more lemurs enter the room.

All five take turns between each of us, taking bites and pieces until the bucket empties. Once the last of the food is gone, the lemurs start making their way back into the main portion of their habitat.

All but two, that is. One with burning yellow eyes and a smaller one with cool emerald eyes stay behind.

They sit in the middle of the table grooming themselves, then each other. It's all very adorable and PG until I see the bigger one with the yellow eyes make his way to the backside of the other.

"Are they about to…" My question is answered when the lemurs…get into position.

I search the room for Nick, hoping this is the part where he ushers us out of the room and allows the animals their due privacy. Instead, he's just watching.

"Get it little buddy!" Says Noah, laughing with Sam.

"Should we leave?" I ask, unable to contain my own laughter.

"It's better to not disturb them and let them finish. It won't be long." Nick says.

I laugh more because I assume he's joking, but after the fourth and final minute of watching the miracle of lemur life be made, I sorely realize Nick was indeed *not* joking.

The lovebirds make their way back into the enclosure and Nick finally opens the door to show us back to the main path of the zoo.

"I hope you all had a good time and learned a lot. Please visit us again here at the Nashville Zoo." He says, before casually walking off.

Our Song

"Did we all really just watch live lemur porn as a group?" Max asks, in tears.

"That felt illegal to watch." Link says.

"I hope they name their baby after me," Sam jokes.

"That's going to be me on a Miami beach next week." Roni laughs crudely before high-fiving Sam.

"I'm glad you had a nice day at the zoo, kids." I laugh.

***

I pull into Edward Recording Studios and put my car into park. I forgot my planner here earlier when we wrapped up the movie song.

I just need to run in and grab it before heading home to have dinner with Noah. I'm already ten minutes late.

It's weird being back in our apartment, even if it's only for a few weeks. I remember when we first moved in, it felt so big for the life that I had known until that point.

Now it feels small, claustrophobic almost.

I'm going to suggest renting something bigger for our down time over dinner tonight. Tour ends in December and I want to be more comfortable and have a little more space when the band writes the next album.

I get out of my car and head inside. When I unlock the mixing room we rented for the week, I'm surprised to see the lights are on.

I must've forgotten to turn them off when I locked up earlier.

I grab my planner from the table and walk towards the booth door where the light switch is and freeze.

I'm paralyzed from the sight of a naked girl straddling Noah in the recording booth.

He's sitting on one of the couches spread through the high ceiling room.

Evidently, he's also running late for our dinner.

His hands are pulling at her hair, face buried in her chest.

Her head is tilted all the way back, eyes closed and mouth open. One hand is behind her on his left thigh, the other is between them.

It takes a few moments, but I eventually recognize her. *Kayla*, the audio assistant that's been working on the new song with them.

I wonder if this is the first time.

I wonder if she's the first.

Does it matter?

I watch a while longer, waiting to be caught. Waiting for either one of them to look up and see me catching them in the act. Waiting to officially become the foolish wife.

But they don't hear me choking back tears behind the glass, they don't hear the rampant screaming in my head.

Then, I do the darndest thing.

I leave.

I get back into my car.

I drive for fifteen minutes.

I run up four flights of stairs, because the elevator would be too slow.

Our Song

I bang viciously on a white painted cold metal door, like an animal in a cage.

When the door opens, I step in without a welcome.

My lips crash into his.

Link's hands find their way to my waist as I pull his shirt over his head between our feverish kisses.

My shirt meets his on the floor next.

Then, my bra.

Chapter 21
August 2024 - Lincoln

The clock on my hotel room night stand reads 3a.m. It takes a few moments for my brain to catch up with my senses. When I smell strawberries, I fully awaken.

I look down at my chest to see Quinn's head laying against it. To my right, I feel my arm wrapped around her small frame. I pull her tighter to me ever so lightly, soaking in the feeling of holding her while she sleeps.

She fits perfectly into place like the last bit of a million-piece jigsaw puzzle.

The room is lit with nothing but moonlight. I can only make out shapes and shadows painted on the wall just beyond the bed. Peering over the edge of the mattress, I see a trail of clothing that starts somewhere around the front door.

When I heard the panicked banging last night, I thought there was a fire. My first assumption was that a neighbor or hotel worker was alerting me to leave, so I didn't burn up in flames.

Our Song

Without thinking, I jumped up from where I was sitting on the couch. I had just gotten back from grabbing food and was about to…*shit.*

I look at the coffee table and see the small baggie of white powder still next to my keys.

I was about to take a bump of cocaine when the banging started. Well, *another* bump.

When I opened the door and I saw it was Quinn, I didn't have much time to hide it, nevermind processing why she was there or why she was kissing me like my lips were her only source of oxygen.

While I've made a habit out of poor decisions lately, I'm not a complete idiot. I will take any ounce of Quinn that she is willing to give me. Whether it be a knowing glance across a crowded room or the skimming touch of our hands in passing.

I want it all.

Never did I think what happened last night would be an option, but she was there, pining at my clothes as I licked off her cherry lip balm.

My shirt was taken off before she even closed the door behind her. By the time she was braless, I was able to use the last bit of common sense in me and reach past her to close it myself.

Our lips locked from the door to the bed that she pushed me onto, not that it took much force or convincing.

"Are you sure?" I had asked her as she fought my belt out of my jeans.

"I'm on birth control." Was her only response before both of our pants were on the ground.

What followed was probably, *no, definitely*, the best night of my life.

I didn't have sex with Quinn. I made love to Quinn and I think she knew that. It wasn't just a hookup, it was a true expression of my love for her.

I've never experienced the feelings I did with Quinn last night in my entire existence. No one has ever made me feel like they needed me, just me, as I am.

I've also never felt so safe and relaxed in the intimate presence of someone like that. I didn't have time to overthink it because I wasn't thinking at all.

Our bodies moved like two lost souls finally driving off into the sunset.

A unionizing of two halves, separated far too long.

I still haven't fully unpacked why I relapsed. I know it's my own fault and that something in me that I thought was healed clearly isn't.

Part of me fears it never will be.

The past few weeks, I've rationalized my recreational use of cocaine. Unknowingly, Sam has been my deciding factor. He has his shit together, and he does a little coke for fun and he's fine, why can't I be too?

I've begun to question if I was so young when I started using drugs and drinking that maybe it only became a problem because I was a child without a support system.

Now, I'm surrounded by good people who care about me. I'm an adult and I've lived more of my life. Most importantly, I don't have unanswered questions about the phantoms that made me anymore.

Our Song

I know who Nancy Hale is and I know I'm better off without her.

I can take care of myself. I've been doing it for years. As a result, I've rationalized that I can handle a bump here and there.

The days after the disastrous Arizona show, I asked one of the roadies, Micah, who gets Sam's supply, to help me as well. An eight ball was delivered to my hotel room later that night.

He asked if there was anything else I wanted and while I was tempted, I was proud of myself that I only asked for the coke.

It was my first exhibit of self control that validated my decision to stay on my current path.

I realize I just need a little something to make me feel better and have more energy. Coke provides that for me.

When the bag was gone after just four days, I realized that maybe I needed to slow down. With that in mind and the assurance that nothing bad had happened, I refilled again.

To monitor myself, I've been filling up small dime bags and not taking more than they can fit with me to rehearsals, shows and band hangs.

This form of discipline made me feel, until this point, this could be a realistic lifestyle for me. But now, I'm lying in this bed hoping to god the woman I love doesn't see the cocaine on the table.

Fuck.

The moment Quinn see's that bag, any hope of us is certainly gone. It only takes me thirty seconds to decide that I'm quitting and getting sober again.

I *will* be the person Quinn deserves.

I try to think quickly. I need to get her off of me without waking her and get rid of it before she wakes. This is one of the many punishments I deserve for being an idiot.

I look to my right and grab one of the unused pillows on Quinn's side of the bed.

Quinn's side of the bed. I like the sound of that. I want to get used to that.

Focus Archer!

I gently lift her head as I expertly replace my chest with the pillow, sliding out of bed like a slinky.

My feet hit the ground as I ease into my body weight, letting it pull me the rest of the way out of bed, all while securing the pillow under her.

When I'm finally out of bed and standing up right, I walk one slow step at a time to the coffee table. My fingers lightly graze the plastic but my pinky knocks into my keys, causing them to make a small jingle and scraping noise as they adjust on the table.

My hand freezes and I can hear my heart beating in my ears. I whip my head around to confirm Quinn is still peacefully living in dreamland. By some miracle, she is.

I turn back to the table and grab the bag without any further hesitation, then I make a B-Line for the bathroom.

I step lightly across the carpet and when I make it into the bathroom, I shut the door, turning the knob first so that once it's fully shut, the least amount of noise possible is made.

Then, I lock it.

My body is shaking and a thin sheen of sweat has formed on my brow. I lean my back against the cool metal door of the bathroom. I can feel my heart beating in my stomach when I look up and see my reflection in the vanity mirror.

I *hate* the man looking back at me.

He's a liar.

He convinced me this was a good idea, assured me that no one would know and that nobody would get hurt.

Before I decide to fist fight him, I walk over to the toilet and open the lid. I peer down at the small bag of white powder laying flat in my palm.

"I don't need you." I whisper to the plastic.

I turn my hand over and reach forward to flush the toilet when I hear the bag hit the water. I watch with confidence as the coke baggie flows in circles around the porcelain until it is finally pushed out of sight at the bottom by the new water rushing in.

I did it.

So why do I feel so bad right now?

It's more than just knowing I made a mistake when I walked back into Nancy's hotel room. I need to truly become better now. When I leave this bathroom I will live every moment of my life making myself worthy for her.

Quinn is the only drug I need to live.

I take a deep breath and open the door, ready to sneak back into bed and start being the best man I can be for Quinn.

All my plans are derailed when I step out of the bathroom and see her standing next to the bed, putting her clothes back on.

"Hey." I say, stepping behind her and pulling her into my arms.

Her back is against my bare chest and I feel her relax into my hold for only a moment before she's stepping out of it.

"Hi". She says to me without eye contact, still zoned into getting dressed.

"You know, you don't have to hurry and leave. We're on a break for two weeks, remember?" I ask playfully while I find my own pants and put them back on.

"I can't. I...I have to go home, Link." She's still avoiding looking me in the eye.

"Sure you can. In fact, you never have to go back there again. You can stay with me in the hotel and we can figure out our next steps." I smile, watching every curve of her body move.

"What do you mean next steps?" She asks, stepping into her pant leg.

"I mean figuring out how we're going to navigate being together and keep the band together. I know Noah can be a lot and that he loves you, but-"

"Lincoln, stop." Quinn says, at a speaking level with screaming agitation.

"What's wrong?" I ask, taking a seat on the bed, giving her space.

"I don't know, I-..." She tries to finish her sentence through tears that are forming, but is unsuccessful.

I watch as she takes a seat on the couch across from me. "I shouldn't have..."

"Please Win, you can say anything you want, but please don't tell me you regret this...us." I say, pleadingly.

Her eyes finally lock with mine and I can see the storms spinning behind them.

"I don't regret it. I don't regret anything we've ever done, I promise, but that doesn't mean I should have done this. At least, not like this. I feel so guilty." The flood gates open and I watch Quinn fight the streams descending her cheeks.

"Don't feel guilty, I don't feel guilty."

Or at least, I don't feel guilty about sleeping with you, but I don't say the last bit out loud.

"But *I* do. I'm no better than him. I should've gone home last night, I shouldn't have come here. This isn't fair to you." She's shaking her head back and forth like she's beside herself on the matter.

"I'll decide what is fair to me, Win. Just tell me what's going on." I say, gently.

"Last night, I went back to the studio to grab my planner that I left behind…and when I got there. Noah was there…"

"If he laid a single finger on you…" I'm standing now, despite the internal fight to keep a calm demeanor for Quinn's sake.

"He didn't, he didn't even know I was there…" She lets out a big sigh, like she's gearing up to tell me I have a terminal illness.

"I don't understand. Why was he even there that late?" I ask.

Her face changes from an expression of sadness to one of non-negotiable hurt.

"He wasn't alone. When I walked into the room to get my planner, he was in the booth…with Kayla."

"I don't understand, why were they…" Then it clicks. "He was having sex with Kayla?" I ask, trying to keep composure.

"Yes, he was."

"And your response was to come here…and have sex with me… Did you use me to get back at him?" I try to keep the anger from simmering into my tone.

"I didn't use you! I would never-"

"So then you're definitely not going back to him, right, if you weren't just using me?"

My question borders on a demand and I don't like it, but I feel desperate. I just got her, and she's already slipping through my fingers.

"I don't know what I'm doing, but I know I shouldn't have done this. Not saying that I shouldn't have slept with you, but I shouldn't have done it like *this*. He doesn't even know that I saw him last night. I need to talk to Noah, okay?"

"What is there to talk about, Quinn? He treats you as an after thought, he has put hands on you at least once that I know of and is literally out fucking other woman. You're his wife!" My voice raises with my last sentence.

"You don't think I know I'm his wife! I know what I did, I know who I married. That was my choice. You don't think I haven't thought about what it would be like if I met you sooner? I wish for everyone's sake it was only ever just us Link, but it's not, and in this current moment, it can't be." She gets off the couch and grabs her shoes.

"Win, please leave him. I'm begging you. Noah loves fame too much to leave the band. We'll get through it."

"NO WE WON'T! Listen to yourself, Lincoln," she yells, "If I go home and tell Noah that I'm leaving him for you, the band ends, my career ends, your career ends." Her words are clipped.

The scared look on her face is what bothers me the most.

"I don't care-" I begin to say, but she stops me.

"Don't Link."

"You don't even know what I was going to say." I argue.

"I do though, you're going to tell me you don't care about your career because you only care about me? Right? Aren't you?"

She looks at me expectantly as I try to think of another answer, because she's right. *I don't care what happens to me as long as I have her.*

I try to muster up the emotional strength to say literally anything, but she beats me to it.

"I'm honored that you care about me so much, Link, truly. But you have worked too hard and have gone through too much to just throw it all away. We both have." She returns to her seat on the couch and begins putting on her shoes.

I know my time to convince her of us is dwindling, and that realization floods me with emotion.

"You can't do this. You can't just come knocking on my door and let me think there is hope when there isn't," I make sure I'm standing in front of her when I continue. "I'm in love with you, Quinn Elizabeth Finch. I'm over the moon, head over heels in love with you, Win.

"Conversations are boring without you. Food tastes bland without you. Colors are dull without you. Music is meaningless without you as the muse. Every day I don't see you is long and insufferable. So please, I'm *begging* you, don't go back to him." I feel the hot sting of my tears trying to escape, but I won't allow them purchase.

"Link, I can't, not now." She states, standing up.

"Then when?! Name the time and place and I'll be there. Please don't shut me out again. I can't survive another day like this. I miss you, Win. I need you."

I step towards her, leaving no more than six inches of space to fill the hollow feeling that lies between us.

"I'm sorry." Is all she says as she steps around me and paces towards the front door.

"You can't come back." I say, immediately regretting the notion.

"What?" She asks, hand on the door knob.

"I can't do this back and forth with you anymore, Quinn. That kiss on the roof felt like every prayer I ever prayed was answered, and then you took it all away so fast, and didn't get a say in it.

"I thought you wanted me and then when we kissed and you ran away after, I hated myself. I thought myself no better than Noah. I felt like I took advantage, so I understood when you distanced yourself. I hated it, but I understood it.

"This, this I don't understand. You drove across town, ran through the hotel, banged on my door and then you kissed me. So now, I thought you finally realized that we were meant to be. I thought that you realized Noah could never love you as much as I do. I thought you realized you loved me.

"Then you give me this magical night where I feel safe and secure with you. I truly felt that you were finally coming home to me, but really, I'm just a placeholder for you when you're mad at your shitty husband." I feel as ugly as my words.

"It's not like that at all. How could you say that?" The look on her face, one of betrayal.

"Then don't go. Stay right now and I'll know, but if you walk out that door Quinn we're done. All of this between us will be done. I can't be *just* your friend anymore, not now that I know how it feels to wake up with you in my arms."

"Link, please…"

"I'm serious, Win. It's me or him."

I immediately regret the ultimatum I issue her, mostly because I know the answer before it's confirmed by the sound of the door shutting behind her.

"FUCK!" I scream to no one but my own frustrations.

I find my phone and text Micah.

> **Me:** I need another ball.

> **Micah:** Got it. Be to you in an hour.

Chapter 22
August 2024 - Quinn

I've been driving around in circles for hours.

I'm numb.

I've never felt so guilty.

I've also never had such clarity.

I need to leave Noah. That seems imminent.

Similar feelings from the first time Link kissed me arise on my drive home. However, they are immediately stifled by flashbacks of last night.

Kayla, naked and on top of Noah.

My heart broke, but I'd be remiss if I didn't admit I also felt freed by it.

The part of me that had felt like it was drowning finally broke through the surface. I felt like I could breathe and I knew exactly where to find my favorite source of air.

Oxygen outweighed logic.

Our Song

Noah's actions still don't justify my own. I should've waited and properly figured out my marriage and split up with Noah.

I've run out of time to think of more hypocritical regrets when I pull into the parking garage of our apartment.

I have no texts or missed calls from Noah, which is alarming. The silence is all too eerie to me.

I'd expected that when he eventually got home last night and realized I wasn't there, he would be mad. I surely thought when I didn't come home at all, he would be infuriated and blow up my phone.

Yet, there's been radio silence between us.

On my way up the elevator, I recount every second from the studio. There was no way he saw me catch them.

He was too busy with Kayla's left breast shoved in his greedy mouth. I debated the possibility that she could have seen me, but her pupils were rolled too far back in her skull for her vision to have worked.

I feel heat creep up my neck when the doors open to my floor. I need to go in there calm and cool. If I go in on the defensive side it will be impossible to avoid an explosive altercation.

I will tell him what I saw and what he did, and that this is no longer working. He clearly doesn't love me if he takes no issue in sleeping with other people. This isn't working for either of us, so we're done. It's simple.

I can remain a capable manager of the band and operate impartially. The only mystery left unsolved is how Link and I will find a path together *and* keep the band intact.

One problem at a time, Quinn.

I unlock the door and see Noah sitting on the couch. His elbows are resting on his knees and his head is hanging low. His eyes seem to be fixed on the shag area rug under the coffee table.

"Hi." I say, shutting the door behind me.

He picks his head up but doesn't move. I walk over to him slowly, taking advantage of every second I have to assess the situation before he responds. I sit on the adjacent love seat and wait.

"Hi." He sheepishly responds.

Is he sad?

I still say nothing, waiting for him to lead the conversation.

"I know you're mad that I didn't come home last night. Please don't hate me."

Did he just say he didn't come home last night?

Does he think I'm just coming home from doing something this morning?

I freeze, unsure of how to proceed.

Do I tell him I didn't come home either?

I could easily just say this is the last straw and leave now. He'd never even know I wasn't here last night, too.

He looks defeated. Maybe this is my chance. My internal debate on honesty ends before I can speak, though.

"I have to tell you something, Quinn." His stare slowly raises to meet my own.

"Okay." I say, flatly.

Our Song

"I didn't come home last night because I couldn't face you. I didn't know what to say to you. I stayed in a hotel downtown by myself."

My mind starts to spiral.

What hotel?

Did he see me at Link's hotel?

Is *he* about to *leave* me?

"Where were you?" Is the only thing I can think to ask.

"I was at the studio last night first. I was working on writing a song when Kayla, the sound assistant, came in. She said she was there, grabbing something from one of the offices, and heard me playing.

"At first we were just talking. She listened to the song I was writing and was giving me some ideas about the different instrumentals for the chorus. One thing led to another and…" He drops his head again, burying his face in his hands this time.

I watch silently as his shoulders start shaking.

Is Noah crying?

I've never seen this man shed a tear in his life. Not when his grandmother died, not when he broke his ankle, not even during that really, *really* sad part of *My Girl*.

But now, here he is, *crying.*

"I'm so sorry, Quinn. I slept with her. I don't know why I did it and I feel so terrible about it. I know you're going to hate me forever, but I am truly sorry. You have to believe me."

His glassy red eyes look up as he reaches forward and grabs my hands with his sweaty palms.

"Noah, I'm d-" I try to speak, but he stops me.

"Please Quinn, you need to know how much I regret it. I don't like the person I've become. I need you to help me find myself again. I know that's incredibly insane of me to ask, but please, I need you. I will do anything and everything to earn back your trust."

I stand up and begin to pace around the living room, making small circles between the entryway and kitchen.

Of all the things I anticipated him saying, a full admission was not on the list by a long shot. I wasn't even prepared to fully tell him my own truth.

My guilt starts to take the lead in the never ending race against my anger.

I should tell him I cheated, too. It's right on the tip of my tongue, but I can't say it.

Shame and fear blend together, creating a sour taste in my mouth. My silence prompts him to continue his pleas.

"It was a mistake, and I will never betray you like that again. I was feeling insecure, and I let that take control. There isn't an excuse in the world for my actions. I was a selfish and horrible husband.

"I know you don't owe me anything, but please just give me a chance to make things better. I will live every day to serve you and love you the way you deserve. I know I've been rash and angry the last few months. Being in the spotlight has made me cruel.

"I've read the things they say about me online, the things they print in magazines. That I'm a talentless hack or an industry plant. People speak about me like I don't have feelings.

"Every day, it feels like I have to prove people wrong about me, so much so, that I've disassociated myself from the real me. Noah Taylor feels like a character I've created on stage now. The role of a man who doesn't care about what other people think or say.

"I didn't realize until it was too late that this person I've created is a villain. I've done you a disservice. I haven't been present like I should and I haven't treated you like you deserve.

"Last night, when I chose myself again, I realized I truly hate the man I've made myself be. So if you hate me, I understand, but please know, I probably hate myself much more." He lets out a sigh as he drops his head down again.

I stop pacing across the room, wondering why it took him sleeping with someone else to say what I've needed him to say for months.

It should be easy for me to own up to cheating at this point, but I still can't get myself to say the words, and if I can't admit to my own infidelity, am I any better than him?

Do I really deserve Link, or anyone for that matter, if I'm just as destructive in my decisions?

The sound of Noah crying again breaks a piece of my soul. I do love this man, even if I somehow hate him at the same time.

I'm not any better than him for what I did, but at least he's admitting it to me. I can't even convince myself to be honest with him.

I've had just as much to do with the deterioration of our relationship as Noah has . I've been distracted and dishonest too. I've had an equal hand in it all.

I've been hiding my feelings for Link for months. I've kept things from Noah. Now, I find myself in this confessional, unable to repent. I'm really no better than the villain he's acted as.

Maybe we deserve each other.

Noah has lost himself in the success and I think I have to. We've both inevitably changed by being plunged into this new life.

In the process, both of us have created new identities to protect ourselves. And if that's the case, don't I owe it to Noah, as his wife, to give him at least one chance to do right by it all?

I am the problem too.

If I was a better wife, maybe Noah wouldn't have felt like he needed to stray. Hell, if I was a better wife to Noah, I could have avoided hurting Lincoln altogether.

I was hoping this break would help me and Noah before I walked in on him and Kayla. Maybe it still can.

I step forward and kneel down between Noah's legs, picking up his face in my hands. We look at each other through mutual tears.

"I think we both could be better partners to each other. That being said, I don't know if our marriage can survive another blow. So I'm here on my knees, begging you to please give me the old Noah back."

He reaches his arms around me, pulling me tightly against his chest.

"I promise you, Quinn, I will never hurt you again. I'll make it up to you. I love you."

"Okay." I agree.

Chapter 23
September 2024 - Quinn

It has been almost two weeks since Noah and I essentially agreed to start over in our marriage.

I've decided to let my night with Lincoln remain undisclosed. The guilt of it all stays at bay by the reminder of everything Noah has done to me as well, in addition to Kayla. It's a contorted balance, but one that I can live with.

Noah and I have stayed in the apartment for our two weeks of vacation. We did a lot of catching up on sleep and watched a lot of movies. It has reminded me of the early days when we were just starting to date.

It's been, I dare to say, *nice.*

Last night, I texted each member of the band a meeting time and place for the buses for tomorrow night. Everyone but Link has responded to me.

I'm sure he hates me for leaving and he would be justified in doing that.

I'm laying in bed staring at the unanswered text when Noah walks into our room.

"Pack an overnight bag and a nice dress." He says, smiling.

"What?" I ask, locking my phone.

"You heard me."

"Why?" I ask.

"Stop asking so many questions and let me do something nice for you," he walks over kissing my forehead, "we're leaving in an hour."

"Where are we going? We leave for the last leg of the tour tomorrow night." I say, concerningly.

"And we will be back by tomorrow afternoon. Now, pack a bag and stop arguing with me." He laughs.

"Not until you tell me where we are going." I cross my arms across my chest in stubborn playfulness, puffing out my bottom lip in a pouting gesture.

"Vegas." He smirks.

"Wait, we're getting on a plane, and flying to Vegas, for one day?" I ask.

"It's cool being rich and famous sometimes, right? I just figured it would be nice to have a fancy dinner and walk Fremont after, if I can keep a low enough profile that is. Maybe we can even pop by and say hi to Batman," He laughs innocently. *I love that laugh*, "Now get moving." He says, walking out of the bedroom before I can ask more questions.

The conversations between us haven't been as real as they have in the last few days for months.

I think we were right, we just needed a break from the fame to find ourselves again, and now that we've found ourselves and know how we lost them, I feel confident we can avoid it from happening again.

***

As soon as we land, we're greeted by a chauffeur and limo, waiting for us outside the airport. The driver opens the door for us and puts our luggage in the trunk before driving us to a house about twenty minutes away from the strip.

I look out the window in confusion as he pulls down a long white stoned driveway that leads to an orange clay shingled house.

"I hope you don't mind. I got us an Airbnb instead of staying on the strip. I just figured having somewhere private to go after dinner would be nice in case I get recognized," Noah says as he helps me out of the limo.

"I think this is incredibly kind and I appreciate your thoughtfulness." I respond, smiling.

"You deserve it, Quinn." He says before pulling me into a kiss.

While we've gotten back into a normal rhythm of conversation, I've held out on any physical contact for the moment. We've shared a peck or two before bed once or twice, but that's really the extent of our affections.

But now, Noah is kissing me softly and deliberately. I find myself leaning into him, giving in to the small butterfly coming back to life inside of me.

"Should we go inside and get ready for dinner? We have to leave here in an hour to make our reservations." He asks, pulling out of the kiss.

"Yes." I say, letting him take my hand in his as he walks us up the driveway towards the house.

We bring our things inside and start to get ready for the night.

I've chosen a form fitting black cocktail dress with matching heels. Noah is matching me in black slacks, a black t-shirt and black sports coat.

"So where are we going anyway?" I ask Noah, as we climb into the back of the limo.

"So many questions. Don't you ever like to be surprised?" He asks through a laugh.

"No, never." I say, smiling.

I spend the ride looking out the window as the city lights approach and grow around us. There's traffic on the strip, but I love it. I vicariously watch the tourists through tinted glass.

Everyone looks so happy and normal. Walking around with friends or family. Taking pictures of the sights, capturing memories together, uninhibited.

I envy those people, but I don't know why.

I have it all, don't I?

My train of thought is interrupted by the feeling of Noah's hand on my shoulder.

"We're here, Quinn."

Our Song

The driver gets out and opens the door for us. When I step out of the limo and look up at the towering hotel, I see a sign that reads The Strat in bright blue lights.

"Is the restaurant here?" I ask.

"So many questions." Noah says in answer, before taking my hand and walking us through the front doors.

We're ushered by a hotel worker to an empty elevator. We step inside and I watch as Noah pushes the button for the top floor.

We hold hands in a peaceful silence the whole ride up. When the doors finally open, I'm greeted with large floor to ceiling glass windows framing the skyline view of the strip.

The city is lit up like a thousand stars.

"I hope this is okay." Noah says.

"Are you kidding me? This is amazing!" I'm still stunned by the view.

"Mr. Taylor, right this way." The host says as he walks us to an intimate round table with two chairs facing the window.

"Thank you." I say, while Noah pulls my chair out for me before taking a seat himself as the waitress makes her way over.

"Good evening, my name's Candice and I'll be your server tonight. Could I start you out with something to dri-"

I look up at young, blonde Candice and notice her eyes grow large as she looks over Noah's face.

"You're Noah Taylor right? Oh my God, I'm such a huge fan."

"I am. It's nice to meet you, Candice." Noah says, extending his hand before shaking hers.

"Sorry, I'm just a little star-struck. What can I get you to drink?" She laughs.

"I'll take a whiskey, neat." Noah replies with a smirk.

It should be criminal how easily he switches into his Mr. Famous persona. I try to quiet my thoughts because Noah hasn't done anything wrong.

"I'll have a Diet Coke, thanks." I say to Candice.

"Perfect, I'll be right back with your drinks." She says cheerily before walking away.

I could be over assessing the situation, but I swear I see Noah watch her as she walks away.

He's done being that guy, I remind myself.

"So what are you thinking, chicken or fish?" I ask, trying to move on from my discomfort.

"Chicken. Do you think I should offer to sign something for her?" Noah asks.

"What?"

"Should I offer to sign something, since she's a fan?"

"Oh, uh I mean if she asks you to that would be nice, I guess."

We sit in a one way awkward silence before Candice returns with our drinks.

"Have you given any thought to what you might want, Mr. Taylor?" Candice says, oblivious to my existence at the table.

"Call me Noah, please, Candice. What would you recommend?" Noah asks her.

Didn't he just tell me he wanted the chicken?

His question feels like an unnecessary excuse to talk to her more. Something akin to jealousy begins to sprout in my chest.

"Oh, I don't know. I'm a vegan, but a lot of people order chicken." She answers.

Of course she is.

I'm realizing now that everything about young-pretty-blonde-vegan Candice bothers me.

It's not her shameless flirting that's agitating me though. It's how easily Noah is feeding into it, fueling it even.

"I'll get the chicken then, but I'll hold you to it if I don't like it." He laughs with her, handing back his menu.

"Are you part of the band, too?" Candice turns and asks me.

I'm too occupied with picturing young-pretty-blonde-vegan Candice falling out of one of the floor to ceiling windows to answer in a timely manner, so instead Noah answers for me.

"She is Compasses manager."

"Oh, that's super cool! Did you want the chicken or fish?" She asks me.

"Chicken." I say firmly while staring across the table at Noah.

I don't even break eye contact when I hand her back my menu.

The daggers I'm casting towards Noah are obvious, I'm sure, but he's too distracted by Candice to notice.

"I'll go put that in for you two and be back to check in shortly." She says in her chipper tone.

"Can't wait." Noah says, with his *stupid* laugh.

I wait long enough for any staff to be out of ear shot before saying something to Noah.

"Are you kidding me?"

"What?" He asks.

"You can't be serious?"

"What are you upset about now, Quinn?"

"Well, for one, you introduced me as the band manager, not your wife."

"But you *are* the band manager. She's a fan. I thought she'd be excited to know your part of the band."

"I just don't understand why you couldn't introduce me as both then."

Am I being paranoid right now?

"Quinn, calm down. It's not that serious."

"I'm telling you how your actions made me feel and you're telling me they're not serious?" I rebuttal.

"Of course, your feelings are serious and important. I'm sorry, I was just trying to be nice to a fan. What's wrong with making someone's day?" He asks innocently.

We look out the windows without discussion as we wait for our food.

I'm plagued with unasked questions.

Was Kayla really the only one?

Was the protection of our bubble the only thing keeping us civil for the last two weeks?

Is this how it's going to be when we're back on the road?

"Alright, here are your orders. Can I get you guys anything else?" Candice asks, putting down our plates while she smiles at Noah.

"We're all good here, thanks." I say, quickly.

She gives me a disconcerting look before leaving us to our meals. We eat in silence, just enjoying the food and view.

All I can picture is Candice in a similar position to Kayla. At this very dinner table, naked and straddling Noah over his chicken.

I wonder if I were to get up and leave right now, if Noah would hang back and rent a room here for the two of them.

I'm simmering by the time Candice returns at the end of our dinner with the check.

"Thank you so much for dining at Top of the World, here at The Strat. I hope you come back soon." She smiles, taking away our empty plates.

I watch as Noah grabs his wallet and replaces the check for three 100 dollar bills before closing the folio flat on the table.

"Ready to go?" He asks.

"Yes."

The quiet follows us down the elevator and to the car park in the front of the hotel.

"Should we head to Fremont for a bit?" Noah asks.

"I'm actually feeling tired. We should go back to the house." I say.

I think it's clear I'm upset, so Noah doesn't argue as he opens the limo door for me.

"Back to the house." He tells the driver.

We sit in traffic on the way back, but the people watching isn't as enjoyable now.

"So, how much was dinner?" I ask.

"Don't worry about it. It was my treat."

"I know, but how much was it?"

"Why do you care, Quinn?"

"It just seemed expensive. $300 is a lot for two entrees, three whiskeys and a soda."

"I tipped well." He says, looking out the window.

"How much is well?"

"Why are you acting like this?" His tone catches an attitude.

"Like what?" I ask, confused why he's the angry one right now.

"We'll talk about it when we get back," Noah says, ending the conversation.

The remaining ride back to the house is slow and grueling. The air in the limo is thick with intensity by the time we finally pull up the driveway.

I don't wait for Noah or the driver to open my door before I open it myself and head into the house.

The cool night air feels like such a relief that by the time I get into the house, I feel suffocated again. I see the back slider on the other side of the living room and walk out to the back yard, needing the relief of the cool air again.

"What is your problem tonight?"

Noah followed so closely behind me I didn't notice him on my heels.

Our Song

"I just want to know how much you tipped her." I say, turning to face him.

"What would it matter? You've clearly decided you're already upset with me. I tip well now because I can afford to. I'm just giving back."

Don't get me wrong, I absolutely believe in properly compensating service workers, but to me it's clear as day *why* he tipped her that well.

"Give me the check."

"What? Why do you need to see it?" Noah's voice raises and when it does, his speech sounds slightly slurred. It's clear he has a buzz going.

"I saw you put it in your wallet. If you're not going to tell me how much you tipped her, let me see how much dinner was."

He stands still, making no attempt to reach for his wallet.

"Quinn, you're being-"

"Give me the check, Noah!" I can't tell if my loud tone is warranted or borderline delusional.

I watch as Noah hesitates before pulling out the check. He pulls it out of his wallet but instead of handing it to me, holds it up for me to see.

When I see the total price of $150, I'm annoyed that he tipped her 100 percent.

When I notice the moonlight shining through the paper, casting a silhouette on the phone number she wrote on the back of it, I'm outraged.

"Are you fucking kidding me?"

"What?" He asks.

"You're telling me you didn't take the check because her number was written on the back?" I ask, even though I already know his disappointing answer.

"She did? I didn't notice, relax." He says, playing dumb and dismissing my concerns.

I want to yell, but more so, I want to cry.

It's not just the drinking and partying that turned Noah into a villainous self loathing liar, it's the fame.

As long as he gets recognized, he's going to be this character and this character is not my husband.

He can't be.

"I can't believe after everything we've tried to work through the last two weeks you would take a girl's number!" I yell louder.

"I said I didn't notice. You're acting insane, Quinn!" He matches my volume.

"Am I though? What reason do I have to believe you?" I ask.

"Why are you ruining this nice night I planned for you?" He asks me, instead of answering my question.

"*I'm* ruining the night? I'm pretty sure you courting the waitress in front of your wife ruined the night." I snap back.

"You're so dramatic, I'm going to bed," Noah says, turning back towards the house.

"And you're a pathetic, cheating liar!" I hypocritically scream.

I reach to wipe away the tears I'm crying, but Noah's hand makes it to my face first.

Our Song

The sheer force and surprise of it knocks me off my feet and I feel the back of my head hit dewy grass as I fall down.

I think he's about to help me up or apologize, but instead he walks another few steps towards the patio door before he turns around to face me again.

"Who's pathetic now?" He says, his voice stone cold.

I watch as he walks back into the house, slamming the sliding door behind him.

I lay in the grass and cry for what feels like hours. I recount the night and start to wonder if I instigated this, if he really *didn't* notice her number.

When I finally pick myself up off the ground, I decide I'll sleep on the couch and we'll talk about it in the morning when he's less buzzed and I've slept.

I pull on the slider but am met with resistance.
What the fuck?
I pull harder, but the door won't budge.
He locked me out.
In the backyard.
In the cold.
Like a dog.

***

I spent the entire night planning how I'm going to leave Noah. I fell in and out of moments of sleep a handful of times, resting against the sliding door.

I'm exhausted and enraged.

My back is still to the slider when I feel it move so I lean forward and turn around.

"What are you doing out here?" Noah asks me, squinting his eyes in the morning light.

"You locked me out!" I yell.

"No I didn't." He says with a straight face.

Does he actually believe his lie?

I decide the fight is beneath me. I'm packing my bag, getting on a plane home and ending my marriage with Noah when we get back.

Not exactly in that seamless of an order though.

I tried to call Link, but he didn't answer me. I probably would've called him a few more times too if my phone hadn't died.

As soon as I see him at the buses, I'm telling him that I'm leaving Noah. I'm sure he's still upset with me for walking out on him at the hotel, but I know we can get through that.

I'll do whatever he wants me to do. We could quit the band and run away together if he wanted, and I would gladly pack my bags.

None of it matters anymore if I can't be with him.

I've spent the last two weeks being the best wife I can to Noah, and he has proven to be an incredible disappointment and a pathological liar.

The limo ride to the airport, flight back to Nashville and Uber ride to our apartment, pass by like a silent film.

There's no indication of what Noah is thinking or feeling, but if I had to guess, I'd say he's unbothered. He probably thinks this is going to blow over.

Our Song

When we get home, we unpack our Vegas bags, then begin packing our tour bags. The vocal reserve remains through the afternoon and seeps into the car ride to the studio where we are meeting the buses.

By the time we arrive at the studio parking lot, I've concluded Noah thinks this one will be swept under the rug like the rest.

We get out of the Uber and are greeted with warm welcomes from Sam and Roni, standing around with a few crew members.

"I've got so much to tell you, bitch!" Roni says, pulling me into a strong hug.

"Sounds like it." I force a smile, enjoying the affection.

"Where's Max?" I ask, watching Noah and Sam unload the bags from the back of our Uber and into the buses.

"Already on the bus, probably busting someone's balls about lighting or whatever he found to complain about," Roni says, laughing.

"And Lincoln?" I ask, trying not to seem desperate for an answer.

"Haven't seen him yet. I'm sure he's on his way." She gives me a comforting smile.

"Hey Roni, come show Noah the riff you wrote!" I hear Sam yell from the door of one of the buses.

"You coming?" Roni turns to me before going over to Sam.

"I'll be right there," I smile, "just taking in home for another minute."

"You're so fucking cute, Quinny. I missed you." She says as she departs.

I sit on one of the parking space bumpers, watching the road for any signs of slowing cars.

My soul feels like it's engulfed in fire. I gave it a shot, a real genuine shot, with Noah and he proved me right.

I don't have guilt anymore.

I know what I want, even if it took me this long to realize it.

My legs feel restless from their nervous bouncing when I finally see a car pull up to the curb of the studio. Excitement floods through me and I shoot up from where I'm sitting.

I see Link step out of the car and my heartbeat quickens.

Looking at him feels like a homecoming I've never felt before. I'm in love with Lincoln Archer, and I'm finally ready to tell him.

I will follow him to the edge of the galaxy if he wants, as long as we're together from now on.

I begin a quick pace towards him when I notice a short red-haired girl get out of the driver's seat and walk around to where he is.

I halt, dead in my tracks.

Who the hell is that?

I watch, standing in the middle of the parking lot as the woman hands Link one of his suitcases and gives him a hug.

Neither of them seem to notice me staring at them. They're in their own universe.

My heart stops when I see him whisper something in her ear and I hear her laugh.

Our Song

I want to know what he said to her more than I want to breathe right now.

Why are they acting so giddy?

Who is this girl?

I watch as Link caresses his hand against the back of her head and kisses her.

Chapter 24
September 2024 - Lincoln

I open my eyes and they immediately sting. My mouth is dry and every muscle in my body is screaming. Victoria's mattress is the most uncomfortable thing I've ever slept on in all my life. The beds on the tour buses have more cushion than this spring-loaded block.

I don't know why I keep choosing to sleep at her place when I have a perfectly good hotel room under my name, downtown.

That's a lie.

Yes, I do.

It's because I don't want to be alone. All my friends had these great plans for vacation. I debated seeing Jason, but I was terrified if I spent too much time around him, he'd know I was using again. I still don't know how I managed to play everything off to him back in Arizona.

Our Song

When I found myself alone, hiding from my only family and watching my friends live their lives on the other end of a screen, I did what I do best.

I played.

I booked a studio for the full two weeks and started a routine for myself.

Wake up, line.

Drive to the studio.

Play, line, play, line…

During the first week of break, I wrote six songs. Each one of them, about Quinn.

I'd come to terms with the fact that I'll never be able to play them in front of her or the band. Despite that, I decided to record them anyway as a really sad sort of diary. They'll never see the light of day or be heard by anyone's ears. It would be too painful and embarrassing.

On my fourth consecutive day in the studio, there was a knock on the door. I opened it, surprised to find a girl around my age impatiently tapping her foot.

"Ugh, Hi?" I said, opening the door.

"Hi." she said, looking up from her phone, revealing her blue eyes.

"Hi." I repeated, unsure of what else to say to this stranger.

"Are you going to let me in?" She asked.

"Why?"

"Because I have your delivery," she said as she tucked a red ringlet of hair behind her ear. "Wait, is this studio 2A?"

"This would be studio 2*B*," I corrected her politely.

"My bad man, have a good night." She said, turning back down the hallway.

"Wait." I said.

I didn't know what else I had to say to her, but I wasn't ready for this peculiar conversation to end.

"What?" She turned back in confusion.

"I don't see any food." Was all I could think to say.

"I make different kinds of deliveries." She smiled slyly.

"Oh."

If life were a cartoon, a giant light bulb would've illuminated above my head.

"Well, have a good night then." She said, starting to depart.

"Wait!" I said again. "I didn't order a delivery, but I would like to."

Something about her smile made me feel good, so I invited her into the studio.

I learned that her name was Victoria, and that she had just moved here. She was helping her brother move some product around the local music scene while taking a gap year before college. She's staying with him in the meantime.

It's more than cocaine, though. It's molly, ecstasy, meth and heroin. You name it, they have it, and if they don't have it, they can procure it.

She's a hell of a sales woman too. I replaced Micah with her after our first interaction at the studio. She saved me some money by convincing me to buy higher quantities for a slightly smaller cost, but to be honest, I just liked her company.

Every morning I'd place an order, whether I actually needed it or not, just to talk to her.

We became friendly quickly and so she would invite herself to come sit and hang out in the studio with me in her down time between deliveries.

It wasn't just transactional. Victoria liked my music and I liked someone hearing it. I even decided to play her my "diary". She doesn't know it, but she will be the only one to ever hear my pain on the subject.

She's made me feel heard for the first time in a long time. The scars from Quinn are still healing, but I know she made her choice, and it was Noah.

I needed to start choosing myself. So when Victoria decided to sit on my lap one afternoon, I didn't stop her.

When she kissed me, I let her.

When she wanted more, I gave it to her.

I got completely lost in her. Call it a distraction or master compartmentalization, but I felt better. I got to be someone else with her and it was so easy.

I didn't have to hide my use. She didn't have a husband. Our lives weren't hanging in the balance. We didn't expect anything from each other but company, and that was all I wanted.

Company.

The last few nights I've let Victoria convince me to have a few percocet. I know I promised myself it would just be a little coke, but the coke doesn't relax me the way the pills do.

I can actually sleep with the pills.

I hear a train pass over the tracks behind Victoria's apartment and am brought back to the present. As I wake up more, last night starts slowly coming back to me. I think I asked Victoria to be my girlfriend.

No, I definitely did.

My memories catch up to my mind and I remember.

We ordered pizza at the studio and she told me she was going to miss me when I left.

So, I asked her to be my girlfriend, just like that. I think knowing she cared enough to miss me caused me to cling to her, even if we would be apart for the next four months. At least I would have someone.

It's a good plan, or at least that's what I thought at the moment. I'm still surprised she said yes.

Now, with the anxiety of seeing Quinn today breathing down my neck, I'm not sure anything will allow me to survive the day unscathed, not even Victoria.

The hurt of seeing her with Noah might deteriorate the progress I've made.

When Victoria wakes up next to me, I try to stop remembering the feeling of Quinn in her spot.

I've done this every morning that I've slept here.

"Hi." She smiles.

"Hi." I kiss her cheek.

"When do you have to leave?"

"About an hour." I answer, noticing we slept until 3p.m.

"I don't want you to leave." She says, holding my face in her hand.

"I don't want to leave either, but it will be a fast four months. Watch. I'll be back by Christmas and we can spend the Holidays together." I say optimistically.

"I'm glad you have it all figured out." She laughs, stretching her arms.

Our Song

"Are you going to drop me off at the studio or should I schedule an Uber?" I ask her.

"Make my *boyfriend* pay for a ride? Never! Now come here, we still have an hour." She giggles, pulling the blanket over our heads.

***

I'm already running about fifteen minutes late. I debate asking Victoria to stop for a coffee that I don't really need, just to prolong seeing everyone a little longer.

She reaches over from the driver's seat and rests a delicate hand on my bouncing knee.

"Are you nervous about getting back on stage?" She asks.

"You could say that," I smile at her, "I like how you make me feel. I wish I could feel that way a little longer." I finish saying as she pulls up to the curb of Edward Recording Studios.

"This should last you until you're back." Victoria says, pulling a small black backpack she and her brother put together for me from the back seat.

"Thanks." I smile and hesitantly open the passenger side door.

I get out of the car and watch as Victoria gets out, grabs one of my suitcases from the back seat and meets me on the sidewalk.

When I turn and shut my car door, I see Quinn in the parking lot and she's making a B-Line towards me.

I know she's pissed I didn't answer her text and phone call. I shouldn't have to check in with her, though. I'm an adult and I can show up on time without her reminders. She doesn't need to look out for me anymore.

She's probably just mad that I'm late, but I don't really care.

I'm late because I was trying to prolong the pain that seeing her has already brought me.

I pretend I don't see Quinn and grab Victoria close to me and kiss her.

I hope it stands as a sign to Quinn that I've moved on and I don't need her to coddle me. The last thing I want is her sympathy.

"Why does this feel like a permanent goodbye kiss?" Victoria asks, pulling back from me.

"It's not, it's a see you soon kiss." I laugh, feeling like a fraud.

She smiles and we hug one more time before I take my bags from her. I stand on the sidewalk and watch her get back in the car and drive off. When I have nothing left to stand around for, I turn back towards the buses.

Quinn is gone, and it looks like the crew is finishing loading all the gear.

First stop, Chicago.

Chapter 25
September 2024 - Quinn

The eight-hour drive to Chicago felt like a million. I just got everyone checked into their rooms at the Congress Hotel, and I'm ready for bed.

We left at 6p.m. to avoid traffic, which I thought was a great idea. Now it's 2a.m. and I can't tell my left from my right.

After Noah and I dropped our bags in the room, I left him to grab water from the vending machines. My current problem is, I can't find the vending machines.

I quietly wander down two endless hallways when I finally see the sign for them. I turn left into the alcove where the machines are and nearly scream.

"Holy shit, you scared the crap out of me!"

"Sorry." Link says.

"You have no reason to be sorry. I'm just half awake." I laugh nervously.

A majority of the million hour drive was spent thinking of my first interaction with Link after leaving him at the hotel.

I mean, sure, I thought about it over break too, but my original plan doesn't seem as smooth now.

I thought coming back was going to be easy if Noah and I were okay.

Yes, putting Link in that situation at the hotel was unfair and I truly regret any pain I've caused him, but I'd hope at least that he would understand.

I could explain that Noah's changed, that he told me the truth, that he really was just having a hard time too. Now that those notions, and the ones of running away together, are out the window, I feel like I have to pretend to be happy with Noah.

Not to make Link jealous but to show, in a messed up way, that his pain wasn't for nothing.

I want to think the friendship we built will transcend the drama, eventually. At the root of me, I love him as a person and always will. I care about him and I want him to be okay.

After seeing Link with that girl, it's clear he's moved on. It hurts, but if I expected him to be my friend when I stayed with Noah, don't I have to be his friend if he's with her?

"What do you want?" Link asks, pointing at the vending machine.

"Oh, don't worry, I can get my own."

"Okay." He shrugs his shoulders, continuing his monotone demeanor.

I should probably mind my business, but when have I ever done what I *should* do?

"So, who was your friend that dropped you off?" I ask, trying to sound more like an inquisitive friend than the intrusive person I'm actually being.

"Victoria."

"And how do you know Victoria?"

He grabs his water from the machine and turns to me. He looks like a mixture of angry and confused.

"The studio."

"Oh, did you record stuff on break? I'd love to listen." I say, genuinely.

"No." He says with an opposing sternness.

"Did you write something with Victoria?"

"No."

"What did you guys do in the studio if you didn't record or write?" I push.

"Why are you doing this, Quinn?"

"Doing what?"

"Acting like everything is normal between us." His eyes look like fixed snipers, ready to shoot.

"I'm just trying to be polite." I say, defensively.

"No, you're trying to play twenty questions with me instead of just asking the one *real* question you want to ask. So go ahead, *ask me*."

I hesitate, but I don't think I could sleep without knowing.

"Is she your girlfriend?"

"Yes."

"That seems quick." I don't mean for it to come out as judgemental as it does.

"No quicker than you changing your mind between me and Noah."

"That's not fair." I say, even though he's not *completely* wrong.

"How is it not? You used me and then you left. I held out hope for days. I stayed up late every night, just in case you knocked on my door again. I thought maybe, somewhere in that infuriatingly beautiful brain of yours, you would finally figure out you're too good for him.

"I thought you'd leave him. You had me fooled, but it's clear that you never will. I refuse to be the idiot who follows around the girl that will never love him back."

It's on the tip of my tongue to tell him that he's wrong and that I do love him. I want to scream how mistaken he is.

But I can't.

He's moved on and pulling him back in again would truly make me the worst person alive. I love him, so I have to let him be happy.

"It's more complicated than that and I wish you'd let me explain that." I plea.

"I don't want to hear your explanation's right now. You broke me." His voice chokes at the end.

"I'm so sorry, Link. What I did is unforgivable. But I really miss my friend, and even if you hate me right now, I hope, eventually, you'll forgive me."

I hope you're okay.

I hope you're happy.

"I need time, Win." He says, walking past me, turning the corner back into the hallway before I can respond.

Our Song

***

I used to get excited about these band outings, but now they just feel like a chore.

Curse me and my never ending ability to plan.

When we first got booked for the tour, I planned out the entire year until August in one night. Then, did the same when it got extended.

That feels incredibly stupid now.

I should be looking at the penguins currently being fed. It's one of the cutest things I've ever seen.

But I'm not.

I'm looking at Link responding to text messages every other minute, all from Victoria, no doubt. I'd commit a capital offense to read their conversation.

When we got on the bus to come to Shedd Aquarium this morning, everyone was in good spirits. It made me optimistic that we could have some quality family time before the first show back tonight.

That seems to be going pretty poorly at the moment. It doesn't feel like we're bonding as a group like our other outings.

Noah and Sam are busy talking up the girl holding a bucket of fish. Link is obviously occupied on his phone. Roni has stayed close to me but also seems to be more invested in her current text conversation. And Max…

Where the hell did Max go?

"Did you see where Max went?" I ask Roni.

"Hmm, yeah, they're really cute." She says, without looking up from her screen, clearly not listening.

"I think I'm going to shave my head." I test her.

"Mmm, yeah, I agree." She fails, still on her phone.

"I'm going to adopt seventy-six cats and move to Oklahoma."

"Love that."

"I'm going to quit the band and rob banks for a living instead."

"Mhmmm."

"I'm in love with Link."

"Wait, what?" She says, finally joining my one sided conversation.

Fuck.

"I'm kidding!" I recoup, "I was saying a list of ridiculous things, and you would know that if you weren't so invested in whoever you're texting right now. Who are you texting anyway?" I ask, changing the direction of the conversation.

"Shame, I was going to start planning your wedding."

"I'm married to Noah."

"People divorce every day, my parents did. Granted, I never thought me coming out of the closet would be the catalyst for it, but my dad and I are better off. And for your information, *nosy*, I'm texting Paige." She smiles, bumping her shoulder playfully into mine.

"Is Paige 'Florida Girl'?" I ask, keeping on the subject.

"Paige is indeed, *Florida Girl*. I don't know what it is about her, but I'm hooked. Usually I like to keep things casual, but with her, I don't know if I can."

"Does she make you happy?" I ask.

"Yes."

"And does she treat you well?"

"Yes, she's one of the nicest people I've ever met. It's weird." Roni laughs.

"Then I say go for it. What's stopping you other than your usual pattern?"

"I guess for so long I just wanted to focus on playing. I've been working really hard to achieve success someday, and now that someday has finally arrived, I don't know what comes next."

"Maybe it's Paige." I say, grabbing her hand in mine.

"Maybe it is." She grins, squeezing my hand.

We stand at the edge of the penguin exhibit holding hands, peacefully watching their feeding time. It's a nice, quiet five minutes of appreciating the little creatures before I hear Sam and Noah approach us.

"Aww, *now* will you two kiss?" Sam asks, laughing at me and Roni's current stance.

"Not until you and Noah play tonsil hockey first." She snickers, turning around to face them.

"We're going to go check out the whale exhibit. You guys coming?" Noah asks.

"I thought we were going to see the Dolphin show at 2p.m.?" I ask.

"But Rachel's about to go give a talk about the Beluga's!" Sam whines.

"Who's Rachel?" Roni asks.

"The nice girl feeding the penguins." Sam says, looking back and waving at the blushing blue-haired girl.

"Ahhhh." I say.

"Yeah and I need my wingman to talk me up to her about how important I am to our *very* famous band. *Pleaseeeee, Mom!*" Sam jokes, changing his tone to mimic a toddler begging for candy.

"Fine, but we need to be back on the buses at exactly 3p.m." I agree.

"You're the best, Q-Tip." Sam says, grabbing Noah's arm and pulling him along to follow Rachel.

Roni and I laugh amongst ourselves, watching Sam follow her like a baby duckling.

"Now that's someone who will never settle down." Roni laughs.

"That's for sure. Now, let's go find this dolphin show." I say, walking towards the exit sign of the exhibit.

"Lincoln, are you coming?" I hear Roni shout behind me.

I turn for only a second to see Link start to follow behind us, eyes still locked on his phone.

We follow a few dark hallways lined with tanks and onlookers. This place is so huge and impossible to navigate, I have to stop and ask a worker for directions.

"Okay, she said it was out this door, but I can't remember if she said left or right." I say to Roni as Link lingers a few steps behind us.

"I think it's left. Maybe it's through that white tent over there?" Roni suggests, pointing at the large canopy.

We walk under the tent and turn the corner to see a large raised pool in the center.

"Well, this definitely won't fit a dolphin."

"No kidding, Roni." I laugh.

When I look around the tent, I see a worker on his phone in a chair under a sign that reads "Touch Tank". Then, I see them.

"It's sting rays!" Roni says, beating me to the revelation. "Can we please pet them, Quinny? The dolphins can wait." She asks, walking up to the worker before I can agree.

As I round the other side of the pool, I notice Max sitting on one of the benches on the perimeter of the tent.

"There you are. I was looking for you earlier. Have you been here the whole time?" I ask.

"I wanted some air, so I stepped out here and saw this tent. I thought it was a quiet spot to take a second." Max explains.

"I get that. Sometimes I need a minute too." I admit.

"This is awesome!" Roni says, elbow deep in the pool.

"At least someone's having fun." I say.

Max and I laugh as we watch Roni have the time of her life.

Shockingly, Link puts his phone in his pocket and joins Roni.

"Come on, Quinny, you gotta pet one of these babies!"

"Fine." I laugh, giving into her request.

I roll my sleeves up past my elbows and reach in.

"Just hold your hand flat and they'll swim against you as they follow the whirlpool current." The worker says.

I do as instructed and wait with my hand submerged. The stingrays feel a lot smoother and a lot less slimy than I thought they would.

It's calming watching them swim round and round. Just floating with their pack.

It seems like a dream to be a stingray. No one expects you to be anything but a stingray. By simply existing, you are doing all that is expected of you, and all you have to do to be happy is swim.

It's kind of beautiful to think about.

"Maxi, you've gotta try this!" Roni yells enthusiastically across the tent to where Max is still seated on the bench.

"I'm good." He says.

"But they're so cool!"

"I said I'm good Roni." Max says with growing agitation.

"What, are you scared or something?" Roni asks, instigating him more, but he doesn't respond. "Shut up! Are you really afraid of the stingrays?" She laughs.

Link and I are both looking at Max now, waiting for him to shut Roni down, but he doesn't.

"So what?" He finally says.

"Max, you're like the scariest dude ever, and you're afraid of a little stingray?" Roni asks.

"You saw what they did to Steve Irwin! He had a family! Poor Bindi and Robert were just babies!" Max says defensively as he gets up from the bench and storms out of the tent.

All of us, including the worker, stand in an awkward silence for a moment. The stillness is broken by the best sound I've heard in weeks.

Link's laugh.

We all join in, uninhibited laughter fills the tent before slowly dying down as a family walks in.

I watch the worker greet them as Roni goes back to petting the stingrays. When I look over to Link, he's already looking at me.

I wonder if he misses my laugh too.

We exchange half smiles before Link removes his hand and walks away to answer his phone.

I don't know why, but that small exchange feels promising and it gives me an idea.

***

The band is about to go on stage for the first time in almost three weeks. The excitement is high and the crowd at Huntington Pavilion is full of energy.

The band is lining up and getting ready to walk out. Of course, Noah is first followed by Sam and Roni. Then Max, and at the end Link.

I've gone back-and-forth if this was a good idea or not since the touch tank, but it's not like he could hate me anymore than he already does.

Right?

I take my chance when I hear the announcer hyping up the crowd. Everyone's distracted, trying to peek over the side to see the audience. I walk up to Link and place it in his hand, then hold my pointer finger in a 'shush' position.

I walk far enough away to not linger, but close enough to still watch his reaction.

He delicately unfolds the napkin and stifles a small laugh as he looks down at my, anatomically incorrect, drawing of Max being eaten by a stingray.

His smile is all too quickly replaced with his usual straight faced disposition. Then he slips it into his pocket instead of discarding it in the perfectly good trash barrel he's standing next to.

Chapter 26
October 2024 - Lincoln

We're in the middle of playing "Sugar Sugar" and the crowd is going wild. Thousands of singing fans form an ocean of faces, but I'm only searching for one.

Last week, I invited Victoria to come to the show we're playing in Washington tonight. I offered to send her the money to fly out and rent a car, but she refused.

"It'll be part of my gap year adventure, plus you can't fly with *certain things*," she argued.

I called her before we went on and she said she was walking into the VIP pit, but I still haven't seen her. I try not to get too anxious, but it's hard when I know what she's bringing with her.

We've been back on tour for almost a month and my backpack is running low. I only use when I'm alone, which is more often on this leg of the tour than the last. Quinn never hangs back anymore. I successfully pushed her away.

I'm not proud of my increase in use. When the tour is over I plan to take some serious steps to cutting down. But, for now, I need to get through the next two and a half months.

I have a few lines in the morning and before the shows, then when I get back from the concert, I take to percocet to make myself crash.

Then I do it all over again.

While a restocked bag isn't the reason, I invited Victoria to this show, it's definitely a benefit.

I don't feel comfortable asking for Micah for anything more than coke. Call me paranoid, but I feel like it would raise some red flags and somehow get back to Quinn.

Rock stars do coke. It's just what we do. No one cares about the coke.

I didn't tell anyone that I invited Victoria to the show, or that I offered for her to stay for a few days. I'm pulling a "selfish".

Watching Quinn and Noah be happy is hard. I'm craving that type of company.

Even though the break was only two weeks, it's taken me twice as long to get back into the routine of things.

I quite enjoyed the bubble Victoria, and I had been in. No schedules or rehearsals. No interviews or talk shows, it was nice. I didn't have to be "on", so to speak.

It makes me look forward to the end of the tour in a cumbersome sort of way. A longer break from the limelight is needed.

I'm not sure what's next, but it seems like another album will be expected of us. Last night, I overheard Quinn on the phone with someone from the label talking about a new contract.

Compass was only signed for the one album initially, but with its success and the tours demand, it seems inevitable a second one is coming.

It's clear they're trying to woo us into staying signed with them by the extra amenities we've been allotted for the last leg of the tour.

For example, we haven't stayed in a hotel since the first week back. The label has been booking us Airbnb houses instead of hotels.

In addition to their generosity of our accommodations, they've also provided two Escalades and private drivers that have been appointed to us to follow our buses.

It seems a little extra, but it's nice not having to always take Ubers when the buses are too distracting.

Quinn calls it a sign of good faith, but I see it for the bribery it is.

It's clear they weren't expecting an *actual* overnight success when they only contracted one album with us.

Now it seems they're trying to secure their spot to produce the next one, and possibly more, before a bidding war starts.

"Phases Of The Moon" is the only song left in "The Top 10", sitting at number nine.

Overall, we had a record breaking streak for a debut album and I'm proud of how long we charted. We achieved Multi-Platinum status last month while playing in Montana, our momentum has started to steadily decline since then.

The song ends and I'm brought back to the moment. The stage lights brighten to a shade of yellow on the crowd as we transition into the next song, "Eras".

It's not much easier to see in this light, but the faces are a little more discernible than the purple hue they were before.

I make my way towards the right edge of the stage and try to get a closer look into the crowd. As the song starts to pick up in the chorus, white strobe lights begin to flash, allowing me half second frames to comb the crowd.

I walk towards the middle of the stage when Noah is busy entertaining the left. Once I'm front and center, it only takes me three seconds to pick her out. Her curly red hair is illuminated by the border of a spotlight, in the back of the first section of VIP.

She's standing on her seat waving to me. I nod and give an air kiss motion to the audience in her direction.

I get confirmation she knows it was for her when I see her catch it and stuff it in her pocket.

****

Victoria and I stumble in the front door of the Airbnb around midnight, or more accurately, *Victoria* stumbles in.

I am acting as a human support beam as she walks with her left arm swung around my shoulder. It's a good thing I haven't taken drinking back up or I wouldn't have been able to drive her car back here.

When the concert was over, I gave my pack and guitar to tech and got the hell out of there. I threw on a baseball cap and met Victoria at the back exit. Then we got into her car and drove to a restaurant on the edge of the city for dinner.

I enjoyed the fettuccine, and Victoria enjoyed the wine. I don't mind, it's nice taking care of her. It makes me feel useful.

The more we spoke over dinner, I realized how much I missed her. I decided on the drive back to the house that I'm going to ask Victoria to stay until the end of the tour.

What's two months, *really?*

We're not cramped and staying on the buses, or even hotels anymore, we have houses now. It's not like Victoria is some random person. She's my girlfriend.

I know Quinn won't be thrilled, but I think she'll be okay. We've exchanged small talk in passing between outings, shows and rehearsals, but I've still been keeping her at an arm's length.

It's hard to talk to her and not immediately want to forgive her, just to stop the fake niceties and have a *real* conversation with her. But, I've held out, it's better for both of us this way.

An additional perk of Victoria's presence is the resources it yields. It's good knowing if my backpack runs low again, her brother probably knows someone to refill, no matter where we are.

I'm doing my best to support Victoria's weight and get her up the stairs, but it's proving to be a challenge, working against gravity.

We're fumbling into the walls, laughing our way up the steps.

I'm thankful the group planned an outing at a bar after the concert. That guarantees we'll have the house to ourselves for at least a few more hours.

That's what I thought at least, until we edged the top of the staircase, and I see Quinn walking down the hall. She looks as surprised as I do.

"Oh, hi….Sorry, I hope we didn't wake you. I figured everyone was at the bar." I say, breaking the silence first.

"No, I have an early meeting, so I had one of the drivers take me back. I'm surprised you didn't see the SUV in the driveway." She says, looking over Victoria like a tactical threat.

"I was a little…distracted."

"I see that. I was curious why you ran out without telling anyone."

"We had dinner reservations I didn't want to miss." I reply cooly.

"Hi. I'm Victoria." Victoria says, joining the conversation in her buzzed, bubbly voice.

"Hi." Quinn says, now switching her focus to me.

I prepare myself to tell Quinn that she's staying, but stop myself as I open my mouth.

Does Quinn look…*sad?*

"You're pretty." Victoria says to her.

"Thank you, it's nice to, um…to meet you." Quinn says with obvious discomfort.

If just the sight of Victoria insights this reaction, who knows what will happen when I tell her my plans? It's too late to start a fight, it's better if I wait until tomorrow.

"Well, I'll leave you two to your evening. I'm at the door at the end of the hallway if you need anything. Have a good night." Quinn offers, before passing us and going down stairs.

I can tell she's faking her unbothered facade. I can't tell if it's covering up for sadness or anger.

Why do I feel like I've done something wrong?

I know things with me and Quinn aren't on the best of terms right now, but I don't want her to be sad. I feel like a bad person even though I know I shouldn't. It hurts me to see her look hurt.

"Which one's yours?" Victoria asks me, pointing at the hallway of cedar doors.

I lead us to my room and get her settled on the bed before changing into sweatpants and a t-shirt.

"Hand me my purse, babe." She says, motioning to where she dropped it on the floor.

I bring it over to her and sit on the edge when she riffles through it.

I should be focused on her right now, but I can't get the look on Quinn's face when she saw Victoria out of my head.

"I brought you something special." Victoria says.

"Oh yeah, what?" I ask.

"This!" she says, pulling out a square of tinfoil, slowly unwrapping it. "I don't do this too often, but tonight feels like a special occasion. Getting to see you play live was awesome!"

Victoria keeps talking, but the world around me is muted when I look down at the heroin in her hands.

"Are you listening to me?" She asks.

"Sorry, I, uh. What were you saying?"

"Come on Lincoln, a little of this and we can have a good time tonight. It'll be fun. I've done it a bunch of times. It's totally safe if you know how much to take." She smiles, batting her lashes at me.

"I don't know…I think the pills are as far as I go."

"Please, don't make me do it alone. It's not as fun. Don't you want to have fun?" She asks.

"I don't-" I try to argue, but she cuts me off.

"Come on, do it for me." She says as she leans forward, melding her mouth with mine. Her tongue tastes like Juicy Fruit gum.

"Fine, just a little." I agree.

Chapter 27
October 2024 - Quinn

"Hello!? Quinn!"

Silence.

"Quinn?!"

I wake to the sound of Victoria yelling through the sound of her fist, hammering on my bedroom door.

What the fuck?

I rub my eyes and see the clock on the nightstand.

2a.m.

"Hello!" Victoria says again.

When I wake up more, I hear the fear in her voice. I jump out of my bed and run.

"What's happening?" I ask, whipping the door open to reveal a teary-eyed Victoria.

"I…he…" She struggles to get the words out.

"Where is he?" I demand.

All she can do is point to his door and I take off to the end of the hallway. I push open the door to see Link lying on the floor, lifeless.

I rush over to him, dropping to my knees to get a better look. His skin looks dull, his body unmoving. I turn when I hear Victoria enter in the room behind me.

"What happened?!" I yell at her.

"We were just having a little fun. I didn't know it would hit him that hard." She says, starting to sob.

"You didn't know *what* would hit him?" I ask, but I fear I already know the answer.

"It was only a little." She cries.

I look down at Link's exposed arm and see the mark.

"Go into my room and grab the blue bag on my nightstand, *NOW!*" I yell.

She freezes, watching me as I kneel over his body and start chest compressions.

"Is he dead…" she cries more.

"VICTORIA! GO. GET. MY. BAG!" I scream.

She turns out the door, taking off back towards my room.

When Link told me about his past, I did a little research and invested in Narcan. Not because I thought we'd ever get to this moment, but because of how life saving it is. You never know when someone might need it. *Especially* in our line of work.

I look down at Link's unconscious body and my vision starts to blur from my own tears, but I choke them down.

"Please stay with me, Link. I love you, please. I need you, please." I beg.

I stop compressions and start mouth to mouth resuscitations. I'm coming up for air, about to start more chest compressions, when Victoria comes running back in the room with my bag.

She hands it to me and I dump it out on the floor with no time to rummage and find the packet. I grab it off the floor and tear it open with my teeth like an animal.

I stuff the tube up his nose and press down, releasing the nasal spray.

We wait a few seconds, but there are still no signs of breathing.

"Help me pick him up." I command Victoria.

"What?"

"Get his feet!" I say, positioning myself behind him and looping my arms through his from behind.

"Shouldn't we call 911?"

"There's a hospital five minutes down the road. I can get him there faster." I yell, already starting to drag him on my own towards the door.

Victoria grabs his feet and helps me. We make quick timing getting him down the stairs, but I can see her starting to lose energy as we near the bottom.

"Should I go get the driver to help us?" She asks, panting.

"No, we need to keep this contained. No one from the label can know it wouldn't be good for him. Now come on, we're almost to the door." I say.

With a second wind, we get Link's body to the back door of the SUV.

"Go get the keys off the kitchen counter when I put him in the back seat. *Run!*" I yell.

I struggle, but manage to get him over my shoulder long enough to push his torso into the car. I run around to the other side of the car and pull him through, then I shut both doors.

Where the fuck is Victoria?

My question is answered by the sight of Victoria running out of the house with the keys and a bag in her hands.

"Here." She hands me the keys, out of breath.

"What took you so long?" I ask, walking around to the driver's side.

"I had to grab my bag."

I stop myself from saying the terrible things I want to say to her for the sake of Link.

"Get in, we need to go, now." I snarl, but she freezes again. "What are you waiting for Victoria? Get in the fucking car!"

"I'm sorry, I can't." She says, before running to where her car is parked.

I watch as she quickly tosses her bag onto the passenger seat and peels down and out of the driveway before she even gets the chance to turn her headlights on.

What the actual fuck.

I want to follow her car and do horrible, well deserved things to her, but I snap out of my fervent thought and focus.

I get in the car and start the engine. I put it in drive and slam on the gas. The tires screech on the pavement as I turn out of the driveway and floor it down the road.

The house we're staying at is on a dead-end street, tucked just behind the city. A few corn fields and a turn onto Main St. and we'll be at the hospital.

Our Song

My foot's nearly flat on the pedal and I start to see building lights appear at the end of the road.

A sudden noise in the back seat almost makes me swerve the car into a ditch.

"What's happening!?" Link shoots up from where he was just laying comatose in the back.

I want to scream, cry and throw up all at the same time. I instinctually settle metal footing the brakes, which almost sends Link flying into the front seat with me.

I pull the car off the road on the edge of one of the fields, shift into park, cut the head's lights and jump out of the driver's seat, slamming the door closed behind me

I walk around the front of the car and into the field and scream. It's pitch black and uninhabited for at least a mile in each direction, so I'm not worried about the time or surrounding houses.

I hear the sound of a car door open and shut behind me.

"Win, let me explain. *Please*."

"How long?" I order, still with my back to him.

"Not long."

"*How long*, Lincoln?"

"August." He finally answers

Two months, he's been using for two months and I hadn't the slightest clue. Have I really been so caught up in my personal bullshit, I couldn't see what was going on right in front of me?

"Why?" I ask, afraid of what he'll say.

"I don't know. Impulse, at first, I think. Then routine. Now, I don't know…"

"Is this my fault?" I ask, turning to face him.

"What? No Win! This has all been my decision. I never thought it would get out of hand like this. It started as just a few lines to help me through the day. Then, I started to take pills to help me sleep.

"I thought I was helping myself. I told myself I could stop anytime, and that I didn't *really* need it. Then tonight, when Victoria offered me something more, I thought there wouldn't be any harm in one time."

"We thought you were dead!"

"I'm *so* sorry I put you through this…wait, where is Victoria?" He asks, looking back at the SUV.

"Oh, your wonderful *girlfriend* decided to get in her car and drive away when I was shoving your lifeless body into the back seat!"

"Well, clearly she's not my girlfriend anymore." He says, flatly.

"Is that all you have to say!?" I yell, frustrated with his relaxed demeanor.

Now that I know he's alive, I have time to be mad at him.

"What do you want me to say?"

"I don't know that you're going to quit and go to rehab because you almost just cost yourself your life!"

"But there's two months left of the tour."

"*Fuck* the tour Link! You almost died. Nothing is worth your life."

"But this is your dream. I don't want to destroy it. All I do is destroy things." He sounds somber, looking down at his feet.

"Why do you care about my dreams? Last time I checked, you hated me." I snap back.

"I don't hate you…I could never hate you, Win. I told you I love you and I meant it. I will love you until my last breath, which, because of you, isn't tonight." He takes a step closer to me, but I keep my distance and step backwards.

He looks hurt, but he doesn't try to come any closer.

"If you loved me so much, then why did you ask Victoria to be your girlfriend?" I ask accusingly.

I know I have no right to have an attitude about it but I can't rationalize any of my emotions right now.

"Because you chose Noah and left. And I don't mean that in a blaming way, but you made your choice, and I respected that. Even if I can't, for the life of me, understand it. I thought she would help me move on, but she couldn't, because she's not you.

"I start every morning trying not to love you and somehow every night, I end up deeper in the abyss where my heart should be. Even when you don't want me, I crave you, Win. I yearn for your company. I ache for your laugh. I burn for your touch…"

There's a ball stuck in my throat and it won't secede to the words I want to say. Unable to speak, I start to sob like the mess I am.

"Please don't cry, Win."Link begs.

He sounds desperate to console me but remains respectfully standing in place.

"Why are you crying?" He asks.

I'm flooded with emotion and so I pull the trigger.

"Because I love you!" I yell, "I love you Lincoln Archer. With every fiber of my being, I love you!"

I don't know who moves first.

All I know is I'm stepping forward one moment and tangled in his arms the next. Our mouths ravaging each other like starved wolves.

The relief of finally saying it out loud makes me feel invincible.

Link slowly pulls back and we stare at each other under the full moon.

"The day we left for tour, I was going to tell you I was leaving Noah." I say.

"What?" He looks confused.

"Shall we?" I ask, pointing down at the plushy grass of the field.

We lay down, side by side, and look up at the stars together, our favorite activity. *I've missed this so much.*

"I was going to tell you I chose you. Yes, it took far too long and way too many unfair choices to get there. But I was ready to leave him.

"I would've done anything you told me to at that moment. But then I saw Victoria, and then I saw you kiss her. And I knew I couldn't tell you anymore."

"Why?" He asks.

"Because you deserve to be happy, Link. It would've been horrible of me to pull you down with me when you were clearly moving on."

I feel him grab my hand and squeeze it.

"Do you still want to leave him?"

"Yes." I respond quickly, not needing a second more to think.

"What do we do now?" He asks.

"Maybe we start by telling each other the truth." I suggest.

I curl into Link, placing my head on his chest as he wraps his arm around me.

I tell him *everything.*

I tell him about my dad dying first, starting pretty much from where we left off. When I tell him about Noah's episodes, I use a little discretion.

I tell him about the yelling and locking me out in Vegas, but keep the rest to myself still. I'm not being dishonest, I'm just withholding small details. It's easier for everyone this way.

Despite leaving so much out, I still have to hold him down to the ground so he won't take the car to wherever Noah is and do God knows what to him.

When I've run out of things to admit to Link, he takes over in divulging his indiscretions. He tells me about meeting his mom and how his habit picked back up. He also tells me how he *really* met Victoria.

It's heartbreaking that he's been hiding so much pain and struggle right in front of me, and I didn't even notice.

I guess it's because I was too busy trying to hide my struggle and pain for his sake too.

What a wreckage we are.

Hurting each other in an attempt to try to protect each other.

"So, what do we do now?" He asks.

"First and foremost, you get clean."

"I agree. I can do it. I don't need rehab. I got myself clean before without it, I can do it again," He says confidently.

We go back and forth for a while, but ultimately, I agree he gets one chance to do it himself, but the second he slips he goes, no argument.

"So that leaves one last thing to figure out, I guess."

"It does. So what are *we* going to do?" He asks, turning on his side to look at me, so I do the same.

"I don't know. There's only two months left of the tour and I'd hate to be the one to risk taking it away from the rest of the band, Noah aside, obviously."

"Hear me out." He says.

"I'm listening."

"What if we finish the tour? When it's done, you tell Noah you're divorcing him, and if he can't handle you being his ex and manager *and* us being together, we leave.

"Then we move away together and start a new life. Everyone gets to finish the shows and worst case scenario,by the next album, they replace us and we live happily ever after."

"I like that idea, but there is just one problem."

"What's that?" He asks.

"I'm willing to give up my job and the life I've built, but I'm not willing to pretend I don't love you for another day nevermind two more months, Link. I can't stuff it back in."

"So don't."

"What do you mean?"

"Be with me. Noah deserves nothing from you, so be with me, too. I don't mind, it's only temporary. Pretend to be with him if that's what's easier for you and keeps the peace. We will make it through the next two months like everything is normal and then we'll be together. We'll never have to see him again if you don't want to."

I want to insist we just leave now, but if this is what he wants to do, I'll do it. *Especially* if that means he stops using.

"It's a plan then." I agree.

"I love you, Win."

"I love you too."

Chapter 28
November 2024 - Quinn

"You made me look so stupid!" Noah yells at me.

"How? All I did was tell the waitress you didn't want another drink and asked for the check." I say, calmly.

"I'm more than capable of deciding when to cut myself off!"

"Are you though?"

We sit in uncomfortable silence as our driver brings us back to the Airbnb. Despite every other thing Noah has promised me and went back on, like regular therapy and basic day-to-day communication, a weekly date night has managed to stay intact.

I have to admit, though, more and more they're starting to feel like hostage situations.

I'm uncomfortably aware that if Noah and I were alone right now, and not in the car with a label provided driver, he would be much more volatile.

Our Song

To his credit, Noah's injustices have remained verbal since the night he locked me outside, but I still fortify myself every time he screams.

This marriage is a landmine and I'm just trying to get out of it without any more casualty inducing explosions.

Every time he has raised his voice at me or instigated a fight in the last four weeks, I've mentally retreated.

I take a deep breath and brace for impact. I let him get it out and I escape to the world I've created in my mind where Link and I live, rent free.

I think of the things Link and I will do and places we'll see when we can finally be together. I know Link's plan includes a working theory that Noah will come to terms with us and let us stay in the band, but I know for a fact he won't.

There isn't a rational bone to be had in that man's body.

Link and I have promised to be honest with each other, but I've kept mention of Noah and I's fights out of conversations. It's easier if he thinks everything is okay, because it eventually will be.

This is all temporary.

I'm not willing to risk Link's sobriety on anything. If he thinks I'm in danger or stresses that our exit strategy won't work, I'm afraid what he'll do. So I keep him in a bubble he doesn't know I made for him.

Sneaking around can be challenging at times, but it's more rewarding than anything. I've never been happier, and honestly, sneaking around is kind of fun.

There's a certain level of adrenaline involved in hiding like two teenagers who can't keep their hands off each other. It's not like it's exactly difficult either.

Noah is obsessed with himself therefore, he pays very minimal attention to me. Every night, show or not, he seems to find a reason to hang out at a bar or go drink in a studio somewhere to write music, or so he says.

I swear in his mind, the fact that he admitted to one infidelity means I'd never suspect him of another.

At the beginning of Link and I's new arrangement, I had genuine guilt at first. I felt no better than Noah with respect to a few other details.

 That was until I saw his phone vibrating on the bed when he was in the shower a few weeks ago. I looked down to see an unsaved number calling him.

Sure, it could've been just some random number calling him, but I'm not a complete idiot.

Keeping an eye on the bathroom door, I went through his texts. I found the unsaved number with text notifications set to "Do Not Disturb".

How clever.

I scrolled through a conversation that was mostly told through pictures.

Nude pictures, to be exact.

Quinn from the beginning of this year would've been devastated. She would've been a mess, maybe even would've retreated home to South Dakota.

But this Quinn, the woman I've fought tooth and nail to become, she doesn't give a fuck.

I mean, why should I?

Noah isn't the same man who vowed to love and respect me anymore.

Our Song

Why would I love and respect him?

I backed out of the messages and locked the phone exactly where he'd left it on the bed. Unbothered, I left for a run on one of the trails near where we were staying and met up with Link.

We spent the afternoon in the woods…in the leaves.

It's the last week of November now and we only have three weeks left of shows. I can see the finish line, and Link is waiting at the end for me.

My prize.

I officially signed a contract for the band for another two albums with Rich Records. We had offers from places like UMG and Republic, but ultimately I decided it was better to stay with the people who helped us get here in the first place.

After signing the deal, I got a call from Grant Madison himself congratulating us on our success and his expectations for our future.

I'll miss the excitement and praise of operating a flourishing band. I'll miss Roni, Sam and Max the most, though. I hope they'll forgive us and understand.

The band's last two weeks of shows are spread out through the state of California. This is convenient because during my call with Grant Madison he also informed me of two, label provided, houses waiting for us there.

Rich Records has dozens of studios and offices across the US. The one located in Los Angeles reserved for their most successful artists. That lot now includes Compass, apparently.

Grant said submerging us in the LA music scene would be the epitome of stardom and that living there would only elevate exposure of the band.

It's conflicting, wanting the worst for Noah but providing him the best. He's lucky that the others are so important to me. Every choice I've made is solely with their benefit in mind, not his.

I want Compass to be successful, and I want Roni, Sam and Max to excel. So I do it for them.

I've spent the last few days communicating with a moving company from Nashville who has started the process of moving everyone's apartments out to LA.

We're set to move in officially next week, but I plan on keeping most of my boxes packed.

We decided to split the houses like we did with the buses in the beginning. Roni, Noah and I in one, Max, Sam and Link in the other, with the boys' house serving as the communal writing space. Especially given the giant grand piano in its living room.

The houses aren't big, but they are fancy. All filled with modern fixtures and appliances. Hi-tech security systems and cameras protected behind tall gates. Each backyard, equipped with an in-ground pool and jacuzzi. By far the nicest place I will ever live.

Shame it will probably only be for two weeks.

"Are you listening to me, Quinn?" Noah yells.

I snap back to reality and realize he is still going on about what I did at dinner. It's so easy to tune him out these days.

I love it.

"I'm sorry Noah, you're right. That was wrong of me. You deserve better. It won't happen again." I offer.

Lying to him is easy these days, too.

Noah's face shifts and he looks confused by my immediate roll over. I don't fight with him because he isn't worth it.

"Well, good…I *do* deserve better." He says, folding his arms across his chest and looking out his window. He almost seems let down by my lack of resistance.

Sometimes, I wonder if I wasn't good at my job as the band's manager and Noah's personal punching bag, if he would still be with me.

I catch the driver looking in the rearview mirror and when our eyes meet, he quickly shifts his stare back to the road.

I'm sure he's thinking I'm some poor girl whose husband yells at her

Only, I'm the one pulling the strings now.

Chapter 29
November 2024 - Lincoln

I might miss doing these radio interviews the least. At this point, we've been asked the same ten questions a dozen times.

What's it like having such a quick rise to fame? What's your favorite part about being on tour? What's your favorite song to play?

So predictable.

"What's your favorite part of being rock stars?" The interviewer from IHeartRadio asks the group.

The ladies, I say in my mind, mimicking Sam's voice.

"The ladies!" Sam answers.

See, *predictable.*

I don't completely hate the routine of it. Routine is what has helped me stop using. I replaced every urge to use with a thought of being with Quinn, and slowly it's gotten easier.

Don't get me wrong. The first week or so was hard on my body.

Thankfully, withdrawals and the flu have the same symptoms.

I haven't slipped once since our agreement. For that part I'm proud. I have, however, had a difficult time *psychically* parting ways with what Victoria accidentally left behind.

I keep the tinfoil square tucked away in a bag, almost as a challenge to myself.

Every day that passes that I don't touch the pocket it's zipped in, I prove to myself that I'm stronger than it.

That it doesn't control me.

 That I deserve Quinn.

"So you have two weeks left of shows, the last two at SoFi stadium. How does it feel to know you're ending the tour in your largest venue yet?" The interviewer, Mark, asks us.

"I think it's a testament to our accomplishments this year and a foreshadowing of what's coming next." Roni says, smiling.

"Does that mean there's another album in the works?" Mark, the interviewer, pries.

Quinn nods to us as a sign of approval from behind the glass where she's watching us.

"It does Mark. We're so excited to begin working on our sophomore album as soon as the tour wraps." Noah says, making sure he's the one to share the news.

My spite for Noah is endless, but the energy I used to put into actively allowing him to be the bane of my existence has slimmed. The distraction of Quinn and the knowledge of what is next for us makes him easier to tune out.

I feel like Romeo and she's Juliet. Our forbidden love story, hiding just beyond the shadows of anybody's watch.

Only in our Shakespearean rendition, Juliet saved Romeo from the poison.

Noah got signed for a brand deal last week for a new energy drink, so he's been busy filming promotional material between rehearsals and shows.

That and his insistent need to go out every night has made it easy to find time for me and Quinn. Moving into the LA houses has allowed us more places to sneak off to.

After tonight's show, when everyone goes out to whatever bar Noah has planned, Quinn and I will say we're going home twenty minutes apart.

We'll take individual rides to the same place and he will be none the wiser. Everyone will think I went back to the guys' house and Quinn theirs, but really, we're meeting at a bar outside of the city.

I found it a few days ago and I really think Quinn's is going to like it. I know she's brunting the harder part of this purgatory by having to pretend with Noah every day.

It makes me try extra hard to find opportunities for her to feel valued and remind her that it's going to be worth it. Whether it be a napkin-note or two hours of alone time in a dive bar no one goes to.

Anywhere is better, when Quinn is there.

***

Our Song

"Where on earth did you find this place?" Quinn asks me, laughing hysterically from the sidewalk.

We're standing across the street from the deepest dive bar I've ever seen. Adorned with a group of forty to fifty somethings smoking in a group down the alley bordering the building.

It has *charm.*

"Doesn't it remind you of Sallys? I found it online and have come here a few times. It's nice." I laugh.

She smiles at me and I give into the need to kiss her.

"It has *some* resemblance."

"Just wait until you see the inside."

I grab her hand and walk us across the street and into the bar. The clever red flashing neon sign above the door that reads Whiskeys invites us in.

"Holy shit." Quinn stops a few steps in.

"Told you. Come on, let's get a booth in the back." I pull her hand.

I keep my head down as I navigate through the Friday night crowd. No one has recognized me here yet, given the older demographic, but I always stay in stealth mode anyway.

Once we are seated across from each other, a waitress comes over and takes our drink order.

"Two sodas with lime, please." Quinn says, ordering for me.

The waitress rolls her eyes and walks away from us. We sit and laugh together.

Just two non-drinkers, casually hanging out at a bar.

"I give you credit, the outside was deceiving. It *does* remind me of Sally's in here." She releases a big exhale as she scans the room.

I only played with them once at Sallys in Nashville before leaving on tour, but that night has stayed with me. It was the first real conversation I got to have with Quinn.

"So why here?" She asks.

"I just wanted to give you a piece of home. I know you've been going through a lot lately, even if you try to put on a brave face for me."

"I do not!" She argues, playfully.

"You do too, and I get that it's who you are, so it would be rude of me to ask you to be anyone you're not. So instead, I'll just try to remind you of how cared for you are."

"I love you." She says, as the waitress comes back with our drinks.

"I love you too."

We enjoy each other's company watching the locals sing on a karaoke setup, similar to Sallys.

"Want to know what I love the most?" Quinn asks.

"What?"

"It's weird." She laughs.

"Well now, you *definitely* have to tell me."

"I find the sound of the pool tables so soothing. Maybe it's some weird ASMR, but the clacking sound just seems to drown out all the other unwanted noise in my head sometimes."

"That's not weird at all." I smile, reassuring her.

"It's like music to my ears."

"Okay, maybe a *little* weird." We both laugh.

"I could write a song to their beat."

"Then do it." I say.

"I haven't written in a while. Not since right before my Dad…" She trails off, her expression turning sad.

A heavy moment of silence sits between us.

"You want to get out of here?" I ask.

"We just got here." She laughs.

"So? We have at least two hours until anyone even considers leaving the bar. Let's go back to me and the guys' house and write a song. I've been tinkering with the piano and I think I've got it down." I say, sugar coating the truth.

I am terrible at playing the piano.

"You taught yourself to play the piano in two weeks?" She laughs.

"Guess you'll have to find out for yourself." I say, sliding out of the booth, extending a bow and my palm to her.

She takes her hand in mine as I drop a twenty dollar bill on the table and we leave Whiskeys.

***

I unlock the front door and turn on the lights. Quinn takes a seat on the couch in the living room, taking off her shoes. I grab my guitar, a pen and paper, then join her.

"Are we really about to write a song?" She giggles.

"Why is that funny?" I ask.

"I don't know. No one's ever asked me to write a song with them."

"But, you're a song writer?"

"You know, you're the first, and only, person to ever call me that."

I lean forward, placing a soft kiss on her cheek.

"Let's see what you got, Win." I say, picking up my guitar.

I show her a few chords I've been working on and she hums a melody to the beat. It's not long before the pens in her hand.

We exchange a few ideas and reminisce about the last ten months together. The good, the bag, the ugly, the even uglier.

All of it from start to finish.

Quinn is writing and scribbling, even ripping out and tossing a few crumpled up pieces of paper. She looks like a mad scientist conducting an experiment in a lab. I can see the gears turning in her mind.

It's almost 2a.m. when she finally puts down the pen and we look at the notebook in front of us.

It's there, three verses and a hooking chorus.

We wrote a song.

"Holy shit." She says, sounding astonished.

"That felt *way* too easy." I joke.

"It really was. I could write epics with you." She leans her head against my shoulder.

"Well, you're the writer. What are you titling it?" I ask.

She looks down at the paperwork with a grin, mulling over the possibilities.

"Story? No…maybe, Epic? No, that's not right either." She says, struggling.

"It doesn't matter what you call it, all that matters is that it's our song." I smile, proud of the art we made together.

Our Song

"Our Song." She repeats.

"We'll, I mean, you can call it your song if you want. You definitely did most of the writing." I offer.

"No Link, Our Song. That's the title."

"Our Song." I smile, loving how it sounds.

I rest my guitar against the couch and pull Quinn into my lap so that she's facing me, straddled over my legs.

"I should get going. Bar's let out soon." She kisses me.

"Five more minutes." I jokingly whine.

"You drive a hard bargain." She says, giving in to my request.

I run my fingers through her blonde hair as it curtains around our faces. The smell of strawberries sending me into an all-consuming universe where only Quinn and I exist.

I know Quinn's just as lost in our kiss as I am because we both don't hear it when someone opens the front door.

The sound of the hinges breaks our kiss as we both look at the entrance. There's nowhere for us to run or hide in time. The living room is in the center of the house directly when you walk in.

Max looks as equally shocked to find us in our current positions, as we do to see him come home early from the bar.

He calmly shuts the door behind him and resumes his deer-in-the-headlights position, silently staring at us.

Quinn moves off of me, standing up to face Max. She looks like she wants to say something. I can tell she's trying to find an excuse or reason that would logically explain why she was on top of me.

I'm also trying to think of the same cover story.

Before Quinn or I can say anything, Max's face shifts into a…

Is he smiling?

"I saw nothing." He says, kicking off his shoes.

"Max, I can explain…" Quinn says, as she approaches him, but she can't get out any more words.

"You don't have to, because I saw nothing," he reiterates, "Have a good night Quinn." He says, hugging her.

Then, he walks by where I'm seated on the couch, sending an approving nod in my direction as he disappears up the stairs.

Chapter 30
December 2024 - Lincoln

Today is one of my least favorite days in the calendar.

My birthday.

It's the one day of the year my childhood trauma always gets the best of me. I'm mentally teleported, against my will, to a time when I was a helpless child.

Every year.

Like clockwork.

It's Thursday night and we have our last two shows this weekend. Everyone went out to a club in the city to celebrate playing our first stadium show tomorrow night.

A little premature, but I understand the excitement. If I wasn't so anxious today, I'd be out with them too.

This year has taught me so much about myself. The lessons have been hard, but the ending appears to be worth it. I'd relive it a hundred more times if I had to, as long as I end up with Quinn.

Two more days and she's mine.

Like she can sense I'm thinking about her, my phone starts ringing on my bedside table.

"Hey." I answer.

"Are you at the house?" She asks.

"Yeah, shouldn't you be out with everyone?" I can tell she's not by the lack of background noise.

"Come outside." She ignores my question.

"What?" I laugh, thinking she's kidding.

"Just trust me, put on shoes, and come outside."

Quinn hangs up before I can argue anymore. I'd be concerned about the spontaneity, but overall she seemed calm, so I rule out anything being wrong.

I put on a hoodie and sneakers, grab my keys and head out the front door. Quinn is parked, sitting in the driver's seat of the new Mercedes she bought herself last week.

"Get in!" She shouts to me out the window.

She looks cute driving the little thing. My long legs, however, don't love it as much as I stuff myself into the passenger seat.

"What are you doing here? I thought you were going out with everyone?"

"I did, and wouldn't you know, the second I got to the club I came down with a stomach bug and had to leave early." She explains, smiling.

"You don't look like you have a stomach bug." I say.

"And you don't look like you should be alone on your birthday."

"How did you kn-" I start to ask, but she answers before I can finish.

"I have my ways. What I can't figure out is why you wouldn't tell me yourself."

"I didn't want to make it a thing. It's not a big deal." I say.

"You're a big deal to me, so it's a thing." She replies, shifting the car into drive.

"So, where are you taking me?" I ask.

"It wouldn't be a surprise if I told you."

"Should I be scared? Is this you taking me to a secondary location before chopping me into pieces?" I joke.

"Someone's been watching way too much Dateline with Roni."

The car ride is filled with seamless conversation. We're talking about where we'd move if we have to leave California, when Quinn turns the car down a windy road, leading us up a hill. As we make it over the highest point, the city's landscape comes into view.

It's just after 10p.m. and every building is fully lit up.

There's no other cars in the parking lot when Quinn pulls into a spot.

"What are we doing here?" I ask.

"Dinner. With a view." She smiles, reaching into the back seat to procure a picnic basket and blanket. "Shall we?"

"We shall." I agree, opening my door.

I follow Quinn's lead as she walks us down a narrow foot path to a small patch of grass that overlooks the Hollywood sign. Despite the city's abundant lights, there are still visible stars scattered through the night sky.

"This is beautiful." She says, impressed with herself.

"You're beautiful." I protest, shaking my head in disbelief that this is my real life.

We spread out the blankets and sit across from each other with our legs crossed.

"The luxury ends here." She laughs, pulling sandwiches in ziplock bags from the basket. "I hope you like peanut butter and jelly."

"It's my favorite." I say, eagerly taking one of the bags from her.

I'm glad it's dark up here so Quinn can't see the tears fighting to escape. No one's really bothered to celebrate my birthday since I was fourteen when Robert indefinitely ruined them for me. I spent the rest of my life actively avoiding it after that.

Thanks to Quinn, I think I might have a new outlook on the day.

"This is the nicest thing anyone's ever done for me, Win. Thank you."

I lean forward and kiss her, even though she's chewing a bite of her sandwich. Her lips taste sweet.

"Well, you deserve it, and more. Next year, I will make sure we throw you a proper birthday celebration." She declares.

"So you plan on still dealing with me this time next year?" I joke.

"And every year after. I'm ready for it, all of it. Which brings me to your gift…"

"You shouldn't have got me anything!" I say.

"I didn't. Well…not in a material sense, at least. My gift to you is a promise. A promise that-. Sorry, one second."

She holds up her pointer finger, as if to put a literal pause in our conversation. I watch as Quinn pulls out her cell phone that I didn't hear vibrating.

"That's weird. It's kind of late for an unknown number. It's an LA area code." She states.

"You can take it. I can wait." I encourage her.

"Hello?" she answers the call.

I can't hear what the person on the other end says to her, but I know it's not good by the way she rockets to a standing position.

She sounds frantic as I listen to this one sided phone call.

"Are you sure?"

"How did it happen?"

"Is he okay?"

"Where is he now?"

"Okay."

By the time she hangs up the phone, she is already grabbing her things off the blanket.

"Can you call yourself an Uber? I have to go, Link." She states, offering no further explanation.

"I can, but what is going on, Quinn?"

"There's been an accident. I need to go."

"What happened?"

"I have to go." Is all she offers as a response.

"Well, I'm coming with you." I say, joining her in packing up the basket.

"You can't."

"I'm not letting you drive alone upset like this."

"Call an Uber, Lincoln." Her tone is cold, and it makes me get defensive.

"No. I'm coming with you."

"No, you're not. It's Noah, he's in the hospital…I don't know what happened. They won't tell me, they just said I need to come."

"So you don't even know what is happening and you're running to him?" I stop picking up our things and look at her.

"Yes."

"I bet it's something stupid like he fell off a table at the bar being a drunk idiot. You don't have to drop everything and run to him anymore, Quinn."

"I need to go." She starts walking back to her car with her arms full.

"Quinn, wait up!" I trail behind, catching up to her on the path.

By the time I make it to her in the parking lot, she's already dumped everything into the back seat. She opens her driver's side door, stopping before getting in, and turns to face me.

"I know you won't understand this right now, but I'm his wife still. I have to go."

"He doesn't act like your husband." I say, I know I sound mad. I am mad.

Not at her, at *him*.

Somehow, he always manages to ruin her happiness and pull her into his bullshit. She's so close to leaving him already. I don't understand why she won't just send someone else for him.

"Regardless of our plans, right now, *at this moment*, I'm still his wife. I know it's hard to think about, but there was a time when he wasn't a complete piece of garbage. Buried deep, there is a man I used to care about who helped me at a time when I needed someone. He helped me get where I am. I owe it to him." She says.

"You owe him nothing!" I bark.

"Noah made me!" Quinn counters.

"You made him!" I yell.

Infuriated isn't a strong enough word to describe the rage I feel towards Noah right now.

He's put her down for so long she doesn't even realize his success is only because of her. And worse, he's manipulated her into believing that.

"I have to go. I'll call you later." She dismisses me.

I don't try to fight her anymore when she gets into the car and drives away, leaving me alone in the dark.

Happy Fucking Birthday.

Chapter 31
December 2024 - Quinn

I'm speeding in my car, replaying the call in my mind.

"Hello?"

"Hi, it's Chad, from Rich Records. I'm one of the producers from the label we met earlier tonight at the club. Listen, I don't have much time to talk, but I need you to get down to LA General Hospital. I was in my car with Noah and we got into an accident, but we're fine." Chad said, sounding slightly intoxicated.

"Are you sure?"

"Yes, but it's important that you get down here…right away."

"How did it happen?"

"I can't really say at the moment. Can you please come here?"

"Is he okay?"

"Everything's going to be okay. We just need to get you down to the hospital ASAP."

"Where is he now?"

"He's being seen by the doctor. When you get here, call this number back and I will come meet you." He instructed ominously.

"Okay."

I have a considerable amount of guilt for abandoning Link, but I know there was no way I could show up at the hospital for Noah with him. Especially since I left the club earlier because I felt "sick".

The strong arm battle between my guilt and curiosity begins to sway as I speed down the highway.

I know Chad was with Noah when they got into the accident, but shouldn't a nurse or doctor have called me?

And why wouldn't he give me any more information?

I pull into the emergency room parking lot after a heart pounding drive. I catapult out of my car and start a brisk walk to the entrance, as I call Chad.

"Hi, I'm here. I'm walking in now."

"Okay, just wait for me. I'll come get you."

"Can't I just give his name and they'll bring me back to you guys?" I question him.

"No, don't do that." He responds, then ends the call.

I wait by the front desk in a contained panic, watching the swinging doors that lead to the patient rooms.

I pull out my phone to send Link a quick text along the lines of, *I'm sorry* and *I love you*, but Chad walks out before I can hit send.

"Hi, follow me." He says, turning back towards the wooden doors.

The pleasantries are nowhere to be found as I follow him into the back area of the ER. A few turns down white walled corridors and finally we arrive at a room with a closed door and drawn blinds.

"The lawyer is with him. Before you go in, we need to talk about a few things." He says.

"The lawyer?" I ask.

"Yes, Mr. Madison likes to protect his investments."

"What are you talking about?"

I'm more confused now than I was on the drive over here

"As you know, we were all out tonight, celebrating the band playing the stadium shows this weekend. A few people from the label, including myself, were invited. Noah and I hit it off pretty good and drank more than we should've. I got a craving for pizza and Noah thought that sounded good, so we decided to leave the club a little early to get a late night bite.

"Against better judgment, Noah and I got into my car. I told Noah I didn't think I could drive and that we should call for a ride, but he told me he was fine, so I agreed to let him drive us.

"On the drive…" He braces himself before telling me the next part, "He was driving…not even that fast, he was in the lines too. He saw a flashing yellow light, but he thought it was just a regular yellow light, so he sped up so we wouldn't get stuck at a red light. When he crossed through the intersection, he hit someone."

"How bad is the other car?" I ask.

"No, you're not hearing me, Quinn…he hit *someone*."

My stomach drops.

"What do you mean…"

"He hit a girl. She was using the crosswalk, and he didn't see her. I didn't see her either."

"Is she okay?" I can feel my palms start to get clammy.

"She is, we're not sure if she will sign-"

Chad is cut off by a tall man in a blue suit coming out of Noah's room, shutting the door behind him.

"You must be the manager. Noah's been briefed. I already talked to the staff and they've agreed to help us. I'm going to talk to the victim now and then I will be back." Suit Man says.

He doesn't wait for a response before stepping into another patient room two doors down.

The manager.

I was called here as the band's manager, not Noah's wife. This is not fucking good.

"What is there to brief him on? And what did he mean by *'the staff are helping'?*" My panic feels like it might drown me.

"We need to handle this situation with discretion, Quinn. If word gets out that Noah was involved with this, this could be the end of Compass."

"How would word *not* get out? I mean, his name's got to be in the police report, right? People will find it."

He doesn't respond as he analyzes me.

It's like he is trying to find a way to explain things to me in a cookie cutter fashion. A switch flips, and I shut off my emotions.

It seems to be my special skill these days.

"Give it to me. Straight up, full truth, *now.*" I demand.

Chad stands up straighter and takes a deep breath before speaking.

"Noah struck the girl and there were, miraculously, no witnesses. We were turning out of a back road with no foot traffic, excluding the girl. When he struck her, we immediately stopped the car and got out. She was lying unconscious on the pavement and her leg was…bent…unnaturally. We lifted her carefully and put her in the back seat of my car and drove her here.

"On the drive over I called Jack, the label's lawyer, who's really more of a fixer. He's the guy that you just saw. Jack met us at the back entrance of the hospital with a team of two nurses and a doctor. They took the girl in and got her looked at.

"She woke up during her exam and the nurses explained that she was in an accident, but the team was instructed not to say anything more until Jack spoke with her directly.

"What I currently know about her from the nurses is that her name is Sasha, she is nineteen years old, she's currently attending West Los Angeles College and Noah broke her right femur."

"Oh my God…she's just a kid." My heart aches for the damage Noah has caused her.

"Don't look upset, this is good for us," Chad says, maniacally.

"What do you mean? How is this good for anyone?"

"She's in college, which most likely means debt. Her broken leg is about to pay for her full tuition and then some."

"I don't understand…are you telling me Jack is in there paying off that poor girl right now?"

"Yes, in exchange for signing a Non Disclosure Agreement."

"And the hospital staff?" I ask.

"Already signed. Like I said…Mr. Madison likes to protect his investments."

My heart is pumping blood at an alarming rate and I feel myself choking down an anxiety attack.

I'm angry. No one should be able to get away with this. I feel like a forced accomplice. I ready myself to start berating Chad for more answers when my phone starts to ring.

"Hi." I answer, holding up a finger to Chad and walking a few paces away.

"Hi. I'm just checking on you. Are you okay?" Link asks.

"I can't talk right now. Things are kind of crazy." I say to Link as I notice Jack in the room across from where I'm standing.

Against my better judgment, I walk further to get a full view of her from the room's hall window. Unlike Noah's room, her blinds aren't drawn with the courtesy of privacy.

She looks so young and scared.

I watch as Jack throws some papers on her lap and hands her a pen. She looks hesitant, but she signs anyway, sealing her fate.

"Hello? Quinn?" I hear Link say in my ear, realizing I drifted out of the conversation we were having.

"I said I can't talk right now, Link. I'll call you later." I say before hanging up.

I feel bad but I need to do something to stop this. I need to tear up that NDA. I need to apologize to that girl. I need to do anything to make this right.

Truly right.

I get two paces in the room before Jack lightly pushes me out as he exits himself.

"Oh no you don't. Follow me." He instructs me like a scorned child.

"Did she just sign an NDA? Shouldn't someone call her parents first?" I ask.

"Keep your voice down." He's all business, not a shred of humanity to be found behind his cold gray eyes. "She is of legal age, therefore there is no need for parents. Also, she is being compensated *very* generously. Because of what she just signed, she will never know the burden of student debt." Jack says in a dismissive fashion.

"All set?" Chad asks Jack as we approach.

"All set."

***

The ride back to our house is silent. When we pull into the empty driveway, I park the car right at the front door and help Noah inside.

Apart from still being intoxicated, he appears to have no other ailments.

"So, are we going to talk about what just happened?" I ask Noah, as he takes a seat on one of the couches in the living room.

"What is there to talk about?" He asks, looking disinterested in the subject.

"Maybe that you should be in jail with a DUI right now or the fact you almost killed someone?!"

"I just broke her leg." He says.

"*JUST* broke her leg? Do you hear yourself? Please don't tell me that the security of a fancy lawyer has allowed you to validate what you did."

"It doesn't," he argues, "but, it's fine now. I won't do that again. It's alright. Can we do this in the morning? I'm tired." He says, moving to a lying position on the couch.

"Can you really sleep knowing what you did?"

"Yes. You heard Jack, I just paid for her to go to college." He says smugly.

"You didn't pay for shit! This crooked label did!"

"Well, this crooked label just saved all our jobs, Quinn."

"Yeah, after you almost ruined them all!"

"I'm not doing this with you. We'll talk in the morning." Noah responds, as he rolls himself over so his back is turned to me.

What the fuck.

I can't bear the thought of waking up in the same bed, nevermind the same house as him. He's lost all his humanity and I can't be around it, not even for two more days.

I decide I'm staying at the guy's house until after the shows Sunday and then I'm gone.

I leave Noah to his guiltless sleep on the couch and head up to our bedroom. I grab my duffle bag and start throwing enough clothes in it to last me for a few days. I pack a few other personal items and start to walk down the hall to grab my toiletries.

I pull out my phone to check the time when I see the missed call and voicemail from Link, about five minutes ago, just after midnight.

It strikes me as odd because he's never bothered with leaving a message before, especially when he knows I'm with Noah. It's too risky.

I head into the bathroom with my duffle as I start listening to the voicemail.

"Hey...Win…Quinn…whatever I'm allowed to call you right now……Hi….did I say that already?...I don't know…I love you...I just thought you should know that…I'm fine…….I know you're busy….I'm fine……Call me back….when…you…have…time……..for me……"

I shut the bathroom door and immediately start calling Link, but he doesn't answer.

I call again.

And again.

And again.

It's clear he's under some influence. Deep down I know which one.

Panic fully sets in as I listen to the voicemail one more time for any clue of where he might be.

That when I hear it in the background of his message, the clicking of the pools tables.

He's at Whiskeys.

I open the bathroom door and stash my escape bag under some towels in the hallway closet.

Our Song

I run back to the bedroom, grab my car keys, and slip out the front door.

Yet again, speeding off in the dead of night.

Chapter 32
December 2024 - Lincoln

When the Uber brings me back to the house, I head straight to my room, not bothering to check if anyone else is back yet.

I feel lost and empty. It's an ache I can't seem to cure. I feel like an afterthought. Second choice to the biggest asshole I've ever met.

I sit on the foot of my bed, trying to convince myself that Quinn is just a caring person to a fault. To my demise, my insecurities outweigh the rationalizations that I'm desperately clinging on to.

My anxiety doesn't allow me to sit still, so I start pacing small circles around my room. I do this for a while, but being left in the dark has made me feel desperate.

I need to call her. I need to know everything's going to be okay. That we're still going to be okay.

I hate that I can't keep my anxiety in check. I work so hard to keep a calm mind these days, but I'm failing now.

Selfishly, I fear if something is seriously wrong with Noah, Quinn would sacrifice her happiness to stay with him and take care of him.

Before I can think better of it, I grab my phone off the bed and dial Quinn. Luckily, she answers right away.

"Hi." She sounds distraught.

"Hi. I'm just checking on you. Are you okay?"

"I can't talk right now. Things are kind of crazy." She says.

"I can't imagine. I'll be quick. In the sake of honesty, I'm just struggling a bit with…things right now. I know it's silly, but can you just tell me you love me and that we're still sticking to our plan? I think I can convince myself to sleep if you do." I say, in a shameful plea for security.

Silence.

"Quinn?" I say again.

More silence.

"Hello? Quinn?"

"I said I can't talk right now, Link. I'll call you later." She says before hanging up.

It's the loudest silence I've ever heard.

Everything hurts.

It's a hot searing pain, with only one antidote.

I feel like I'm floating.

I'm having an outer body experience,watching myself walk to my closet.

I grab my bag, *the bag*.

I order an Uber and head to Whiskey's. I don't want to do this here.

On the ride over, I premeditate my dose. Clearly last time was far too much, that's why I'll only do a quarter of that. Just enough to make it stop.

It hurts so badly right now.

I'll sit in a back booth until they kick me out at closing time. There will be plenty of time for me to sober up before the show and maybe it will even let me be able to sleep.

I need help to sleep through the hurt.

The Uber pulls up to the curb.

I enter the bar and head straight into the single stalled men's room, locking the door behind me.

I unzip my backpack and take out my supplies and the foil square. I line everything up in a neat row on the edge of the counter.

I pace more.

I talk to myself in the mirror.

I hurt.

I'm burning.

I scream.

I cry.

I hurt more.

I fill the needle.

I lose my sobriety.

I start to feel better.

I feel lighter.

I don't hurt.

I put everything back in my bag and take a seat on the floor, absorbing what I just did.

I feel paranoid…

Our Song

I need to call Quinn….

I need to tell her I love her…..

I'll wait for her longer, if she wants me to…..

I don't want her to leave me…….

My arm starts to feel heavy as I pull out my phone to call her.

It rings and rings, then it goes to voicemail.

"Hey...Win…Quinn…whatever I'm allowed to call you right now……Hi….did I say that already?...I don't know…I love you…I just thought you should know that…I'm fine…….I know you're busy….I'm fine……Call me back….when…you…have…time……..for me……" I hang up…

I hurt again….

She's too busy for me….

I throw my phone and hear it smash against the wall…..

I hurt more……

I need more…………..

***

"Lincoln! Lincoln, wake up!" Quinn's voice sounds like it's underwater.

I can barely open my eyes, the fluorescent light burning.

"Baby….you came!" I say.

She smells like strawberries…

I see her crouch down to me.

My arm stings, but I can't feel much else.

I'm so tired, she's yelling at me, so I try my best to focus.

"You need to get up. Come on, put your arm around me. We have to go *now*." She says.

I nod and do my best to find my footing as I lean against her when I stand.

I'm walking…

She is talking…

I can't hear her….

I'm too busy walking…

I feel my body falling, but not far…

I'm in her passenger seat…

I open my eyes as much as I can and I see Quinn….

She looks sad…

She buckles me in and shuts the door…

I'm so tired….

***

Wind on my face.

Cold wind on my face.

I'm awake.

"Where are we going?" I look over to Quinn, eyes focused on the road.

"Do you not remember the last ten minutes?" She asks.

I remain silent because it seems indefinite that confirming it would only upset her more.

My mouth is dry, but my pants are…*wet?*
Did I pee my pants?
Jesus Christ.

"I remember your hair smelling like strawberries." I grin at her like a guilty puppy.

I use every bit of energy I have to slide my hand across the center console and into her lap. I place it gently on her inner right thigh. Just holding part of her helps me sober up.

She's real and she's here.

I need to be here for her. I need to explain it was a mistake. It got the best of me. I won't let it happen again.

"Don't be mad at me, please don't hate me Quinn, I fucked up, I didn't mean to. It was one more time, I swear." I plea.

"I'm not mad at you, I could never…" She stops herself, like she doesn't know what to say to me. I'm sure it's hard to convey the amount of hate she must have for me right now.

"Does he know you were with me earlier?" I ask, trying to change the topic.

If she showed up at the hospital and he somehow knew we were together, I know what he's capable of, no matter what condition he may be in.

He's a monster, he'd find a way.

"No, but you can't keep doing this to me, to us....I'm sorry, I'm not mad, no one knows. But I need to know…why did you do it again?"

I sit up straight, removing my hand from her leg to fix my hair and rub my eyes. The cold wind from the highway isn't enough to keep my focus anymore.

Why did I do this?

"I just…I don't know. I hurt and I didn't want to hurt anymore." I whisper.

"I don't want to hurt anymore, either." She says.

Chapter 33
December 2024 - Quinn

We're five miles away from the airport.

I know Link was still coming to consciousness when I told him where we're going, but I don't have the heart to repeat myself.

On my drive to Whiskeys I called Chad's number and got Jack-The-Jackasses number. I told him he had to do one more job tonight, and he didn't ask anymore questions.

I gave him a list and instructions and he said he would make it happen.

When I was getting Link in the car, Jack texted me the address of a private airport and flight number for the jet the label uses.

He'll be waiting for us on the tarmac.

Next on my drive to Whiskey's, I called Jason, Link's the closest thing to family. Link refers to him as a brother, so I treated him as one.

Instead of just sending Link off to a rehab, I need to send him home, to family.

I explained to Jason what was going on and that I needed him to make rehab arrangements back in Arizona.

Away from this.

All of this has broken him. All of us have contributed to where he is right now. Especially me.

This isn't good for him.

I'm not good for him.

I make a mental note to call Jason for an update when I get back to the house.

"I never got to tell you my promise, Link." I say, trying to keep him awake and spill my guts before sending him off.

"What?" He asks, confused.

"Before I got the call, your birthday present…my promise to you." I explain.

"Oh, yeah. What is it?" He says, starting to sound more coherent.

"My promise was that no matter what the next few weeks bring us, I will do everything in my power to do what's best for us so that we can be together…now I guess it just might be longer than we wanted…"

"Why? Where are we going again?" He asks, this time fully upright, taking in his surroundings.

"Where here, actually." I say, pulling up to the barbed wire fence.

"Is that a plane?" He asks, gaping at the aircraft parked behind the chain link.

"A jet."

"Are we at an airport?!"

"Yes."

"Are we leaving?"

"No."

"Then why are we at the airport, Quinn?" He says, his confusion growing into frustration.

"*You're* leaving." I say, putting the car into park before getting out.

I start to walk towards the security guard box, not having the heart to discuss it any further, when I hear the passenger door slam.

"Wait, Win! What are you talking about?" Link says, hesitant to catch all the way up to me, like I might drag him the rest of the way by his ear.

I take a deep breath and ready myself for the heartbreak we're both about to experience. When I turn to face him, he already looks on the verge of tears.

"This jet is taking you back to Arizona. I already called Jason, and he's made arrangements for you to-"

"You called Jason? You told him….about my sobriety?" He asks, with an expression of betrayal.

"I had to Link. I'm sorry but you need to go to rehab. We tried it your way and look at where we are! There isn't an argument to be had. We're doing it my way now." I state firmly.

"I'll go to rehab, fine! I just don't understand why you need to send me away."

"Because you were fine when we met the day of the audition. The only thing that has changed since that day is *me*."

"*Everything* has changed! *I've* changed! Please don't blame yourself."

"Don't bail me out of this one, Lincoln. If we never met, this wouldn't be happening to you. You have to go."

"If we never met, I would've stayed the miserable person I was. You showed me colors in the grayscale life I was living. You offered me compassion in the midst of chaos. You taught me how to breathe. You made my life better. *I* did all of this to *myself*." He argues.

"You're going home, Link."

"You're my home."

"Please get on the jet." I beg.

"No."

"Get on the damn jet, Link! Please! For me!" I break down and let the ball in my throat drop, unable to choke back any more tears.

Link rushes up to me and pulls me into a desperately needed hug. I feel him shake in my arms as he starts to cry, too.

"I hate to break this up, but we need to take off before the next plane is scheduled to land." Jack-The-Jackass interrupts us.

"Who is this?" Link asks, sizing him up.

"This is Jack-The…the lawyer…from the label. He's going to be escorting you to Arizona. Jason will meet you on the other end and take you to rehab. We will figure things out when you're done, I promise. I need you to take care of you right now, for me."

"How am I supposed to survive without you with me?" Link brushes a gentle thumb across my cheek in an effort to wipe away my tears, but it's no use.

"Aren't you married to the singer?" Jack-The-Jackass asks.

"Not what you're paid for, Jack. He'll meet you there in a minute." I say, dismissing him.

I watch as he walks back through the now open gate.

"You need to go." I say.

"Okay." He finally agrees.

"I love you, Lincoln."

"I love you too, Quinn." He says, kissing my forehead before turning towards the gate.

"Bye." I say, in a teary-eyed whisper.

"No…see you soon." He corrects me.

***

By the time I make it back home, it's 4a.m. The clouds are starting to turn to a shade of light blue before the California sun colors them orange.

There's no other cars in the driveway which leads me to believe the driver that was with Roni took her back to the boy's house. At least Noah's in a deep drunk sleep on the couch.

I can grab my bag, finish packing it and slip out before he wakes up.

Even though my plans with Link are paused, that doesn't mean I'm not leaving Noah anymore. I'll stay in a hotel for a while if I have to, just to avoid him being volatile. First, I need to remove myself safely from this situation.

I'll say that Link and I are sick for this weekend's shows and that we must have picked up the same stomach bug. I'm sure the label will help find someone to play his part for this weekend.

Then, this week, I'll text Noah that I want a divorce. Maybe texting is a copout to some, but for me, it's safe on the other side of a screen with a paper trail as a conversation.

As for Link and I, I haven't figured out that far yet.

All I know is that I'll do whatever needs to be done for him to get better, whether or not that includes me in his life anymore.

My plans crash and burn as soon as I open the front door and see Noah sitting upright on the couch. My duffle bag is on the floor, its contents dumped on the coffee table.

About two dozen napkin-notes from Lincoln are scattered across the glass top.

The corny jokes, the cute doodles, the poems, the professions…everything, written out in black and white on full display.

Fuck me.

"The funniest thing happened, Quinn. I woke up from my nap on the couch and decided to take a shower before joining my wife in bed. But, when I opened the hall closet to get a towel, I found this bag buried underneath everything. Well, not buried well enough, obviously." There's a heavy pause of silence before he continues.

"So, do you want to tell me how long you've been *screwing Lincoln?*" He asks, standing up from the couch.

I stay in the entryway, unmoving. It feels like someone took away my ability to speak.

"No? Okay, do you want to talk about how you think you can just pack up and leave me? Because this is what this is, right? A getaway bag?"

Our Song

His condescending voice makes me want to scream, but still I can't find any words Fear strangling my ability to communicate. The look in his eyes shakes me to my core.

I've seen it a few times before.

"I ASKED YOU A QUESTION, QUINN! YOU THINK YOU CAN JUST LEAVE ME?!" He roars in my face. His hot breath wreaking of liquor.

I rule out fighting back. It's time to *run.*

I turn to open the front door, just as my finger tips graze the doorknob they're quickly pulled away.

I feel my neck snap back as Noah grabs me by my hair and pulls me from the door.

"Where do you think you're going? I told you, you can't leave me!" He shouts in my ear.

I squeeze my eyes tight, bracing myself, as he spins me around. His hand is on my throat, but he's not clutching down on it just yet.

"Tell me how long," He demands, shaking me.

Instinctually, I step back and out of his grip.

"Answer me Quinn!" He yells, as his hand finds its way back to my neck. This time pinning my shoulder against the front door with his other hand.

"Let me go!" I muster.

"Answer my question!"

I open my mouth to yell more, but my words fall flat when the hand that was on my throat hits my face, knuckles first.

Then once more.

After the first you don't really feel it anymore, your face is too busy tingling, trying to catch up with the pain.

I isolate the stinging and use every bit of energy to jerk my leg up and knee Noah right in his crotch. He retracts long enough for me to open the front door and run out to the driveway.

I turn back to face the house and stop. I see Noah getting back up and walking towards me.

If I run fast enough, I might be able to make it to my car.

But I don't.

"Stop hitting me!" I scream, standing in the driveway.

"Stop deserving it." Noah says, fast approaching.

I close my eyes again and take a deep inhale, bracing myself again.

He shoves me with full force and my back hits the pavement.

"YOU! DON'T! LEAVE! ME!" He screams, crouching down on me before landing another blow.

Then another.

I close my eyes and focus on playing dead in a final attempt to make it stop.

After what feels like an eternity, it does.

I feel Noah get off of me. I keep my eyes closed and hold my breath. Then I hear the sound of the front door slamming shut. It finally gives me the courage to open my eyes.

He's inside, but I don't know for how long.

I roll myself on my side and hoist myself up on my shaking knees, barely managing a standing position.

Our Song

I limp as fast as possible to my car and get into the driver's seat, immediately locking the doors. When I pull out of the driveway, I pull up my phone's GPS.

I drive down Santa Monica Freeway, clutching my side.

I think he broke a rib when he was kneeling down on me.

Fifteen minutes later, I pull into the paved lot and put my car in park.

I grab my phone and head up the steps to the large red brick building. I open the door and walk up to the front counter.

"Ma'am, are you okay?" The officer standing behind the front desk of the LA Police Department asks.

My jaw hurts too much to speak, so instead, I unlock my phone and place it screen side up on the counter.

I slide it across and hit play on the video I queued up on the drive over.

I look at the cop's face as she watches in horror, Noah beating me in our driveway through the lens of our doorbell camera.

Chapter 34
June 2025 - Lincoln

Today marks six months clean.

It's been one of the hardest times of my life, but I'm getting myself through it.

Every day, one day at a time.

I stick to the program; I go to meetings; I play.

That's all my life is now, and that's okay.

I didn't deserve the fame. I definitely didn't deserve her.

The last time I saw Quinn was on the tarmac. It's not her fault, and I'm slowly trying to accept it's not entirely mine either.

Life just kind of happened to us after that.

When the jet landed, Jason was waiting for me as promised. He checked me into Cactus Valley Rehab Facilities an hour outside of Flagstaff.

It was a ninety day treatment program with no contact allowed, except for one incoming phone call from home a month.

Our Song

After my first thirty days, I was so relieved to hear Jason's voice, but I'd be a liar if I said I hadn't hoped it would be Quinn's instead, but I understood why it wasn't.

When I asked Jason about her and the band, he just told me it was best for my sobriety if I worry about the outside world once I actually return to it. I resented him for that at the beginning.

After sixty days and me and Jason's second phone call, I was itching to ask about her, but didn't.

I knew the answer would be the same. I needed to show my progress and prove to him and myself that I was ready to be back. That I wasn't reliant on her actions for my sobriety and that I could do this whether she was waiting for me on the other side of this or not.

Two weeks before my release day, the facility manager pulled me into their office to tell me that Jason had passed away.

He had an aneurysm in his brain. It killed him in an instant. One minute he was standing in line at the grocery store, the next, he was dead.

Grief is a funny thing.

I'd expected it to crush me and set me back even. But instead it's pushed me, it has motivated me, every day.

One day at a time.

The devastation has lingered, but I keep it together for him.

When release day came, I took a taxi to the cemetery where Jason was buried and said my goodbyes.

I spent a few hours at his grave talking to him, figuring out my next move.

I had no family, no phone, no one's numbers, nothing.

All I had were the clothes I went into rehab in wearing, which were a little tight on me, and my wallet with twenty dollars cash and my debit card in it.

The last time I had checked the balance before rehab was sometime over the summer, and it only had $300 on it.

Quinn set up and managed the accounts for everyone with all the income from the band. I never really needed to pay for much. Everything was always covered some way or another.

I figured whenever I was done going through my savings from before the band, I'd ask Quinn to get me a card or move money over.

With nothing but hope and that debit card, I walked to the nearest gas station and bought a pay-as-you-go phone. It wasn't the fanciest thing, but it made calls and could download apps, that's all I needed.

I was relieved when the purchase went through. At least I could try to find anyone on social media. I never believed in it before. It always made me anxious to be accessible online like that, but I needed to find a way to contact her.

When I powered on the phone, it had enough juice for a few minutes at best, nowhere long enough to sleuth the internet for signs of Quinn.

I needed to find somewhere to stay for the night, and somewhere to charge the phone.

I called the number on the back of my debit card to check the balance, hoping desperately I'd have enough for at least one night at the Motel 6 that I passed on the walk here.

Our Song

I dialed the number and followed the prompts before the robot's voice read my balance. *"Your last deposit was made on December 15th 2024 at 9a.m. for the amount of three million. Your current account balance as of today, June 15th 2025, is three million dollars and fifteen cents."*

I think I had actually stopped breathing for a bit

Three million dollars..

It goes without saying that I was able to comfortably pay for my one-night stay.

When I got settled in my room and plugged in the phone, I made an Instagram first, then a Facebook and a few others after that. All using a fake name, Archibald Link, as not to draw attention to my online presence.

When I pulled up Compass's pages across every platform, there hadn't been any activity since December 10th, right before the stadium shows.

Then, I searched for Quinn, no results. Then Roni, same thing. I know each of them had social media before, so I was growing fairly worried by that point.

I found Sam and Noah's but theirs hadn't been active just as long as the bands.

Max was like me and never took an interest in having them.

When I ran out of people to search for on socials, I opened Google. My first search for just the band name alone proved to be very informative.

I read an article published by ENews! Titled, "The Quick Rise and Faster Fall of Compass".

It detailed the mysterious circumstances of the twelve hour cancellation notice of the band's two biggest shows to date.

It touched on the vague announcement that was posted and then promptly deleted from social media after only twenty-four hours.

It expanded on the suspected dynamic of the band's state that may have led to our demise. All pure speculation.

At the bottom of the article, there was a hyperlink for another article titled "Compass: Misdirected Madness".

That article detailed the arrest of the lead singer of Compass, Noah Taylor. They outlined his arrest for the assault of his wife, Quinn.

Wrath laced my veins and I wanted to hunt Noah and give him a taste of his own medicine.

The article went on to talk about how the arrest ultimately resulted in the cancellation of the last two shows and suspectedly the cancellation of the band's contract with Rich Records.

All other members of the band, besides Noah, were named MIA in the article. Not a single word of me going to rehab.

I checked the date on the article and it was from January of this year.

I Googled just Noah's name next and found out he was six months into serving a two year sentence.

Two years is a fraction of what he deserves and I don't even know exactly what he did.

I searched Quinn's name along with everyone else's, but nothing of significance came up from after December. Just articles from gossip sites speculating where we all are now.

Our Song

With no luck in my digital search, I decided to rent an apartment back in Los Angeles.

It was the last place where Quinn was, so that's where I decided to go. Solely in the hope that if she never returned to social media that maybe I would at least be able to bump into her.

I've been here for three months now.

There's been no sign of her online, so I stick to my back-up plan in having faith that the universe will put us back into each other's paths.

So for now, I will do what I do best.

Play.

Chapter 35
June 2025 - Quinn

My alarm wakes me up as the song "Karma" by Taylor Swift plays on my phone.

After snoozing it two more times, I finally silence it and rub my eyes awake. I desperately needed that nap before going out with Roni tonight.

It's my first night going back into a bar since last December and it makes me very panicked. This is something that needs to be done, though. It's part of my healing.

I unlock my phone and see a text from Roni.

Roni: Be there in 30 minutes. See you soon!

I let myself get lost in the routine of getting ready, letting my mind drift off as I shower and do my hair. Twenty minutes later and I'm walking out the apartment door to my car.

I plug the bar's address into my phone's GPS and put my car in drive. I turn the radio on and let my mind wander again.

Nearly every day for the last six months, I've replayed that night in my mind on repeat.

After Noah's arrest, the cancellation of the tour and Compass's contract for the next album pulled, the band and I moved back to Nashville.

Sam moved in with his brother Harvey.

Max rented a house downtown.

Roni was prepared to go to Florida, but for reasons I still can't understand, decided to stay with me in Nashville instead.

We only lasted there for two months before I told her I couldn't be home anymore, that for me it wasn't home anymore at all.

Noah's lawyers worked out an agreement that he could serve his time at Nashville Correctional. All Tennessee became was a constant reminder of my life with him.

Considering his sentencing and my active restraining order, there was no issue with the judge when I requested a divorce. It was finalized in just under two months.

As soon as I got everything settled in court, Roni and I packed our cars and drove back out to Los Angeles. We're currently renting a two-bedroom apartment together.

What haunts me the most about that night is Link's face when I left him on his birthday, how *hurt* he looked. Followed by what Noah did to that girl and how corrupt the label actually was. What Noah did to me and what I did to Link.

I think about Link the most.

Jason was in contact with me for most of his rehab treatment. He felt it best not to disclose where he was getting treatment but assured me when Link was done and out, he would give him my new number and let him make the decision to reach out to me.

It stung, but I respected him for it. I knew Link would want to call me, so I tried not to stress about it too much.

Two weeks before his release day, Jason stopped taking my calls all together.

I realized I contributed to a large portion of why Link was in his current situation. I couldn't be mad that Jason clearly decided I wasn't worthy of his time.

I accepted that he ghosted me and hoped that when Link got out, he'd call me somehow.

The label canceled the service on our phones they paid for shortly after our contracts were pulled, so any hope of contact with my new number relied solely on Jason giving it to him.

I removed my presence from social media two months after Noah's arrest and a rather large mental breakdown at the advice of my new therapist who I see twice a week.

All I did was look up what people were saying about me and the band. It was too much, but now and then, I still search Link's name in case anything pops up.

The last six months have been filled with fucked up trials and tribulations, but tonight I put that all aside for Roni.

Our Song

She's performing at an open mic at the bar I'm driving to. She says it's good to stay practiced with a live audience and would double as an opportunity for me to recruit members to the band we are trying to build.

I haven't agreed to manage it, but I have promised my assistance in scouting for talent, so at least Roni can be in a band again.

I'm pulling into the parking lot when my phone buzzes.

Roni: What's your ETA, you need to get here ASAP!

I hurry myself as I grab my purse and lock up my car. I don't know what the urgency is for, I know it's been a while since she's performed in front of an audience, but she can't be that nervous, *she's Roni.*

I show my ID at the door and walk into the bar. I begin searching the crowd of people for Roni when I'm stopped in my tracks, not by what I see, but by what I hear.

I desperately move myself through the crowded bar.

My heart is pounding violently with anticipation as I comb through the groups of people, making my way to the back where the stage is.

When I break through the horde, I see Roni, eagle-eyed, watching the stage.

I look up to see it myself, confirming what my ears had suspected.

It's Link, and he's playing Our Song.

Epilogue
December 2028 - Quinn

I'm on the left side of the stage watching the band perform. I can tell they're feeding off the crowd. It's not every day you get to play New Year's Eve in NYC, especially as the ball drops.

They're on the last song before the countdown begins and they perform their finale at midnight.

It's cold this time of year, but I'm bundled up. The band, on the other hand, will always choose fashion first.

Max is in a mesh black jersey with the band's name, End Game, across the back in thick red letters.

Roni is in a tight red dress with knee high Chuck Taylors.

Stevie has a t-shirt with a cat on it, because well, Stevie does what Stevie wants. He's the weirdest and kindest man I've ever met.

After all, Link wouldn't be sober without his help too.

They met at an NA meeting shortly after Link moved back to Los Angeles. Stevie's actually the one who brought him to the open mic night that served as our reunion.

He's helped him stay on a good path with his advice, but I think the friendship they've formed has helped the most.

It was through their hangouts and shared hobbies that Link figured out Stevie could sing. The rest of the pieces just fell into place after that.

Roni and Link had been practicing together ever since fate, with an assist from Stevie, brought us all to that bar in LA.

They played a few small shows with a few different drummers, but ultimately decided to stroke Max's ego. They begged him to join their new group and move back to LA.

Shockingly, it worked.

They tried to do the same routine when they reached out to Sam, but by some miracle, Sam found a girl and asked her to marry him, so he politely declined.

I never thought I'd see the day.

Despite the loss we all experienced, I feel like the universe has put us all where we are supposed to be now.

I scan the stage to find my husband.

I love saying it, even if it's just in my head.

My husband.

He's dressed in a leather jacket and henley. It's good to know becoming a father didn't entirely transform his sense of style.

Sure, he wears his New Balance sneakers and jorts on the weekends when the band isn't touring the world, but on stage, he'll always be a rock star.

After we reconnected and caught up, we made a plan forward together.

Link was still following his program and had six more months before he could be in a relationship. His sobriety means the world to me, so I waited for him.

Hell, I'd have waited a decade if it meant we would be together at the end.

We still hung out every day, and got working on recording an album for End Game titled *Novus*.

Nine of the thirteen songs on the record were written by me.

Everyone was shocked that it did better numbers than *Invisible Horizon*. The world rallied around the former members and their new singer, taking them all to the top again.

The rest is history.

On December 14th 2025, Link asked me to be his girlfriend.

On December 14th 2026, we got married in Paris.

While Link's birthday may have been the worst day of his life almost every year before, I personally vowed that it would only ever be the best day going forward from then on.

August 21st 2027, we welcomed our first son together, Jason Maxwell Archer. His godmother, Roni and godfather, Stevie, were just as excited about his arrival as we were.

We've also gained Kendelle, Stevie's wife. Piper, the new manager, and Paige, Roni's soon-to-be wife, AKA Florida Girl, in our little growing family.

As for Max, I could be wrong, but I think he might actually have met a girl, or at least I think so by the way he's been more attached to his phone than his sticks lately.

Our Song

End Game just finished the European leg of their stadium tour at the end of November. It's been nice being back home in the states.

We start writing the new record in the next few months and I couldn't be more excited. Letting someone else be the manager has proven to be a lot more relaxing this time around.

All I have to do now is write and be happy.

The song ends and all of Manhattan roars in applause. The countdown starts up on the big screen and I see Link running across the stage, over to me.

"What are you doing? The next song starts in ten seconds!" I laugh, looking at the ticking clock.

"I'm sorry. You don't really think I'm not going to kiss my wife at midnight, do you?"

I laugh but am cut off by his lips.

"It's not midnight yet." I tease, breaking away and looking at the timer with four seconds left.

"It's always time to kiss the woman I love, and that's you, Win."

He kisses me through the sound of the crowd counting down.

"THREE!"

"TWO!"

"ONE!"

"HAPPY NEW YEAR!"

"Happy New Year, Mr. Archer."

"Happy New Year, Mrs. Archer."

Invisible Horizon by Compass

Track 1: Embark
Track 2: Phases Of The Moon
Track 3: Deep End
Track 4: Heartbeats
Track 5: Catastrophe
Track 6: Saturdays At Sally's
Track 7: N.S.E.W (North South East West)
Track 8: Tiny Boxes, Big Feelings
Track 9: Let It Ride
Track 10: Red Lights
Track 11: Sugar Sugar
Track 12: Tailor Made
Track 13: Era
Track 14: Disembark

Our Song

"Our Song" by
Quinn Finch & Lincoln Archer

I'd set myself on fire, just to keep you warm
Life's a condition, like weather to a stone
Make your hopes greater than all your fears
Don't seal your fate for the sake of cheers

Were finding our way
We'll dawn a new day
Won't let them hold us back
Creating new paths
Secrets unwrapped
Nothing can slow us down
Time's too short, so let's spend this life singing our song

No matter how good the view, I'd risk it all for you
Forbidden love findings, we bottled the lightning
It's now or never, it's make or break
My heart and soul are yours to take

Were finding our way
We'll dawn a new day
Won't let them hold us back
Creating new paths
Secrets unwrapped
Nothing can slow us down
Time's too short, so let's spend this life singing our song

K. Nies

We'll draw up a map
and never look back
The future is clear,
as long as you're here
Like wind takes the sail
our love will prevail
Through little white napkins
and city rooftops

Were finding our way
We'll dawn a new day
Won't let them hold us back
Creating new paths
Secrets unwrapped
Nothing can slow us down
Were finding our way
We'll dawn a new day
Won't let them hold us back
Creating new paths
Secrets unwrapped
Nothing can slow us down
Time's too short, so let's spend this life singing our song

If you, or someone you know, is struggling with addiction call the Addiction Helpline: 844-990-6996.

Suicide and Crisis Helpline: Dial 988.

For access to information on the use and accessibility of Narcan please visit:

https:///www.narcan.com

Q&A with K.Nies

When did you first know you wanted to be a writer?

My freshman year of high school, I had a really cool English Lit teacher who stressed the importance of not only reading and understanding literature but also writing it.

Our initial projects included a short story, where I went beyond the assigned word count.

As far as the imagination piece of writing, I feel as though I've always had that. Since a very young age, I would stay up late at night past my bedtime, close my eyes and escape to different worlds that I built in my mind. Every night I would live different lives with characters I made up in my head.

What inspired you to write this book?

I've always had this idea to write about a band. My all-time favorite movie is The Runaways. I think seeing such an inspiring, but equally heartbreaking, journey was very influential to me. The basis of balance, and not being able to have good without the bad is moving.

Who is your favorite character?

Lincoln Archer, hands down.

Once I started writing his narrative, I felt an uncanny familiarity with him, like we shared a long history. Only when I was nearing the end of the book did I realize why I feel so close to him.

In so many ways, Lincoln reminds me of my dad, Edward. He lost his battle with addiction when I was six years old, but that isn't what I remember him for. I remember him for his unconditional love for me, for his love of playing the guitar in his band, Back Alley Sally, and for his love of life.

Though he had his vices, he was a good man, taken from us too soon, with so much left to experience. Lincoln allows me to live out his full potential, for which I'm incredibly thankful.

Which character do you relate to the most?

Quinn Finch.

Similar to Lincoln's character, I didn't grasp the connection until I was close to completing the writing. I'm Quinn in the same way so many women are Quinn.

At some point, we've all faced challenges in a world that tries to make us feel powerless or voiceless. But, as women, we endure, we rise and we conquer.

I had to emancipate myself from my mom at sixteen because of her physical abuse, drug use, and alcoholism.

My personal experience with parental trauma and leaving home heavily inspired the storyline of starting anew. One of Quinn's key attributes is loving people so much, even when it hurts, and that's foundational to me.

What was the hardest part about writing this book?

I think when I tapped into my personal traumas and allowed my voice to bleed into the storyline. Giving parts of my personal experiences to these characters was almost cathartic. It's only one side of the sword, though. Writing about your trauma can feel like letting go, processing your emotions in written words, and accepting that you don't have to hold on to it anymore is rewarding, but it can also be draining, and that's okay.

What did you learn from writing this book?

I've realized the validation of actually letting the stories out of my head and onto paper.

I've experienced the freedom of setting my truth free.

I've learned that the toughest climbs are always worth their view.

Our Song